Praise for Diana Rivers

"Rivers is an accomplished writer who expands and deepens the still inspiring tradition of good lesbian-feminist speculative fiction. *Daughters of the Great Star* is an engaging and emotionally authentic adventure into a world where strong loving women struggle, grow and triumph. I loved her flawed s/hero, and fully-drawn characters, and the way that they contend with each other so ferociously. I loved the sex scenes. I especially loved the fast-paced action scenes that led up to and away from the raid on the city. This is an exciting and rewarding read."
— Sally Miller Gearhart, author of *The Wanderground*

"Rivers' writing is a rush to read, and her characters, rather than carved from wood, are complex, flawed and intriguing. And, my goodness, lusty." — Lambda Book Report

"Ms. Rivers' fantasy land of women shows great imagination (I certainly wouldn't mind living there) and great attention to detail. I would certainly recommend it to lovers of fantasy. If you've never read fantasy, this is a great place to start."
— Cleve Boutell in *Dimensions*

"*Journey to Zelindar* deserves its place as a great lesbian/feminist fantasy along with Marion Simmer Bradley's *The Shattered Chain* and other books about the Free Amazons of Darkover. Highly recommended." — Women Library Workers

Also by Diana Rivers

Journey to Zelindar

Daughters of the Great Star

The Hadra

Available fall 2002 from Diana Rivers and Bella Books

The Red Line of Yarmald

In this climactic sequel to *Clouds of War*, the Zarns' armies are now arrayed before Zelindar, the coastal city that is the heart of the Hadra world. Working together, Noya, Amairi, and Jolaina struggle to create an unlikely alliance between the Hadra, the Kourmairi, the Wanderers and the Thieves Guild to defend the Yarmald peninsula with a magical line of power that cannot be crossed by an enemy force.

Clouds of War

DIANA RIVERS

Bella
BOOKS

Ferndale, Michigan
2002

Bella Books, Inc.
P.O. Box 201007
Ferndale, MI 48220

Printed in the United States of America on acid-free paper
First Edition

Cover designer: Bonnie Liss (Phoenix Graphics)

ISBN 1-931513-12-0

For Path, the companion of my life's journey who eagerly listened to many bits and pieces of this book while it was in progress, and who endured with patient understanding my frequent mental absences whenever I wandered off into this other world.

For Susanna who edited my words with such loving kindness and close attention, and who discussed with me the meaning and ideas in this book with a keen interest and intelligence.

For Rehea who helped me bring the Hadra back to life and who has worked so hard to keep them alive in the world.

Also for every woman who has given me hope, inspiration and encouragement by asking persistently when the next Hadra book was going to be published.

Table of Contents

CLOUDS OF WAR

Book 595 of the Hadra Archives

In this time of great trouble and upheaval the three of us have written our own personal accounts of events as they were happening. Then I, Noya, have taken it upon myself to weave them together into one story and in some places to make room for other voices. The facts and times may not all mesh together smoothly, but what follows in these pages has the great advantage of having been written in the moment. Immediacy will have to substitute for polish. We thought it important to set everything down on paper while it was still fresh in our minds.

Noya, Councilor of Zelindar
Amairi the Wanderer, also Elvaraine of Maktesh
Jolaina, advisor to the Zarna of Maktesh

1

Section I:
War Clouds Gathering

Noya

Just a few short notes as I sit here in this tower chamber above the Zildorn, looking out over the city of Zelindar; a few words written in the early morning before I dash off to do the thousand things that need doing this day.

Last week I was chosen to be Councilor for the city and I must admit that it frightens me. Garlian, our past Councilor, says she will stay to help me through the transition before she leaves for Mishghall and a much needed vacation from her duties here. Even so, my heart beats faster every time I think of what lies ahead. It is not so much being Councilor that frightens me, though admittedly that has its own terrors; it is the possibility of war and what it would mean to lead us through such a time.

As I look down on everything women have built in this special place, I am full of doubts and questions. Can I keep us safe here? Can I guard what we have made? What skills do I have for war? For strategy? For the infliction of deliberate and organized harm? But then what skills do any of us have for war? War is not Hadra work. Our powers forbid it. We cannot do harm to another without that harm coming back to us. We certainly cannot kill in anger or cruelty or for sport. And yet war keeps being thrust upon us.

Perhaps I was chosen out of all the Hadra because I was the one who warned the loudest about the possibility of war and now most believed it was coming. Garlian spoke for me saying I had spirit and fire and we might need fire at this moment more than wisdom. Did that mean she thought I had no wisdom? Yes, I have spirit and fire, but is that enough to ward off this terrible threat?

She keeps telling me, "Have no fear Noya; you are not alone in this. You have the Council to rely on. You also have Pathell to help carry out your plans and your companion Vranith for comfort and support. It will not all be on your shoulders."

I know I can depend on Pathell. I do not mention to Garlian that Vranith will give me no support at all in the matter. Surely she must see this talk of war is making a deep rift between us. Vranith thinks it my own personal madness or some quest for power unbecoming to a Hadra. She is sure the Zarns' guards will never press this far into Yarmald.

Garlian has been almost like a mother to me since my own mother died. She pushed hard for my choosing and has much influence here, but Jallin and Linyate were very much against it. Jallin, who sits on Council, has always disliked me. She said in a mocking tone, "Are we going to choose a child to lead us through this coming trial?" Then her companion Linyate added spitefully, "And a child with no experience at that?" But the younger women were for me . . . except Vranith, of course. In the end, after several hours of heated discussion, it was the younger women who had their way.

During these last few days I have just re-read Tazzil's accounts of the beginnings of Zelindar and her experience of being first Councilor here, looking, I suppose, for some wisdom and advice from the dead. Of course, as children, we all had to read and study *The Daughters of the Great Star* and *The Hadra*, but sitting here in Tazzi's place it means much more to me now. Besides, there is something very personal for me here. I am Tama and Pell's great-granddaughter. Their daughter Laisha was my beloved grandmother. In these pages she is just a baby. She actually remembered Tazzil and told me many stories of her life.

Tazzil's second book lies open here before me at its very last page. There she warns us that the peace we have enjoyed all these years may not last forever. I fear she was right. *Tazzil, Tamara, Rishka, Pell, all of you; I wish you were here with us now to give me help and guidance. I fear the world you created is about to be torn apart and I am not sure I have the strength or the wisdom to hold it together.*

The last time there were rumors of war this tower room

was built at the top of the Zildorn to be able to look out in all directions. Then, before their war even started, the Zarns fell to fighting among themselves over the supposed spoils. Now there are rumors of war again and this time I fear they are true. The reports from our spies in the Shokarn cities is that the Zarns have been meeting together and amassing troops, not for each other this time, but for us. Or at least three of them have. So far, the Zarn of Maktesh has steadfastly refused to join their plot, or rather the Zarna, for the ruler of that city at this moment is a woman named Aranella. Perhaps she is not as bent on killing as the men, though any woman who has gained such a place of power can hardly be kind and gentle. Who knows, as things turn, if she will be friend or foe. Only time will tell.

Amairi

Just this morning I promised myself that if he ever hit me again I would leave him, though I have no idea how I would do such a thing or where I would go. Not home to my parents, I know that, not with my brother Nhageel there. He was the one who pushed me into this hateful marriage. I have no doubt he would return me instantly into Horvath's hands. My parents are aging fast and have little power now in that house, certainly not enough to protect me against Horvath's wrath. It was my brother who wanted me out of my home so he could take over the estate and his wife, Lalaini could take over the house, both of which I had been running quite efficiently since my mother's illness.

Our parents had children when they were well past their youth. I had been taking care of them since I was very young and expected to go on doing so until they died. With no ambitions to marry, I would have been quite happy to end up

7

"the daughter of the house" as they say, but my younger brother, the one I had raised so lovingly, had other plans for me — or rather for himself.

He told me I should be very pleased with the husband he had found for me. How would he know? Horvath had probably been his drinking and whoring companion. I doubt that Nhageel had ever felt the force of that man's hard hand across his face. The one time I complained to him, he said, "But sister, you must try not to aggravate him or test his temper. He may be quick to anger but he is also a kind and generous man. Look at all the clothes and jewels he buys you. Except for the Zarna, you are probably the best dressed woman in the whole city of Maktesh." As if that is what matters to me!

When I worked around our family estate I wore sturdy, brown wovenwear and was perfectly happy with it. My interest was not in being admired but in doing my work well and efficiently. I wore clothes that gave me the freedom to move about. When there was a plentiful harvest and everyone was well fed and happy, that was where I took my pleasure and found my worth, not in being decked with the latest fashions. Besides, most of the money for such purchases is not even his! It comes from the dower I brought with me into this loveless marriage. And it is certainly not out of generosity that Horvath buys me clothes and jewels, but out of pride. Regardless of my comfort he insists I wear such tight-fitting clothes that they pinch and cramp and hinder my movements. Whether sitting or walking they leave me breathless and miserable. He also loads me down with jewels that are too heavy for my neck and ears. When we go out I feel dressed for adornment like a bejeweled doll, a brainless thing of beauty. If I complain Horvath gets angry and calls me ungrateful. I know if I say more it will come to slaps and then to blows so I keep my silence.

My husband knows he has married above himself. It makes him both vain and very insecure. We go to parties so he can show me off. Those parties are a torture for me. I am supposed to keep up a lively inane chatter so I will be noticed and admired. But I am not to talk too much to the women for fear they will corrupt me. And I have to be very careful never to flirt with the men. All the while I must pretend to be comfortable in those awful clothes, not an easy task and one which I often fail. If I am silent he is angry. If I am too lively, as if for a single moment I really am enjoying myself, then he is angrier still.

There is always a little critique after the party of how I failed to please him. It often ends in blows, especially if his jealousy flares up. "I saw you talking sweetly to Daimin and looking into his eyes. Do you have an assignation with him? Tell me! Tell me!"

Such foolishness! He thinks I want another man when what I want most is to be left alone. I cringe when he summons me to his bed for what is politely called an act of love. It is an act certainly, but there is no love in it. It is more like an act of conquest or of war. Afterward my body is full of pain and anger and feels like my enemy. I only pray no children come from such a foul joining.

The worst of all this is that I have lost my parents who once were so dear to me. Now I can never talk to them alone. Horvath is always with me on visits. If he must absent himself for some reason, then he makes sure Nhageel is there to spy on me in his stead.

And my brother tells me I should be grateful!? Why should I be grateful for being married off against my will to a man I disliked from the start and have grown to hate and fear? What kind of a life is that? And almost as bad as living in fear is the endless boredom. I can do nothing useful. Every time I try turning my hand at some useful task my husband stops me, saying, "That is why we have slaves and servants. Do you want to disgrace me by having people say my wife does the work of servants?" Of course I do not argue for I know how that will end. But perhaps the boredom is even worse than the blows.

9

All my life I have been a useful, active person. Now I am reduced to this living death. At least I have my books for escape. I brought them with me over his objections. Even so, if I did not have this little journal of pages to scribble in while he is away, I think I would really go mad or die. But I am very careful to always keep it with me in a little secret pouch at my waist. I do not grudge him his time away, drinking or gaming or whoring. It gives me some peace. But I fear if he ever found I was writing this in secret he would kill me. And sometimes I think that might be for the best. Then at least this misery would be over.

Oh Goddess, how to rid my life of this man without having to die myself? My brain turns frantically in my head like those poor squirrels in their dreadful gilded cages, running for the amusement of rich bored ladies. Twice I was shocked to hear a voice in my head saying, *Kill him!* The first time I recoiled in horror. The second it did not seem quite so terrible. Desperation is making me evil, forcing me to turn in any direction that might offer some hope of freedom.

There are rumors of a war against some strange women called Hadra in a city on the western coast. Sometimes I think that is how Horvath will go out of my life, though it seems cruel to wish him on others. I have nothing against those women. They never did me any harm.

His eyes gleam with greed when he speaks of their city. "A man could make his wealth there. I hear there is vast treasure in Zelindar for the taking. Those women are all enemies of the Shokarn and hold power on the coast. The world would be better off with less of them. My sword and I would not mind dis- patching a few." At that he laughs wickedly and I shiver. I can see he is very eager to go and acquire, by whatever means, some fortune of his own. He wants to be off to the fabled city of Zelindar, but I think the Zarna will not allow this war and her advisor Jolaina is said to be very much against it. When I mention this to Horvath he answers with a sly grin, "Well, she may not be Zarna for much longer and that Jolaina woman may soon be gone as well. Those women stand in the way of a man and his sword."

Hearing those words, it goes through my mind that I should try to warn them, but I have no idea how to do such a thing without being discovered by Horvath. I am not even sure what I could say to them. *Then my own life takes a sudden turn and rushes me headlong on another course . . .*

Jolaina

How quickly life changes. Last night I had been the trusted advisor to Aranella, Zarna of Maktesh and a power to be reckoned with in court. I had also been Aranella's lover, a fact unspoken but quietly understood and acknowledged by everyone. Now, since morning light, I have become a hunted fugitive, fleeing from men on horseback. As it is, if her nurse-maid Dharlan had not warned me in time I might already be lodged in prison or perhaps be in the hands of the torturers.

Lucky for me I started life as a farm girl and have not always been a fine court lady. I could not imagine any of them being able to ride so hard, or run so fast or so far, not even to save their lives. And I was suddenly very glad for all the body training Aranella had forced on me, all the hours of acrobatics and sword play and unarmed combat.

Dharlan had awakened me with a warning that my life was at forfeit. Urging me to hurry, she had tossed me a bundle of men's ragged old clothing to put on for disguise, along with my knife and my coin pouch. In a hasty whisper she told me that Khundorn and his faction were planning that day to accuse me of being a witch and using my sorcery to put an evil spell on Aranella. How Dharlan found all this out was a mystery to me, but I did not for one moment doubt her word.

I knew of course there were men who were very jealous of my influence in court and especially put out that it was a

11

dark-skinned Kourmairi who had the Zarna's ear. They wanted to wrest the power from Aranella and put a man in her place, someone who would go along with their plans for war against the Hadra. With me out of the picture or, better yet, in their hands, they had much more chance of controlling her. I might have taken this threat far more seriously had the different factions not been struggling so fiercely among themselves. Khundorn — I should have known! I should have seen it coming and not kept myself buried in my work. Actually I think Dharlan had tried to warn me sooner but with the arrogance of youth I had ignored her.

As it was, I got out through the gates of Maktesh just in time. Another few minutes and they would have been closed in my face. As I rode through I could already hear men shouting, "Close the gates! Close the gates! Fugitive loose!" The great gates crashed shut in back of me. Then, moments later, my pursuers were shouting and cursing for them to open again. Too late! Once closed those gates are not so easily re-opened. It was that closing that allowed me a little time and so saved my life — or at least gave me a chance to flee.

Amairi

Well, I finally got up the courage to tell him this morning and he laughed in my face. At least he didn't try to test my resolve by hitting me. I chose this moment because he was in a good mood, very pleased with himself for having won a big sum at cards the night before. But the harshness of his laugh was almost like a slap. "So you are going to run away from your husband? What a joke. What would you do? Where would you go? Home to your family? Your brother is my friend. He would send you right back. Go on the road? Travel with the Wanderers? A fine lady like you, used to every luxury? You

12

would not last one week on the road. Why are you trying to foul my good mood with such nonsense? Go see that my breakfast is ready before I lose my temper."

Well, it had been said. Things had been set in motion. I turned quickly so he would not see the smile on my face, the look of triumph. He had given me the answer! Why had I never thought of that before? The Wanderers! Now I knew what I was going to do, where I would go, what I should plan for. That very day I set to work on it. I hid a pack with some rough clothes, some food and those few coins I could lay my hands on. As the days went by I added a sparkstone, a few candles, a little map I had cut out of a book, some stout shoes, more coins and a small blanket. Now, when the time came, I would be ready.

Goddess knows, things seldom go as we plan. I thought myself well prepared and had decided to make my escape the next time he left me alone for an evening, not even waiting for him to hit me again. Why wait since it was so inevitable and I was sick of living with the constant fear? Instead, he came home in the middle of the day in a rage over some bad dealings he had made. With no warning he hit me across the face and then threw me against the wall. Usually there was some gathering of his anger before the blows came. This time it was instantaneous. I was flung so hard I hit the corner of the bookcase and fell to the floor with a pile of books tumbling over on me.

Suddenly he started laughing with that hard, cruel humor of his. "There you are, all dressed in books. Perhaps that is what you deserve. I never saw much use in those things anyhow, but you insisted on bringing them with you. Well, now I suppose you are going to leave me, put a pack on your back and go down the road, begging from place to place. You can be sure you will not get any money from me, not one cent."

"Please, Husband, do not hit me again," I pleaded in a

quavering voice. "Those were only wild foolish words. I did not mean them and I will never repeat them. Only let me try to please you and better do your will."

I had never begged before, only suffered his blows in angry silence. I could see my begging pleased him so I went on with whatever sniveling drivel came to mind while some other part of my brain rejoiced: *Yes, I will go on the road. Even being a beggar is better than this. Surely I can find something to turn my hand at once I am free of this man.* The very thought of speaking when I pleased and saying what I wanted filled me with such a rush of happiness I almost laughed aloud, but I was not out of his grasp yet. I was sitting, splay-legged on the floor with books piled all over me. My lip and nose were dripping blood on the pages while I begged mercy from my attacker.

That evening we were to go to a party. I thought this would be my chance for freedom. Surely he would not want me to be seen with my face in such ruin. I knew he would have to go as this party was very important for his business dealings in the city. I planned to slip away as soon as he left. Instead, he sent my maid, Yani, up to me with orders to cover my bruises with powder and paste and help dress me in my new blue gown.

I could not move without groaning in pain. Yani cried when she saw my face. It pleased me to see how her tears left large dark stains on that detested gown. Though my own face was hard with anger, I petted her hand to comfort her. Inside I was weeping with frustration at this lost opportunity. I suppose Horvath did not dare let me out of his sight now for fear I might bolt. I realized too late that I had been a fool to tell him of my intentions. It had not curbed his violence as I had hoped, only made him more watchful.

Now I have written all this, sitting here in this torture of a dress, all powdered and rouged, waiting for his summons to a party I shall despise. People will surely notice my face in

14

spite of all that paint. What will they think? I suppose he does not care so long as no one speaks of it. And no one will. It would not be polite, though you may be sure they will gossip with relish later. Maybe he will even want me to make some excuse about my clumsiness, tell some ridiculously transparent story of how I had tripped and fallen against the furniture. *Well, Goddess, soon this will all be over; soon I will either die or leave. One way or the other this can not go on much longer.*

Jolaina

Spattered by my horse's blood, I tore across the field with my legs aching and my heart thudding wildly against my chest. The woods ahead were beckoning safety yet seemed impossibly far away. I ran on anyhow, expecting at any minute to be cut down by an arrow in my back or by the throw of a knife. They had shot my horse out from under me so perhaps they wanted to capture me alive. At that moment it did not seem a much happier prospect.

In back of me I could hear men cursing and shouting angrily and the sound of their horses' hooves pounding ever closer. Fear lent me more-than-human speed. The line of trees loomed dark in front of me. When I reached them I flung myself headlong into their shadow. With no regard for the sting of thorns and branches, I plunged on desperately, forcing my way into the thickest part of the forest. I knew that where the woods were hard going for a woman on foot they would be impassable for men on horseback.

I would have that one brief moment of advantage. They would be dismounting now, cursing, tying their horses, arguing about which way I had gone, making a plan. I kept running, hoping I was going straight and would not accidentally circle back into their hands. Soon I could hear them crashing in the woods behind me, far off still, but steadily gaining ground.

The woods were closing in around me, branches clawing at my face. Struggling for breath, I slowed my pace a little. Clearly I could not keep going for much longer at that speed. I was very grateful they had not thought to bring hounds or the game would already have been up. Hounds — far swifter than a woman in the woods — would probably be baying at my feet by now or perhaps they would already have brought me down like a deer or a boar. Not a very happy thought. The cries of anger and frustration from the men behind me were getting louder. In those hands it was not likely I would get back to the palace alive, not even to be used as a tool to force Aranella's will.

Looking around frantically for some means of escape, I saw, not far ahead, a huge tree whose upper branches were hidden in a mass of leaves. If I could get to the top of that tree perhaps they would pass under me, unseeing. I rushed in that direction only to find all the branches out of reach. Three times I threw myself at the lowest branch, desperately trying to get a grip on it. Each time I fell to the ground with the breath knocked out of me and each time I got up to try again. The fourth time I got my hands around the branch, held on for my life and began hauling myself up, branch over branch.

None too soon. I could hear their steps close below me now. Pulling myself up as high as I dared, I sat very still and tried to quiet my panting breath. The top of the tree was swaying wildly. I feared they would look up and notice me. Instead they rushed by beneath, shouting to each other, "Which way now?" "That way you fool!" "Idiot, you should have killed her when you had the chance." "Hurry! He will have our necks for losing her!"

When I could no longer hear them, I slipped out of my tree as quickly and quietly as I could, ready to retrace my steps and see if I could steal a horse. There was no need to worry about finding my way back. It was easy enough to see where so many men had passed. When I reached the edge of the woods, I stayed in hiding for a moment or two to observe the scene. They had tied their horses to the outer line of trees. Luck was with me; no one was on guard. In their place I would not have been so foolish. I suppose they thought me a quick, easy catch. After glancing around to make sure it was safe, I cut myself a switch with a quick slash of my knife. Then I slipped out of the concealment of the trees and went along the line of horses, cutting their reins and switching them hard on the rump to send them running off.

When I reached the last horse my legs were shaking from fear and exertion. This one was a tall black creature who looked built for speed. He was nickering anxiously as his companions dashed off in different directions. Speaking softly to him, I undid his reins. Then, with difficulty, I hauled my reluctant body onto his back.

I had just congratulated myself on getting clear away by some miraculous combination of luck and skill, and was leaning forward to switch one of the other horses into motion, when I heard the sharp twang of the bow and the whistle of the arrow. One of those men must have returned and seen me at my work. The bolt came from the edge of the woods and hit me in the left shoulder. Likely it would have caught me in the middle of the back if I had not leaned forward at just that moment. With a cry of pain, I dug my heels into the horse. As he leapt forward with a snort of surprise, I hunched over his neck, gasping in pain and biting my lip not to cry out again.

No matter how fast we flew, flaming pain pursued me. For a while I rode in mindless terror, only wanting to put some distance between me and those men. When my wits returned, I slowed the horse and turned him from the road. I had to get rid of the arrow that tormented me and also marked me. Anyone wearing a red arrow with gold painted feathers was easily marked as a fugitive from the guards and so became any man's lawful prey.

17

Soon I found a little path into the woods and could hear the sound of running water. Tying my new horse to a tree, I made my way to the stream with staggering steps. After only a moment of hesitation I walked straight out into the water. It instantly turned red around me from my blood and the blood of my dead horse that had soaked into my clothes. With a groan, I plunged my face into the cold water. That brought back a measure of sanity. Then I sat down on the bank to work on freeing myself of the arrow. My good luck in the midst of my great misfortune was that the arrow had hit at an angle, going through flesh rather than into bone. The arrow head was actually jutting out in front. Clenching my jaw against a tortured scream, I pulled the arrow forward a little to where I could hack off the arrowhead with my knife. Then, pressing my arm against a tree to keep the shaft steady, I set to work.

The pain was excruciating. Several times I had to stop and put my head down in order not to lose consciousness. Twice I went back to the stream and soaked my head. When I finally could break off the last remnant of wood, I groaned with relief. Then, fumbling one-handed, I tied the arrow to a tree with a piece of vine and threw myself forward. The shaft pulled free of my arm. Blood spurted everywhere. Terrified that I would really faint from loss of blood, I staggered back to the stream and dug some clay out of the bank with my fingers. My hands were shaking as I plastered both sides of the wound to stop the bleeding and tore a strip from my ragged clothing to bind it.

Afterward I sank down on the bank, letting water run up to my knees while I sobbed with relief and pain. Then, before I left, I threw the arrow in the middle of the stream and watched it float away, hoping it would travel for a long way, bearing false witness to my whereabouts.

The first part was done, but there was much more I needed to accomplish before I could be free of pursuit. Among other things I had to totally change my appearance, get rid of my torn bloody clothes and trade my too obvious horse for another that was more common. In spite of the terrible ache in my arm, I started by clubbing my wild wavy hair together in one fist and hacking it off with my knife. One less thing for them to know me by. As I watched my hair float off on the water I felt as if I were watching the strands of my past life float away. Nothing but danger seemed to lie ahead. And if they were trying to kill me what could they be planning for Aranella? I knew I had to find some way to get back to her.

Amairi

I am writing again, hoping to catch up with the present. This is the first chance I have had since that evening that changed my life forever. Much has happened in that time, more than I could possibly have imagined and I need to set it all down while I can still remember.

We went to that party and it was even worse than I had imagined. Horvath drank to excess and was insulting, so of course he ruined the chances that mattered so much to him. And yes, he had even contrived some story for me to tell about how I had slipped on a rug on the stairs and I was supposed to recount this in a convincing manner. I actually enjoyed the looks of shocked disbelief on people's faces as I stiffly recited his little lie word for word. Much to my amusement, they gave me their awkward and confused sympathy. This was all an act, a performance. Underneath my heart was singing, *Soon I will be free, be free, be free.* I would soon be dead or gone. At that moment it mattered little to me as long as I never had to sit through such a party again.

There was much talk that evening of Jolaina's treachery

and her astounding escape from the guards, talk so filled with anger and vengeance and blood-lust that it turned my stomach. It was as if some animal were being hunted, not a human being. Of course I said nothing on the matter, but in my heart I wished her speed and safety. There was also some talk of Khundorn coming to power in Aranella's place, talk that chilled my heart. I had met the man and I shuddered at the prospect.

To my disgust Horvath's voice was one of the loudest raised in Khundorn's favor. With each outburst he downed yet another glass of strong spirits. Even through my own fog of misery I was shocked at this talk. To my ears it sounded like treason. It was one thing for Horvath to hold forth this way in his own home, but quite a different matter here. Were they really all so very sure of their plots and plans that they could feel safe talking this way in a semi-public place?

Finally my fool of a husband was so drunk that he fell asleep in a corner and the master of the house had to call two of his servants to carry him out to our carriage. Our host patted my arm while saying with patronizing kindness, "I think it is time to take your husband home, dear Lady. He seems to have enjoyed himself to excess." I nodded with downcast eyes and followed Horvath's limp body to the carriage.

When we reached the house, Thairn, our carriage driver, went in to fetch the servants. As soon as they had my husband out of the carriage and into the house, Thairn came back to offer me his arm. I had been sitting there, numb and bemused by the events of the evening. On sudden impulse I said, "Wait!" and flung myself out of the carriage without using his help. I could hear the hem of my gown ripping as I dashed across the cobbles. In an instant I had my secret pack out from behind the sacks of potatoes and was rushing back to the carriage, hoping no one had seen me. As Thairn helped me back in, I said breathlessly, "Drive on! I must go to the herbalist for some tonic for my husband. When he wakes tomorrow he will have a fierce headache and be very out of sorts." Thairn set out down the familiar streets. After a few blocks I said, "No, go toward the West Gate."

"But Lady, the herbalist is in the other direction."

I started to order him as Horvath would have done. Then something in my head said, *From this moment on everything will be different.* And so instead I said gently, "I know Thairn, but there is a better one the other way."

We drove for a time in silence while I tried to collect myself and decide what to say. This had been a very sudden decision, not at all like my careful plans. Before we reached the West Gate I blurted out. "Thairn, I am leaving tonight. Goddess willing, we shall never meet again. If we do, may it be far from here. I want you to leave me off near the gate. Find a deserted place where we will not be observed. Then go to the East Gate, but not so close to the herbalist that trouble will come on him. There you must raise the alarm, saying that I directed you to the herbalist, then leapt out of the carriage well before we got there and ran off so fast you were not able to catch me. Make sure to be seen and to remember the name of the street where I supposedly fled and whatever else you need so you will not be blamed. After that go home and raise the alarm there. Hopefully Horvath will be too drunk to do anything till morning and I will have one night on the road to walk and find a place of hiding."

"And then . . .?"

"And then, who knows? Whichever way the road turns me, whatever life presents."

"Lady, do you have any money?"

"The little money I have I desperately need, but I would gladly give you my jewels for your silence."

"Oh no!" he said, horrified. "I meant to give *you* some

money. This will not be an easy road you go by, Lady. I know what has gone on in that house and I wish you well. Yani and I often talk about it. She cries for you and we both feel so helpless." With that he turned and thrust a little sack of coins at me. "Here, take this and do not argue; it is all I can do for you." Then he added, "And take the old cloak that is rolled up under the seat. It smells of horses and is dirty and threadbare, but it will be just the thing to hide your fine clothes and get you safely out of the city. Put it on and make ready to get out at the end of this block if there is no one about."

"Goddess bless you Thairn, I wish I could give you something in return. My jewels . . ."

"No, they would be my death sentence. Now be ready."

With trembling hands, I did as he said. The carriage paused. I stumbled out and suddenly found myself standing alone on a cold, dark, windy corner in the city of Maktesh, listening to the sounds of the carriage driving off into the night. Quickly I drew the rough smelly cloak around me for warmth and protection and started walking toward the West Gate, my first steps of freedom. I was too numb with surprise even to be afraid.

When I reached the gate I had the hood pulled low so it partly covered my face. I hunched myself forward and spoke in a quavery old voice. The guard who opened the gate scarcely looked at me except to say, "You are traveling late mother."

I mumbled something unintelligible in response and shuffled through the gates of Maktesh with Thairn's smelly old cloak hiding my blue satin party dress and shoes. Once I was safely through the gates I had to restrain myself from running or dancing or shouting for joy. After going down the west road for a short way, I suddenly found myself shaking in terror at the realization of what I had just done. There was no going back. That piece of my life was over and with it all the privileges as well as the misery. Who knew what lay ahead? I was free, nameless, homeless and almost penniless on the road to nowhere.

Jolaina

For the next day or so I stayed off the cobbled roads to avoid the guard. Following back roads that were no more than wagon tracks winding through the countryside, I kept my eye out for what I needed. Finally I saw just the right combination: a line with simple farm clothes hanging up to dry, and a large pen with several small cart horses enclosed with the cows.

I had planned to trade horses, but I was uncertain whether it was more dangerous to try stealing the clothes or to try buying them. I called out softly. No one seemed to be about so I went quickly to the pen. There I exchanged my beautiful, swift black horse, gift of my pursuers, for the first cart pony that came over to me, a non-descript little brown creature that rubbed its head against my arm. I had fastened on the bridle and was just cinching up the saddle when I heard a cry of anger and looked up to see a man hurtling out of the barn. The dog at his heels was barking wildly.

The game was up. Propelled by fear I got myself up on my new horse, rode full speed at the clothes line, cut it, rode to the other end and cut that too. Soon I was riding off with a line full of once clean clothes trailing after me in the dust. I was determined to have some clothes better suited for the road and for public view then the wet, ripped, bloody ones I was wearing. Those would surely make me a target of dangerous stares and questions wherever I went. Even riding hard, I managed to pull two shirts and two pairs of pants from the line.

The man had taken another of the little horses. With only

a rope to guide it, he was riding hard after me. I let him gain on me. When he was close enough, I raised the clothes line full of clothes and released it so that it flew back, enveloping him and tangling his horse. Then I shouted back at him, "If you raise a cry you will not get to keep the black horse and may even be taken for a thief. I will gladly pay you for your trouble and your clothes." Quickly I took some coins from my pouch and tossed them back. When I glanced over my shoulder, he had stopped to untangle his horse. There was a little trail of bright coins in front of him. I did not think he would continue the chase or raise an alarm.

Food was my next pressing need in this strange new game of staying alive. I knew that if I did not have more to eat than a few quickly snatched berries and the last remaining scraps of trail bread Dharlan had packed for me, I would soon faint from hunger. Once I was dressed in my farmer clothes and riding on my little cart horse, I thought it safe to drift into a town. Though I still had the pain in my shoulder, at that moment I was feeling quite pleased with myself, as pleased as one could feel under such dire circumstances. I had evaded my pursuers, buried my old clothes under a big rock, found new clothes and a horse and still had my little stash of coins, only slightly depleted.

Amairi

As soon as I was well out of sight of the gate, I stopped to put on the rough work clothes and solid old shoes I had hidden away. With trembling hands, I rolled up my jewels and those useless, fancy, blue shoes in my dress. Then I quickly shoved it all in my pack, not sure if it was more dangerous carrying it with me or trying to hide it by the side of the road. In the end I decided to carry everything, though I was shaking with exhaustion by the time I had finished changing.

It was hard to walk in those shoes that were bent to someone else's feet. My ribs ached painfully from Horvath's blow and I was already wishing I had eaten more of that wealth of food at the banquet or at least carried some of it off in a napkin. I had been too sick at heart to eat much at the party except a little for appearance's sake. But then I had been a rich Uppercaste lady with every luxury available. Now, only an hour or so later, I was a poor, ragged fugitive who would soon be very hungry.

Most of that night I forced my body to keep going, trying to put some distance between myself and the city. The next morning I begged a wagon ride from a farm family on their way to market. They must have thought me very strange as I answered almost none of their questions. Instead, with my head nodding, I dozed among the bags of onion, potatoes and apples. Then, without a word, I slipped off the rolling cart when they neared a small town. As soon as they were out of sight I gratefully devoured the two apples I had stolen. After that I rested a while, hiding between some large rocks until I had gathered enough strength to go on.

With some part of my brain I was perfectly aware of being tired, lonely, hungry and probably in grave danger. I should have been despairing. Instead I was feeling elated. I had escaped! I was free! Nothing that happened now could be as bad as being Horvath's wife. If he recaptured me he might kill me or I might even kill myself, but I knew I would never live with him again.

Toward evening I came around a bend in the road and suddenly saw a big fire with many horses, wagons and people circled around it. The camp had been set up in the middle of a clearing a short way from the road. I stopped and stood staring at that circle of activity. Filled with such a combination of fear and yearning that it took my breath away, I found myself unable to move toward the camp or to go on past it. This was sooner than I had expected to find them. Was this really the Wanderers that I was in search of or only a gathering of farmers on their way to or from market?

Soon dogs began to bark and I knew I had to do something. The moment I stepped from the cobbled highroad and began down the little dirt lane toward the camp, I felt I was being watched and followed, yet when I turned to look, I could see no one. It was a struggle to keep my footing in the semi-dark over that rutted way.

By the time I reached the camp they were all watching me, a circle of rough, strange faces lit by the firelight and turned in my direction. I was suddenly very frightened, wishing I could grow wings and be gone from there. Then one man stood up and reached out his hand to me, his dirty face breaking into a smile full of kindness. "My name is Vondran and I am what passes for leader in this camp. Be welcome among us stranger. Find your place at our fire. There is food and shelter here among the Wanderers if you want."

This Vondran was a striking looking man, big and broad shouldered, with curly red hair and beard, and penetrating green eyes. He spoke a rough and stilted Shokarn. I reached out to clasp his hand in return. Instead I collapsed at his feet.

Coming back to consciousness, I heard a woman's kindly voice saying, "She has been badly beaten. No doubt she is very hungry as well as being exhausted and frightened, but nothing, I think, that will not mend." She was bathing my face with a cool cloth and smiled down at me when I opened my eyes. As she leaned forward, her hair hung down like dark wings on either side of her face. "I am called Mhirashu," she said softly. "You have been mistreated and are in need of shelter. Here with the Wanderers you will be safe. Many women come to us that way. Do you want to sit up now?" I nodded and she helped me sit, propping some cushions in back of me. "We have bathed you and changed your clothes and put a healing compress on your side." So I had been naked before the eyes of strangers. In my former life I would have blushed for shame. At that moment, after all that had happened, it hardly seemed to matter.

A young woman brought me a cup of tea, saying, "I am called Nastal and I travel with the Wanderers. This tea will help with the healing. It is a little bitter, but I have added much honey. Try to drink it all." She was very beautiful and her smile, as she bent over me, was full of concern. My hand shook a little as I took the cup from her. I was trying not to cry from this sudden rush of kindness after so much cruelty in my life. Then Vondran came to squat by my side and said firmly, "I can understand that you may not want to talk yet, but I sense danger here. I must ask for your story if you are going to shelter with the Wanderers as we might have to . . ."

Mhirashu quickly interrupted, "Must you so soon, Vondran? She has just recovered consciousness and is still so fragile."

"All the more reason. She could faint again. We must know her story for her safety and ours as well. Perhaps she is being pursued."

I nodded. "I understand and you are right. When you hear my story you may even want to send me away again. I am sure that by now I am being pursued." And so, in a halting voice, and with much encouragement and support from Mhirashu and Nastal, I told my whole story while several of the women muttered angry and insulting things about Horvath and his entire ancestry. As I spoke Vondran nodded, saying, "Yes, yes, I see . . ."

When I finished Vondran stood up and said decisively, "This is even more dangerous than I thought. We must move quickly. Pursuit could come at any moment. If you still have your clothes and jewels and other personal things with you, turn them over to Rhondil. He will carry them off to a Wanderer hiding place. Later, when it is safe, we can pass the jewels through the Thieves Guild. They will take them apart so they cannot be identified and we can get some of their worth back for you. For now there must be nothing of yours here in the camp."

Nastal handed me my small pack. I quickly took out my money and a few other little things. Then I passed it to Rhondil. He gave me a slight nod of his head and without a word slung the pack on his back. In an instant he was mounted and out of the camp, riding fast away from the highroad toward the deep woods and darkness. At that moment an old woman with a pipe came forward to stare at me appraisingly. Nodding her head and cocking it from side to side, she puffed vigorously a few moments before saying, "We must totally change her appearance. Even with those old clothes on, anyone would know her at a glance for a Shokarn lady."

"Well, work your magic on her quickly, Old Nairth. We may only have a little time for it."

"Fist your hair; braid it and we will cut it off. Then I will give it a new shape. I hope you are not more attached to your hair than to your life. Sometimes fine ladies cry when they lose their hair."

"Take it!" I spoke fiercely though my hands shook in the braiding. "Cut it all off! I want nothing left of that old life." Nastal knelt behind me to help with the braiding. When she said, "Done," I answered instantly, "Do it! Cut it now! Let me throw it in the fire."

Soon the scissors began chewing away at my hair. Then Old Nairth dropped the braid in my hands. It lay there like a heavy, yellow snake and I felt a sudden rush of cool night air on the back of my neck. Mhirashu asked if I wanted her to put the braid on the fire for me. I shook my head. "No, mine to do!" In spite of my forceful words I groaned aloud when I tried to stand and several hands reached out to help me. I had a moment of dizziness as I stood staring into the fire. Then I steadied myself, took a deep breath and threw in the braid. "Done! Over! Finished! Gone!" I shouted as the fire flared up and a terrible, acrid stench filled the air.

I would have stood there watching my hair burn, oblivious of the heat, if Mhirashu had not drawn me back to sit down. "You can celebrate later. Right now time is essential." Two other women, Yurith and Stobah, had come with a pot of stain and a dark grease marker. They set about darkening the skin on my hands and face and altering the shape of my eyes and eyebrows while Old Nairth snipped away at my hair. As soon as she was done someone brought her a jug of dye and she began brushing it through my hair. I shivered as cold dribbles ran down my back and she admonished me to sit still.

When they were all done with their work, Nastal held up a small hand glass for me to see. I gave a little cry of surprise. I would not have recognized myself on the street. I had dark hair, dark skin and dark rimmed eyes that gave my face a totally different expression. A stranger was staring back at me from the glass. I looked like a Kourmairi farmwife. Stobah shook her head and said with a mocking laugh, "No one would mistake her now for a Shokarn Highborn."

Vondran, who had been sitting on a log watching the whole process intently, now stood up and said decisively, "Well, we have changed her appearance and now, just as important, we must change her inner being if she is to be a Wanderer and travel with us. And first I must ask you, Lady, is that what you really want?"

Mhirashu interrupted, "But how does she know, Vondran? She has only just met us. How can she tell this quickly if that is what she wants to do with her life? She has probably heard terrible stories about the Wanderers."

"But I do know! Yes! That is what I want! I want to be a Wanderer. Now! Quickly! Tell me, what must I do?" My voice was shaking with eagerness.

"If that is what you really want then first you must separate from your husband. You cannot be a Wanderer and be bound to such a man." Vondran sounded almost stern.

"Gladly, but how . . .?

"Say three times, *Horvath out of my life, I am no longer your wife*. Say it loudly and mean it. Each time you must throw a handful of this herb on the fire and turn your self around leftward, unwinding the bond."

I did as he said with a fierce joy in my heart. My words of freedom! I had no problem saying the words loudly and meaning them. It felt like a new voice coming out of me or maybe the old one that had been silenced for so long or maybe both together. The smell from the herbs was even more acrid then the burning hair. To me it was like perfume and I breathed it in deeply. It was the smell of freedom.

"Good," Vondran said. "That is the first part of it done. In the eye of the Cerroi you are not a married woman any more. You are no longer Horvath's wife. Now for the next part. Do you truly wish to be a Wanderer? If so you must obey the Cerroi and take that as the guide in your life."

"But what does that mean? I know nothing of this Cerroi." I felt a sinking in my heart. Perhaps this could not be done so quickly or easily after all.

Vondran nodded and gave me an encouraging smile. "There is much to learn, many teachings. If you wish to be one of us you will learn in time. But right now, time presses. In its simplest form the Cerroi is the law of return. *You will do no intentional harm to another. If harm is done to you, you will not return it in kind. Instead you will try to transform what has happened into something new.* That last part is the hardest and takes some practice, especially after having been so badly treated. You may understandably long for justice or even vengeance."

"Vengeance has no interest for me. I long for freedom and to be done with all that past. I long for a new life that will let me speak openly and move in my own way and dress as I please and use freely whatever skills I have." There was a burst of applause from the women around the fire. Mhirashu shouted, "Well said!" And Old Nairth called out, "Give her the oath, Man. She is ready to be one of us and time is passing."

Vondran held out his hands, palms up and gave me a nod. "Put your hands in mine, look me straight in the eye, repeat what I say and mean every word or do not speak. When you are done you will be a Wanderer." Very slowly he said, "I will do no intentional harm to another; if harm is done to me I will not return it in kind."

I said every word and meant it with all my heart. When I was done there were more cheers and they all rushed in to hug me, saying such things as "Now you are one of us," "Welcome home Wanderer," "May you always find a place at the fire," "May your hands be empty and your cup and bowl be full," "May the Cerroi be with you all your life."

Finally I stepped back to catch my breath. "I cannot believe you have welcomed me into your family this way and I have never even told you my name. I am . . ."

"No!" several of them shouted.

"Do not speak her name here," Mhirashu told me, putting her hand over my mouth. "That woman is gone into the fire with the braid. Choose a new name and never speak the old one aloud here. Then we can truly say she is not here among us."

A new name? Nothing came to mind. I looked around at them all for an idea and they all looked back at me in silence. Finally the young woman named Yurith stepped forward, the same one who had helped to dye my hair. At first she seemed shy and hesitant. Then, gathering her courage, she said with conviction, "Amairi, that is the right name for you. Amairi is what I hear when I ask in my head. Amairi was my older sister who died at birth. I never knew her and now she is here among us."

The others were still looking at me expectantly. After a moment's hesitation I nodded. *Why not,* I thought. I liked the sound of it. It was nothing like my old name and I could think of nothing better. "Amairi," I said softly, trying it out. "Amairi the Wanderer." Yes, that had a good sound. "Amairi!" I shouted into the darkness and was answered by a chorus of echoes from the Wanderers, *Amairi! Amairi! Amairi!*

"What about the Wanderer brand?" Stobah asked. Though she was speaking to Vondran, her eyes suddenly turned on me, full of mockery and challenge. I felt a little tremor of fear. I had already noticed that several of them had the letter W branded on the back of their left hands though some, like Nastal, did not. Afraid or not I was prepared to look Stobah in the eye and hold out my hand. Vondran shook his head. "Too complicated; a protection and also a danger, something that cannot be hidden or undone. Let us wait a little while on that." Then he called out loudly, "Now it is time to drink and dance and make music. A new Wanderer has just been born this night. And use her name often, say it to her over and over so we bless her with it and she remembers it in her heart."

"Amairi, would you like some of this brew?" "Do you want to borrow my shawl against the evening cool, Amairi?" "Amairi, do you know this song? Will you sing it with us, Amairi?" "Sit by me Amairi, there is a place for you here on my mat." This is how they greeted me into their tribe and their lives. It was as if I had never had another name and among these people I never had. I was now Amairi the Wanderer. That other self was a pale ghost of little substance.

At her invitation, I went to sit by Nastal. She put a sheltering arm around me and said, "You are my sister now. I am also new among the Wanderers. I came because I did not want to marry the man my family chose for me. In fact I did not want to marry any man at all. I ran off the day of the wedding. My family is very angry at me. I can never go back. But I am happy here and I think you will be too."

"You do not want to marry?" I asked in surprise.

"Marry! What for? Would you have chosen to marry if you had been given a choice?"

I thought for a moment in silence, my mind spinning with memories. Then I shook my head. Still I felt impelled to say, "But surely your family will forgive you after some time has passed."

She gave me a strange look and said curtly, "I think not." Then her face turned closed and sullen, full of secrets. For that moment she said nothing more.

After a while I gave myself over to the music and the fire. Never in my life had I sat outside by a fire, watching its flashing red and yellow magic, listening to music people made for themselves. The murmur of Wanderer voices lulled me. It sounded like wind or running water. If they spoke directly to me I could easily understand their strangely accented Shokarn, but when they spoke to each other, in what sounded like a combination of Shokarn and Kourmairi and something else, the meaning seemed to evade me and my mind drifted away. Looking up, I could see the starry night sky like a giant dome, a slow wheel of light turning overhead.

Just as I was beginning to relax into the pleasure of being there I heard a sharp, shrill whistle and someone came galloping into camp. A young man leapt from his horse in front of Vondran and reported, "Four armed men riding fast this way. I fear it may mean danger for us."

Vondran jumped to his feet and turned to me. "Well Amairi, you have three choices and the decision is yours." Gesturing at the young man who had just ridden in, he went on, "You can flee into the woods with Larameer, though if they catch you there we cannot protect you. Or you can hide in the false bottom of one of the wagons, but that could be a trap as much as a safety. Or you can remain in camp and trust that he will not recognize you. If that is your choice then you must stay calm no matter what happens. Just keep remembering how very different you look. Truly I do not think even your own mother would know you now."

"I will stay here among you," I answered without hesitation. "Frightening as that sounds the other possibilities sound even worse. I could not stand being shut up in a box that way and I am sick of running. But what of the danger to all of you? Perhaps I really should leave and take my chances."

Mhirashu said quickly, "It is not the first time we have faced an angry man looking for lost property."

And Vondran added instantly, "And it will not be the last."

Jolaina

Though there were many Shokarn in evidence, Zanzairi was mostly a Kourmairi town. The look of it gave me a sudden unexpected tug of homesickness. It seemed to be decked out for a festival or a procession. The main street was lined with banners, food stalls and crowds of people. The smell of food pulled at me painfully. First I stopped to buy a farmer's cap of the most ordinary kind to cover my cropped hair. Then, by visiting a few food stalls, I quickly filled my pouch with nuts and dried fruit. With a fruit pie in one hand and a meat roll in the other I pushed my way up to the front of the crowd. Soon I found myself next to a shepherd who, with the help of one dog, was trying to keep his small flock under control. Between hurried bites I asked, "What is happening here?"

He gave me a startled look. "Every one knows what is happening. The Zarna is about to go by on her way to the summer palace." Then he lowered his voice and said in a conspiratorial way, "It is earlier than usual this year and she is under heavy guard. They say it is for her own protection since her advisor is a dangerous and powerful witch. But I think it is more that the Zarna is a prisoner of sorts and they are about to make some changes at the top, though I suppose it matters little to small fish like ourselves. I am driving my sheep there hoping to sell them to the palace kitchen as I have done in previous years, but if things are so different who knows what my luck will be. Aha, here they come now."

There was a fanfare of music that grew steadily louder. The musicians appeared first, then a large company of guards, then the royal carriage decked in red and gold, drawn by six black horses. Aranella! So close and under guard! I tried to keep my face impassive and cheer with the others. Inside my heart was aching. This was so very different from those other times when we had set out for the summer palace together, full of gaiety and waving to the crowds, welcomed by the people and glad to be out of the city in the heat of summer.

As the carriage came level with me I saw that the curtains were closed. With fear tight in my throat I wondered if Aranella was really in the carriage or if this was all show and sham. Was she even still alive? Then, just as the carriage was about to pass me, the curtains opened slightly. They were quickly jerked closed again, as by another hand, but for just that moment I saw her lovely face, very white and strained. The mass of her gold-blond hair was covered with a dark cloth. I doubt if she saw me nor would she have recognized me if she did. Yet, at that instant, if the carriage had been open, I could have reached out and touched her. Then she was gone and the rest of the procession was rolling by. Full of yearning, I watched the carriage as it disappeared down the street and wondered if her sister Nhuriani was with her. That at least would have been some comfort to Aranella. It seemed more likely that Khundorn would have taken the child away.

There was a sudden commotion next to me and I turned to see that some of my companion's sheep had bolted, probably startled by the loud music. His dog was rushing about trying to round them up. I caught two and brought them back to him, each by an ear. When I returned his sheep he was immensely grateful and began gushing with words. "Thank you lad, you must have a way with sheep. My son

35

Uris, he should be the one helping me with this, but he has gone and gotten himself conscripted into the guards. Most times they only take Shokarn into the guards. Right now they are not so fussy. I hear they are taking everyone who is young enough and has two good legs.

"Word around is that they plan to mount a raid against the Hadra city of Zelindar. Well, nothing but a bunch of muirlla there anyhow, so I say good riddance to the lot of them. But why does my only son have to go? You may be sure a Kourmairi farm boy will get no part of the treasure there. Well, the ways of the Highborn are a mystery to me. Sometimes the ways of the low-born are too. My cousin Gwain, the one who is not very bright, he was supposed to help me when Uris was taken. But he went and volunteered himself and so he has probably gone off to war too. He heard there was a whole city of women and thought he would have some fun there."

"I doubt he will have much fun with those women," I said sharply. "I hear they have their own kind of protection." Then a sudden thought hit me. "Conscripted?" I hissed in a whisper to him. "Conscripted by who? Not the Zarna's men surely."

"By the Shokarn of course," he answered in the same sort of whisper. "When the Shokarn come to your village you try to stay out of their way if you can. If not you do what they tell you. You certainly do not ask if they have an official 'by your leave' signed in the Zarna's own hand. She can hardly help herself, she certainly could not help the likes of us." Then he glanced around warily to make sure no one was listening. I suppose he had trusted me because of my dark skin.

It was much worse than I thought if they were already conscripting for a war the Zarna had forbidden. I suppose they were only waiting for my death and Aranella's capitulation to openly set it all in motion. Then a blood bath would wash over Maktesh and perhaps all of Yarmald as well. I thought of all those people who had helped us and sided with us and who would likely be a target for Khundorn's wrath. Everything

Aranella and I had tried to build would be wiped out in weeks, perhaps days. It was not just my life that was at stake or Aranella's, but everyone we knew and so many we did not, as well as any chance for things ever to be different. The old tyranny would come back even stronger than before. Many would die in the process.

I snapped back to the present aware that the shepherd was looking at me strangely. On instant's inspiration I said, "Perhaps I could help you with your sheep since I am also going in that direction." This was the best disguise I could have asked for.

His face brightened. "Why not. What is your name, lad?"

Caught unprepared I blurted out, "Gwain, like your cousin."

"Now there be a great coincidence! Who would imagine it?" He gave me a sly look to show he did not believe a word of it. "Well, you shall be my dimwitted cousin Gwain and I am Gairith. Gwain and Gairith and Gotha, we shall herd the sheep together. Gotha is the dog and she is probably the smartest of us all. See to it that you herd my sheep, not steal them, Gwain. Gotha is quick and well trained and has very sharp teeth."

Suddenly the guards were pushing roughly through the crowd on horseback, shouting that the Zarna's muirlla was a fugitive and there was a hundred silverpiece reward for her capture. They passed so close they could have laid hands on me with ease. I thought to slip away quickly and disappear into the crowd, but Gairith suddenly gripped my arm in his broad strong hand. Trying to break loose would have called too much attention to myself.

Gairith was staring at me with calculated greed in his squinty little eyes and a gloating smile on his lips. "So, that is who you are," he whispered in my ear. "In spite of your shabby clothes you did not seem like one of us; you speak too fine." He was nodding and looking me up and down. "I thought there was something familiar in your face. Nothing

37

personal in this, but that is more money than I could make in three years of driving sheep. Can you pay me that much to keep my silence or shall I call them back?"

"Come out of this crowd where we can talk."

"Why not? This show is over anyhow and it was not much of a show at that. In my humble opinion, a closed carriage is not much to look at anyhow. Now this had best be a lucrative talk or I shall call the guards back instantly. And do not try to run. I can easily sound the alarm." With that he made some complicated hand signals to the dog, saying, "Gotha, keep the sheep together right there."

We had no trouble finding a private place to talk as most people were still watching the procession. I turned to face him, saying, "Release me, Gairith, I will not run. As you say, you have the upper hand; easy enough to call out and denounce me. But first there is something you should hear, not just for my sake but for your own as well. I am far more like you than I am like those fine folk. I grew up on a farm as a Kourmairi dirt-child. But I know the Shokarn and what they do. In these past years I have lived among them and watched their ways. I have seen much more than I care to remember of how they deal with people like you and me.

"If they take me they will no doubt take you too. You think you will see one coin of that reward? Not likely. Do you think your dirty little hide is worth a hundred silverpieces to them? Far cheaper to accuse you of being my accomplice, throw you in a cell and have you executed than to pay the reward. And easy too. Who would dare to object? Who would come to your defense, especially now that you have been seen talking to me and did not denounce me instantly? Believe me, I have heard them plot such things. I have seen it happen, not once but many times with the poor fellow calling out for his reward when his only reward was going to be the torture chamber or the hangman's noose or both. You had best not call any notice to me or you may find yourself keeping me company in the same cell. In fact they are more likely to keep me alive because they need me to help bend the Zarna's will. You will have already served your purpose."

"I believe I have just lost my fortune."

"Not so! Think of it this way Gairith, you have just gained your life and a helper on the road."

Amairi

At that moment the dogs started barking again. Soon I heard the thunder of hoof beats. I quickly withdrew to the far edge of the circle as Horvath and three other men suddenly burst into the Wanderer camp. "Who is leader here?" He shouted in a loud, belligerent voice. "I am looking for my wife and have reason to think she may have come to you." His angry words might have set me to trembling, but at that moment a sharp breeze blew across the fire. I smelled again the acrid stench of herbs and cut hair that marked my freedom, separating me forever from this man.

Vondran had already sat down. Now he got up again and held out his hand. "I am the leader here. My name is Vondran. What is your name, good sir? And what is your business with us?" He spoke with such exasperating slowness as to almost appeared dimwitted.

"I care nothing for your name and mine is none of your business. I am looking for my wife, the Lady Elvaraine. If she is here, I demand her immediate return."

"There is no one here by that name, Sire. There are only Wanderers in this camp. I sympathize with you. It must be very vexing and troubling to lose a wife, but your wife is not among us. You are free to look around the camp if you please or in the wagons."

Mhirashu added sternly, "Remember, there are children and babies sleeping in those wagons."

Horvath pulled up one of the torches stuck in the ground. He swung it all about so that it touched on every face in the circle, even my own. For just one moment he looked straight at me without the slightest flicker of recognition. Then, as his men began searching the wagons, children started to cry and babies to wail. The women who leapt up to comfort them grumbled loudly, showering insults on the intruders. The dogs set to barking ever more fiercely while the Wanderers shouted uselessly for silence. Even the horses that had been dozing peacefully suddenly grew agitated, snorting, whinnying and trotting about nervously. All at once that quiet peaceful camp was in turmoil. I glanced at Vondran thinking he might be upset, but he was watching it all with a crooked little smile and seemed almost pleased.

Seeing the utter frustration on Horvath's face and in all his gestures, I found myself caught between amusement and terror. What if he acted on his anger and hurt someone because of me? What if he recognized me with a closer look? It was not long before he came back in a fury to face Vondran. "How do I know she is not concealed in a disguise?" His eyes were on Nastal at that moment, staring hard. And in truth, if not for her dark skin and a gap in age, there was a marked resemblance between us.

Stobah said indignantly, "We cannot ask every woman here to strip off her clothes for you. Would you not know your own wife no matter how she was dressed?"

Horvath was still staring at Nastal. Suddenly Nastal stepped up quite close to him and said right in his face, "Man, it seems you cannot keep your eyes off me. I am tired of being stared at. Do you really think I am your wife in disguise or do you just want some excuse for seeing my naked body? Either

40

way, if I satisfy your curiosity, will you set your eyes elsewhere and let me be in peace? Surely you would know her body from all other bodies." So saying, she began rapidly stripping off her clothes and dropping them carelessly on the ground until she stood naked before him. Her young ripe body was incredibly beautiful in the firelight and certainly looked nothing like mine. For one thing she was dark all over and not just in selected patches as I was.

Horvath stepped back, stammering apologies and actually blushing. Nastal took another step forward and went on relentlessly, "Well, now you have what you wanted. Look carefully. Is this your wife's body before your eyes or is it some stranger's? This is the body the Goddess gave me in this life and to my knowledge I have never shared it with you. But maybe you have not seen enough to really know, to be sure, to set your mind at rest. I need to show you everything."

With those words she raised her arms and slowly turned around, continuing to talk over her shoulder, "And then perhaps you did not come here for your wife at all, perhaps you came here to see naked Wanderer women because you heard we were easy. Well you can look all you please, it matters not to me. But do not think to touch or I will have a knife in you quicker than you can see. I have not been among the Wanderers long enough to put all my trust in the Cerroi." Something flashed in her hand. Even stripped naked she had managed to keep hold of her knife. Some of the other women were smothering giggles. Old Nairth had taken her pipe out of her mouth. She was rocking back and forth, laughing outright and slapping her knee. Horvath was in total confusion, his face flushed and beaded with sweat. "No . . . I did not . . . I never meant . . . I only wanted . . ."

"Nastal, put on your clothes and sit down," Vondran said sternly. "Do not torment our visitor with the loveliness of your body. He is grieving for the loss of his wife." Then he made a wide gesture with his hand. "You can see that your wife is not here among us, but you and your men are welcome at our fire.

41

There is always room in the circle for one more and food still hot by the fire. We were about to make some music. If you care to join us perhaps you have something to share."

I was terrified that Horvath might actually accept this invitation. His men appeared very tempted, but Horvath shook his head and said angrily, "I am not out for an evening's entertainment. I am searching for my wife. If I find that you have lied to me Wanderer I will . . ."

He never got to finish his words. Vondran had leapt to his feet. Taking several steps in Horvath's direction, he was shouting in a thunderous voice, "Wanderers do not lie!"

Horvath backed away and mounted his horse almost at a run, calling to his men, "Come with me!" They all headed back for the road at a gallop, leaving even faster than they had come. The sounds of laughter and mockery followed them, echoing around the Wanderer camp. As soon as I could no longer hear their horses I came forward to thank the Wanderers and for the second time collapsed in their camp, crumpling in a heap on the ground.

When I came to again I was lying on a mat with my head cradled in Nastal's lap. She was gently stroking my hair. Someone had covered me with a blanket. "Is he really gone?" I whispered to her. "Is that possible?"

Smiling, Nastal leaned over and whispered in my ear, "He is really gone. The sight of my bare breasts frightened him away." Then she laughed, a lovely, musical, mocking sound. The Wanderers meanwhile were all making music around the fire as if this were just any ordinary evening and nothing unusual had happened. Vondran was saying to Stobah, "Well I did not exactly tell a lie, but I surely did not tell the whole truth either." And she answered, "In the Circle of things, in the larger picture, I think you will be forgiven. We certainly could not give her up to him. I shiver to think what he would have done to her." Smiling, I let myself drift off again,

42

listening to their music. It was the first time in years I had felt safe.

Jolaina

For the rest of that day I traveled with Gairith, helping him keep his sheep together. When we stopped to eat, I passed as his not too bright cousin Gwain by keeping my head down, my voice low and saying as little as possible. When any tried to engage me in talk, I pretended to be slow witted and simple. Gairith had little money. I was afraid to let him know how much I had so I followed his example and put down only enough for soup and bread and beer.

While we walked together, if there was no one else about, I talked to Gairith; I talked for my life and for Aranella's too, trying to bring him over to our side. I needed to enlist his help or I stood little chance of getting near her. She was too well guarded. I told him what we were trying to do, the great changes we had been trying to make in Maktesh and how it would affect his life for the better. I said we would not have taken his son and cousin to fight the Hadra, but instead would have made peace with the coast.

At first he scoffed and gave me bitter mocking answers. After a while I could see he was beginning to listen. "Ah, I see you are very clever, trying to tempt me into helping you in these grand affairs. But I am a simple man. The affairs of great folk do not concern me." Even as he spoke I could see the gleam in his eye, the pleasing thought that he might help in foiling the proud and powerful and so have his own small part in spoiling their plans.

That night the Zarna's entourage camped in a huge field. Aranella's carriage was surrounded by guards. There was no chance of getting near it. I never even caught a glimpse of her getting in or out. But Gairith sold a roasting lamb to some Guardsmen and came back to tell me they were stopping the next night at the Crossroads Inn. If I did not reach her there it would be too late. The following day they expected to push on for the summer palace and to be there before nightfall.

Gairith and I took turns walking and riding on my little horse. I even became friends with Gotha. When I walked she trotted at my side with her nose in my hand if she was not herding the sheep. All that day I fluctuated between hope and despair. Was there any chance of seeing Aranella? How could I possibly hope to get past all those guards, especially when I myself was a hunted fugitive with such a large price on my head? I had talked myself out the day before. Now that I had a hope of securing Gairith's help I went in silence, deep in my own thoughts. Gairith did not seem to mind. He chatted on whether or not I answered or even listened. I suspect he could as well have talked to the horse or the dog.

We followed close after the royal procession, part of a long train of those following, and so reached the inn just at dusk. The courtyard was a bustle of activity. Torches were just being lit, horses were being stabled, people were rushing about, looking busy and efficient. The inn was a big rambling building with many doors, windows, archways and entrances and that gave me some hope. It would be hard to guard every entry point.

For me the inn was too crowded, too expensive, too noisy and far too dangerous as a lodging. Gairith and I sat on a stoop outside the kitchen, sharing my nuts and dried fruit and staying safely in the gloom. Later he planned to roll out his mat under the trees. He had already penned his sheep in a temporary pen and paid the fee. Gotha was lying at our feet. She growled suddenly and in the next moment a big burly guardsman burst out of the kitchen door, shouting, "On your feet, you lot!" as he kicked Gairith. Instantly I had my hand on Gotha to prevent her from biting this fool and so making all kinds of trouble for us. "We have to move a big tub to the Zarna's room and we need strong backs," the man went on gruffly. Light from the open door had suddenly flooded our little private spot. I was terrified of being recognized.

Gairith jumped to his feet. "You can count on us," he said amiably, as if he had not just been kicked in the rump. "Show us the tub."

I followed after them, shuffling along and keeping my head down. The tub was a long, deep, metal box. It had a two-sided lid that closed down the middle with a hole toward one end to go around a neck. It even had a latch. This was an old fashioned device called a modesty tub that was still sometimes used in public places. A grand lady could bathe modestly under that lid in a room full of courtiers. I immediately saw possibilities there that had more to do with concealment than with modesty.

Earlier that evening I had circled the inn, taking the dog with me and pretending to look for some lost item. In my rounds I had seen a big tree with branches close to the window. Though there were guards posted there, I still thought that might be my way out if only I could find a way in. Now this tub might be my entry. The guard was just saying, "You will need at least three other men."

Gairith hefted one end of the tub and groaned. "I will need at least six altogether, no less."

"Well find them yourself and get on with it. I have more important things to deal with. Look for me later and you will each get a copper for your efforts. And hop to it quickly. It does not do to keep the Zarna waiting for her bath." Though the words were respectful enough, the tone was mockingly suggestive.

After he left, Gairith and I were alone for a moment with the tub. "The answer to your prayers," Gairith whispered. "You can help carry it up and so gain access to her room."

"Yes, but then I will be put out with the rest of you. I need to be able to stay. Put me inside the tub and fasten the latch on the lid."

His eyes grew wide with fear. "Are you very sure? It looks more like a coffin than a tub to me. You could not pay me enough money to get in there. You are either very brave or very foolish or you love her very much."

"She is my life," I said simply. Then I took some money from my pouch and held it out to him.

"I do not want your money," he said quickly, taking a step back. "I do this out of my own heart."

"I know you do, but I want to give this to you anyway. You have contributed to my life and now I want to contribute to yours, which I know to be a hard one. This may be the last time I see you. An honest bargain among honest folk. But do not refuse me twice, Gairith. I will not offer a third time. Money is not easy to come by on the road."

"Done!" he said, taking the money with a quick flash of his hand and speedily slipping it away. Then, in low voices, we quickly made our plans for getting me out of the room again so I could make my escape.

"Now get me into this thing before I lose my courage altogether. And find some very strong men who are not too curious," I whispered urgently. Then, trying to control my fear, I climbed in. He lowered the lid and latched it. As I heard him walking away, I lay there sweating in the cool night air as if I were lying under the midday sun. If anything went wrong I was dead. If he did not come back I was latched in and helpless. I could not call out. And what if he decided now was his moment to betray me? He would never have a better chance. He could even say he had captured me single-handed. And what if one of those men decided to lift the lid? My only weapon would be surprise and that would not last long. The questions spun in my head. I began to regret my rashness. After what seemed like hours I heard harsh male voices and suddenly I was being roughly hefted up.

46

"You said it was heavy but I had not expected anything like this," one voice grumbled and another answered, "My Lady must have locked all the jewels in the kingdom in this tub. Perhaps we should look and see."

"The guard has expressly forbidden us to open it. There are some very personal belongings of the Zarna's in there." Hearing that I breathed a deep and silent sigh of relief. He did not mean to betray me after all. I was even beginning to feel hopeful. Perhaps this was going to succeed after all and in just minutes I was going to see Aranella face to face.

They hauled and bumped me along, grumbling the whole way, none too careful about corners and doorways. Suddenly I was at a slant, obviously going up the stairs. I braced my feet and stiffened my back, trying not let all my weight slide to the low end. They bumped me on several steps and then I was being carried flat again. I heard some discussion, probably with the guards outside the door, then the sound of a door opening, a few more steps and I was unceremoniously dropped to the floor. The pain in my arm almost made me scream aloud. Only fear kept me silent.

Next I heard Dharlan's voice saying, "Thank you lads. Set it over there under the spigot and take that other one away with you; it is much too small for my Lady. Here is a pence each for your trouble." With much clattering of metal my wheel-less carriage was moved one last time. Then there was a little tap on the lid and Gairith said, "I trust her Ladyship will enjoy this tub and its contents." I suppose that was his way of saying good-bye.

Amairi

Traveling with the Wanderers was certainly full of surprises for me. Some things only took a little getting used to and others shocked, at least at first. Chief among those that shocked me was the casualness and ease of personal relations between men and women. Among the Shokarn of Maktesh sexual connections were strictly regulated, at least for women. Any deviation from the rules was harshly punished. Of course, much went on in secret. There were always whispers and innuendoes, slander and malice. Among the Wanderers there was much good-natured teasing and banter but little gossip. Everything was out in the open. Indeed, secrets were hard to keep when everyone traveled together that way.

Several of the men found me attractive. They teased and flirted quite openly, something I had never experienced before. After all, I had gone from working on my parents' estate and never thinking of myself as a sexual being to finding myself married to a man who was brutal in bed and violent out of it. At first I was embarrassed and confused and even frightened, but I watched how other women did and listened to their lewd jokes and comments. After a while I learned a little of the game. I soon saw there was no harm in it and that, in fact, it was quite safe. No man among the Wanderers would think to touch a woman without her permission. It would go against the Cerroi.

Two men in particular, Ethran and Morghail, seemed to favor me and of the two it was Ethran I found most attractive. Though he had a rough appearance, he seemed gentle and kind. I liked to watch the nimble way his hands moved on the ferl. The music he played on it went right to my heart. Sometimes, now that I had healed, I even wondered how those hands might feel moving on my body. One morning I met Ethran by accident at the edge of the woods where I had gone to gather berries and he said, "Lady, if I tease too much you must tell me. It is only that I find you most desirable and my foolish mouth does not know how to be quiet."

"Ethran, I have to confess that I am drawn to you also. But after all that has happened to me, I am still too fearful. Besides, I have no experience with this game of love. I was married against my will to a man I loathed. He used his sex as a weapon. That is all know of closeness with men."

"I grieve for what happened to you, Amairi. Such things would never have happened at my hands. If you ever decide you want company in your bed, rest assured, I would be kind and considerate and most of all I would give you pleasure, something it seems you have never had."

"But I want no children!" I blurted out.

"Wanderers only have children by choice. We know how to prevent quickening. This life is too hard to have children by accident and carelessness. How could that be fair to a child?"

I put my hand on his arm and looked him straight in the eye saying, "If I ever change my mind Ethran and decide I want that kind of company, you will be the first to know, I promise." Then, on impulse, I put my hands on both sides of his face and stood on my toes to kiss him on the forehead. I was immediately overcome with embarrassment. With my face burning red, I rushed back to camp.

For the next few days we were on the road. I saw little of Ethran as he was in charge of the extra horses. But when we stopped at a place where we were planning to camp for several days I remembered his offer with a little shiver of excitement and suddenly thought, *Why not? After all, I am my own person now. I no longer belong to Horvath and I am certainly not a proper Shokarn lady anymore. Why should I obey their rules? Why not please myself?*

Feeling very daring, I went to look for Ethran. He was talking to a group of men. I blushed with sudden shyness and was about to slip away again when he looked up and saw me. With a nod of his head he left his companions and came to my side. "You are looking for me, Lady?"

"Please call me Amairi, Ethran. Lady reminds me of all that past. I came looking for you because I thought . . . perhaps . . . you said . . ." I blushed again and was so overcome with embarrassment I could not go on.

"Ah . . ." he said softly. With no further words he took my hand in his and kissed it lightly, starting at the finger tips, going on very slowly to the palm, the inside of my wrist, up my arm and ending with the inside of my elbow. By the time he finished I was shivering all over. I had never felt so aroused.

"Come," he whispered, holding my hand in his. He collected some blankets and gave me something to drink. "For safety," he murmured. Then he led me further out into the field, away from camp, where he spread the blankets over the damp grass.

"Now will you show me what you know?" I asked, still in my daring mode.

"Whatever you want, Amairi."

I nodded eagerly. Yet when he had me down on the ground and began kissing and touching me, I panicked. Quickly I struggled out of his arms and sat up, panting with fear. "No, please, I cannot! This was all a mistake! I never should have asked you. Let me go!"

Ethran held up his hands. "But I am not holding you," he said quite reasonably as he sat up next to me. "And you know I would do nothing against your will."

Suddenly I was shaking all over and sobbing wildly. "Oh you do not know . . . you can not know . . . so much pain . . . never pleasure . . . never any kindness . . ."

"Amairi, could I hold you just for comfort? It is very hard to see you cry that way and not be able to do anything." He looked about to cry himself. I nodded. Very gently he put his arms around me. Then I turned my face against his shoulder and soaked his shirt with my tears.

When I was calmer, I pulled away and said sadly, "I am sorry to have brought you here for nothing. I thought I wanted you to show me, but I am too afraid."

"Why not show me what you like instead of my showing

you? I am here. Do what you want with me, anything you please."

What an amazing idea! I stared at him in surprise. Suddenly the fear slipped away and the spirit of daring reawakened in me. "I think I would like to kiss you. Yes, I have wanted to do that for a while now. But you must not move; you must not touch me; you must let me do it all." I kissed him softly on the mouth, then on his cheeks, his forehead, his closed eyes, then down the tender curve of his neck. I could feel him trembling under my lips and it thrilled me with a sudden sense of power. I wanted more. I laid him back down and began unbuttoning his tunic, kissing his chest as I went until I had him bare above the waist. He was visibly shivering. Suddenly I wanted to press my bare breasts against his chest. Not bothering with the buttons, I tore open my shirt and hastily slipped out of my trousers. Then I lay down on him, feeling the thrill of flesh on flesh, pressing hard, my hands clutching at his sides, sweat rising between us. "Touch me! Touch me!" I growled in his ear. "Put your hands on my body! Now!"

There was an ache between my legs that needed easing and a fierce ache in my throat. He did as I told him, slipping his hand between my legs. Then, at my body's invitation, he began sliding his fingers inside, sliding them in and out of the amazing wetness that had suddenly blossomed there. The feelings shook me to the core. As his fingers moved, sensations I had never felt before kept rising up through my body until I had to cry out and dig my nails into his back.

Next I wanted his sex inside me. I could feel it throbbing against my leg. I spread my legs and opened wide for him, gasping, "Now! Do it now! I want you inside!" This was nothing like what I had felt with Horvath. There I had been dry and tight, terrified and repelled, and most of all, violated. This was of my own free will, glorious and wild, my body thrusting and surging and grasping for more. The sound of my own voice split the night. Afterward I lay against Ethran, wet and panting, satiated for the first time in my life. Nothing had ever felt so fine.

Jolaina

Over the muttered thanks of the men I suddenly heard Aranella's voice, sharp and peevish. "Why did they have to bother with such a fancy tub. Clean or dirty it matters not to me. I am still their prisoner. I cannot think they care much how I smell as long as I do not try to escape." She spoke in that petulant, aggrieved tone that used to irk me so. Hearing it now made my heart beat faster with love and eagerness. I wanted so much to reach out and touch her, to tell her I was there, but I knew it was not yet safe to move.

Then I heard Dharlan answer, "Take what you can in this life, my Lady. The road ahead of you has many uncertainties. Right now this bath is here and certain. Perhaps it can give you some comfort for what lies ahead." Then she clapped her hands and said sternly, "Out, all of you. Men cannot be present at my Lady's bath. It would be disgraceful. That goes for the guards too. Wait outside."

"But we were told to . . ."

"Out!" she shouted. "You can wait right by the door until it is time to come back. Surely you do not think she is going to fly out the window. There are more guards posted by the foot of the tree."

I could hear the men grumbling and the thud of heavily booted feet. There was some talk with the guards in the hall, then the sound of the door opening, shutting, and being latched again. Next there was the sound of footsteps coming toward the tub. I readied myself, hoping it was Dharlan. Now was the time, before she opened the lid, before she screamed and brought the guards charging in. I was glad they were still talking loudly outside the door as it might serve to cover the sound of my voice. "Pssst, Dharlan, I am here in the tub. Help me lift the lid."

I heard her suck in her breath, but she made no outcry. Soon there were several hands fumbling with the latch. The lid opened and light came in. Then I saw Aranella's beloved face peering down at me with Dharlan looking over her shoulder. As soon as I pushed back the lid all the way and sat up, I noticed someone else in the room. Behind Aranella a little serving girl was staring at me with her mouth open and her eyes bugging out. "Hush!" I hissed in a fierce whisper with my finger to my mouth. "Do not cry out or it will cost our lives and yours as well. And say nothing to anyone of what you have seen here, not ever, not even to a lover, or death surely will follow." Though I did not say whose death, I saw fear flash across her face as she quickly shut her mouth.

Aranella was on me in an instant. She pulled me to my feet, out of the tub and into her embrace. I held her for a moment, crushing her body against mine, hungry for more. Then, with resolve, I pushed her away and said in a low, urgent voice, "I must talk with you this instant and be quickly gone from here. We only have a brief moment of time before my signal comes. Dharlan, run the water to cover the sound of our voices."

Dharlan turned the tap on a large water tank and steam quickly filled the room while Aranella and I talked in hushed tones. As fast as I could I related to her what had befallen me since we were last together. Then she told me in hasty whispers of the plot that had unfolded with Khundorn's rise to power and her imprisonment, all under the pretense of saving her from my evil influence. At the end she said, "The worst of it is that they are holding Nhuriani in some secret place. If I try to escape, they threaten to torture and kill her. On that I have no reason to doubt their word. So as you see, I am their prisoner in more ways than one."

"But I have an escape plan. Come with me, Aranella. I can get you out of here tonight and together we can find a way to free Nhuri."

"I have no idea where she is. If it were only my own life at stake, I would gladly go with you this night and take my chances. But with Nhuri in their hands I am helpless. They say that if I go against them I will only see her again one finger at a time."

Shuddering at her words, I shook my head. "No matter what, I cannot leave you here!"

"But you must! Understand Jolaina, I am not going with you. And if you are captured then everything is lost. With you free we have a little hope."

"And what is to be done? This is a war, Aranella, and they will use everything they can. All the talk on the streets is of the Zarns gathering troops. This time they intend to crush the whole of Yarmald, destroying Hadra power forever and bringing all the Kourmairi of that region under their yoke."

"That is all the talk here too. Listen Jolaina, they are planning a huge gathering on Midsummer Day at the Parade Grounds halfway between Eezore and Maktesh. The Zarns are hoping to consolidate their power and force Maktesh to join the alliance. Khundorn is prepared to help them in this — for his own advantage, of course. He means to use me as his unwilling tool. On that day, before everyone, I am supposed to declare for Khundorn, give him my blessing and, in effect, make him Zarn of all Maktesh. Everything we worked so hard to build will be destroyed. When I said I would do no such thing he smiled at me in that humorless menacing way he has and asked, 'Zarna, have you forgotten your little sister?'

"They intend to have Nhuri stand beside me so I can declare for both of us. Then I am to be retired to the summer palace for the rest of my life. That will probably not be long. Soon, if not right away, I will likely meet with a much regretted fatal accident. Once I am done away with, Nhuri will also die. They cannot afford to let us live. Alive, we would always be a challenge to their power. I am too popular in Maktesh. That is why they need me to publicly pass on the power."

"Please Aranella, come away with me and we can . . ."

"No! Save yourself, Jolaina! They are looking for you everywhere. It is very dangerous for you to be here. You can still go free and make another life; my fate is already sealed. There is no way I can escape their plans for me as long as they have Nhuriani."

"Not true, Aranella. You said yourself that if I am free there is still hope. Do not give up. I will be there on Midsummer Day with many others. I am going to the Hadra for help. This concerns them also. Watch, listen, pay close attention for any signal. Listen for anyone saying *Otta*. That is what I will call myself until this trouble is over and I can afford to be myself again. Somehow I will have you both safely out of their hands, I promise. Now I must be quickly gone."

She shook her head and there were tears in her eyes. "Kiss me, Jolaina. We may never see each other again."

"Oh Aranella!" I wrapped my arms around her and fell into that kiss like a beggar at a banquet. Before I was altogether lost in her embrace I heard my signal. Warning bells were ringing and shouts of, "Thief! Thief! Stop that thief!" rose from the other side of the inn courtyard. Soon there were more shouts from other directions, much noise and commotion and the sound of many people running. In an instant I was at the window peering down into the gloom with Aranella at my side. Those guards who had been on watch below her window were now dashing around the corner and out of sight. It was time, the only chance of escape I would have. I gave Aranella a quick kiss, swung onto the branch and slithered down the tree at reckless speed. When I dropped to the ground and rolled, the pain in my shoulder made me gasp for breath.

I found my little horse nearby and rode off as quickly and silently as I could, very glad for the commotion on the other side of the inn. In my heart I was thanking Gairith for his good work and hoping no harm came to him. I rode for a short while and then turned off into the woods where I found myself a hiding place and lay for a while in the leaves, resting and listening to the sounds of pursuit, going out and coming back.

If they had known they were chasing the Zarna's muirlla instead of a poor sheep thief they might not have given up so easily. When all was quiet again, I rode on through the dark hours, making my plans. I would find my brother, Douven, and send him to the Hadra of Zelindar for help since I was too weak now to go myself. I could think of nowhere else to turn. There was certainly no one in Maktesh I could safely ask for anything even if I could find my way back into the city without being caught. Anyone I spoke to would be endangered by my presence and might well betray me. Aside from Aranella and Dharlan, Douven was perhaps the only person in the whole world that I trusted.

Amairi

Something had awakened in my body, some dragon of desire and now I was the one pursuing Ethran. I was insatiable. Finally he said to me one night, "Amairi, I am a man, not a bull, and I have a man's limitations. If you desire more than I have strength for you should seek another."

He was laughing, but I was shocked and hurt and shamed. With a cry I sat up and burst into tears. "You do not want me any more. I thought since we were lovers we would be only with each other. I thought we might marry soon."

He sat up next to me and tried to put a comforting arm around my shoulders. When I shook him off, the look he gave me was one of tender amusement. "Among the Wanderers, we gift our bodies freely," he said thoughtfully. "We do not own each other. Some marry, but that is a very solemn promise made for life, not taken lightly or for the body's needs. I do not wish to hurt your feelings, Amairi, but in truth I am your first passion, not your life companion."

"You would not be angry or beat me if I took another lover?" The very idea amazed me.

He shook his head. "I would never raise a hand against you no matter what you did and I might get more sleep if you shared your passion elsewhere. The book of the body has just opened for you. There are many wonderful stories in it. You need to read far more of them before you try to find your life's companion. Then you can remain true to your promise for only then will you really know. Otherwise you would always be longing and wondering."

"But you will still share love with me sometimes?"

"Gladly, with pleasure," he said, hugging me to him. "But not every night."

And so, for the first time in my life, I was released into the passions of the body to make my journey of discovery there. Morghail was waiting and ready for me now that I no longer shook my head at him, and he proved himself to be a skilled, attentive lover. Even young Ablon, who had just joined the camp with his mother Shamu, was glad to share my bed. I found him gentle and playful, as new at this game of sexual pleasure as I was. I was shameless at that time, casting my eyes in all directions.

The only one who rebuffed my advances was Douven, a beautiful young man who seemed to drift in and out of the camp, always staying at the fringes of things. I found myself watching him hungrily, but he would not return my looks. He was lame and I think it made him shy of women. As for Vondran, he and I circled around each other, yet we did not connect in that way. There was a powerful attraction there, along with an even more powerful warning of danger. I sensed that this was not a safe man for me to play with.

My body was no longer my enemy. It was my friend and we were on a wonderful adventure together. In Maktesh I would have been called a whore and worse. If I were still married I would have been stoned to death with no mercy. Here people smiled on me with fond indulgence. I even grew used to the lewd banter they seemed to enjoy so much and occasionally added my own voice to it. All this while I noticed Vondran watching me with a strange, unreadable expression on his face. It made my breath catch and my stomach flutter with desire.

One night Nastal came and sat next to me at the fire circle. Soon she was leaning against me sleepily. After a while she asked if she could lie down with her head in my lap. When I nodded, she did so and even shut her eyes. I thought she was asleep though she kept moving and shifting her body against mine as if trying to make herself comfortable. Suddenly she opened her eyes again. Staring up at me in a most disconcerting way, she whispered, "Do not give it all away to the men, Amairi. Give women a chance too. Some of us might find you most desirable. I know I do."

"Wo-wo-women?" I stuttered. When the meaning of her words sunk in I blushed deeply. My skin burned. I would have jumped to my feet and been gone from there in an instant if her weight had not held me fastened to the ground. "Muirlla," I whispered in shocked surprise. I looked down at her lovely young face and felt a strange mixture of revulsion and desire crawling up my spine.

"Puntyar, that is what the Kourmairi call us," she said bitterly, staring back at me, her large dark eyes full of pain and longing. "That is why I could not marry. That is why I fled to the Wanderers. Wanderers make no judgment on the nature of love, only that there be kindness and consent on both sides. Do I frighten or revolt you? You left their other judgments behind. Can you not leave this one too?"

I kept looking into her eyes, feeling drawn in as if into a pool of water. Part of my mind kept saying, *Leave! Get up and go! Right now! Right now!* Instead, never taking my eyes from hers, I kept leaning forward very, very slowly until my lips touched hers and her arms slipped up around my neck. Then I sank into that kiss as if I had waited for it all my life. With our lips together, I slowly slid down into her embrace and the voice in my head was silenced. Miraculously, people moved away until we had that part of the fire circle almost to ourselves.

That night we did nothing more than kiss and hold each other. But soon after, when we could find a place to be alone, Nastal showed me a whole other way of being lovers and introduced me to the mysteries of a woman's body. When she caressed my body with hungry hands or took my nipple between her lips and then between her teeth, it was not like a stranger exploring my body; it was as if she knew me already, knew me from the inside. It was as if I were guiding her hand or her mouth with my own longings and desires.

When she finally put her head down between my legs and her tongue touched my sex, I thought I would die right then and there of fear and shame. Then everything shifted suddenly and I thought I would die of pleasure. Men had tried this and I had always pushed them away. They had accepted my refusal. Nastal was far more persistent, pressing my legs apart with her arms and moaning with desire. As soon as I let myself accept the gift of her mouth on my flesh, I found myself moaning with her, carried into a world of sensations I had never even imagined, sensations that sharpened and deepened until I heard my voice crying out like some wild creature and felt my whole body shuddering with release.

Afterward she held me in her arms, stroking my hair and whispering gently to me while I wept for what my body had endured at Horvath's hands. There could have been so much pleasure, if only there had been some love and kindness. Later, when I reached out to love Nastal in the same way she said softly, "Not now, next time. For tonight just let yourself gather in all this pleasure and feel it and sleep on it. Later you can turn it back again, though I must tell you, this one night of loving you has given me more pleasure than anything else in my whole life."

Jolaina

This was certainly a strange way to return to my natal village. I crept into my family's home like a thief in the night, praying that my stepmother and my two little half-brothers slept soundly. I had circled the village, staying far enough away to not set the dogs to barking, and left my horse tied to a tree. When I had crept close to the house, our old dog Tolli had rushed out in a flurry of barking. But as soon as she was near enough to smell me she had come to press against me and lick my hand. Stroking her head, I was suddenly touched and warmed by this one friendly contact in such a hostile world.

I will never forget my father's look of terrified surprise when I woke him by pressing my hand over his mouth and holding a candle up in front of his face. Nor will I ever forget the sudden rush of ugly pleasure it gave me. I leaned over and whispered in his ear, "Be silent and follow me. We must not wake your wife."

Soundlessly he slipped out of bed and followed me into the next room where I set the candle on the table. "Jolaina, this is very dangerous," he whispered urgently. "They are looking for you everywhere. They have been here twice and will no doubt come back again. If they find you here we are all dead."

"All true," I whispered back. "I came here looking for Douven. As soon as I find him I am gone again, with luck as secretly as I came."

"He is not here. He has gone with the Wanderers again."

"Oh, curse the luck!" I whispered louder than I intended.

"Hush, you will wake the children. They must not see you

here. Small mouths tell big stories," my father whispered as he held up a finger for silence. "The Wanderers were here only a few days ago. They are headed for their trading ground by the Burnt Hills. You can probably catch up with Douven there. Now, I beg of you, leave quickly and do not let yourself be seen."

Just as he said that, I heard sounds from the bedroom and slipped back into a shadowed corner. A young woman in a long white bed dress appeared in the doorway. "Who are you talking to, Husband? I thought I heard voices."

"I got up to relieve myself and was talking to the dog. Go back to bed Aniya; it is late."

"But I thought I heard another voice answering."

"Wife, are you questioning my word? Go back to bed now. It is too late to be standing here arguing with your husband."

She turned meekly and left, but not before casting a quick, curious glance around the room. Luckily she did not see me in my dark corner. I certainly had a chance to see her well enough, caught in the candle light, anxious and innocent, very pretty and very young, not much older than Aranella, not much older than his own daughter for that matter. The old goat!

I had a sudden flash of jealousy for my dead mother's sake, all the stranger since I had not been very kind to her myself. In fact I had held her in contempt for her meekness and timidity, and hated her for wanting me to be the same. Or perhaps, truth be told, I was really jealous for myself. My father had not been cruel to me, he was not really a bad man. He had never beaten me. There had always been food on the table and clothes to wear. But I think he never really loved me. I was his useful tool and Douven, with his crooked leg, was his embarrassment. All his love, all his hope and his longing had gone to Korzil, the first born, the bad seed, the one who should have been his pride and was instead his shame. In his yearning disappointment he had nothing left for the rest of us.

And now he had this new family, this pretty young wife who had birthed him two perfect little straight-legged boys and I was nothing but a danger to them. He did not even wish me well or safe on this terrible, frightening, dangerous journey that might easily cost my life. He only wished me gone. He had given them his love and I was left out and bitter with jealousy. Ah well, I am not in these few pages going to try to solve the puzzles of the human heart.

I waited until I heard Aniya settle in the bed and her breathing turned steady. Then, with only a nod to my father, I slipped out as quietly as I had come in. Moments later the candle was blown out and I was slipping through the darkness with Tolli's cool nose pressing itself against my hand. At least my old dog loved and remembered me.

I rode away in the night with the information I needed and no one stopped me. Either they were not watching at that moment or I had been cautious and silent enough to avoid them. For the rest of that night I rode toward the Burnt Hills, keeping to the side of the road and off the cobbles. Each time, when I heard someone coming, I slipped off my horse and into the trees and each time it was more of an agony to re-mount.

Once, as a small company of guards was passing, my horse nickered. Instantly my blood froze. I thought I was surely done for. But they were talking noisily and went by without stopping. Though I rested the next day deep in the woods, I could not sleep. The raging pain in my shoulder flashed up and down my back and I was in a fever from it. By dusk I was almost delirious. It was a struggle just to get to my feet. When I rode on I could tell I was getting weaker. I had to find Douven and entrust him with my mission before it was too late; otherwise all my struggles were for nothing.

It was probably close to midnight before I reached the Wanderer camp. From the shelter of trees at the edge of the cobbled road, I looked longingly across the open field at the great fire and the circle of wagons. Scraps of talk and music floated to me on the wind and occasionally the smell of the fire and even the smell of food which made my stomach clench with hunger. I dared not cross the field. If there were guards watching for me I would get myself quickly caught and probably endanger the Wanderer encampment as well. I was so close and yet so far. Suddenly I wanted to cry, a luxury I had not allowed myself since this all began. I think it was the fever weakening me. All my reserves were gone and I still had this last dangerous piece of work to do.

Amairi

Nastal did not love in the easy, open way the Wanderers did, without jealousy or the desire to possess. Indeed, she did not fit the Wanderer mold. She was bold and abrupt, impatient with subtlety and unwilling to be bound by any rules. Almost like a child, she was easily hurt, quick to anger, rarely tactful and often rude, full of her own newly emerging power. Young, vulnerable, and prone to erratic changes, she was certainly a challenge to my patience. Yet, with all that, I still found her very appealing, though we were not without our differences.

To me, being a Wanderer came naturally, like breathing or walking. Whether I stayed with them or not, whether I eventually wore their brand or not, I would always be a Wanderer in my heart. These were my people. I saw in their ways what I needed to know for my life. For Nastal they were only a temporary refuge. Now that she had connected with me, she wanted me away from them. She even talked of visiting the Hadra city of Zelindar and made me very curious, though I thought it might only be a ruse to separate me from my other lovers. Like a ferocious dog she managed to keep most of them at bay. Still, since she satisfied me so thoroughly, I did not much care. No one had ever loved me so fiercely. It was both very gratifying and a little frightening. I let myself be carried along by her desires and so did not try to change the course of things.

One morning, I woke with the imprint of her body still upon mine. Nastal had slept all night curled against me, her legs pressed into my legs, her arm a pleasant weight around my waist, her breasts pushing soft and insistent against my back. She must have left only moments before. The warmth of her presence was still cooling in the morning air. I sat up quickly, feeling bereft. I wanted the deep comfort of that contact back again, that warm closeness that was so new and unfamiliar to me and was becoming so necessary. Looking around, thinking to call her back, I saw her in a heated argument with Vondran, gesturing fiercely.

Quickly I slipped out of our shared bedroll and went to her side. Her face was flushed with anger and her eyes flashed when she turned to look at me. "I want to take you with me to Zelindar and Vondran is insisting we must take other Wanderers with us as if I could not keep you safe. He wants Morghail and Comanth and even Undaru to come with us and he wants Morghail to choose some others. Why do we need a whole troop to get from here to the coast? Why do we need Morghail who cannot keep his eyes off you?"

"Nastal, you are being led more by jealousy than wisdom," Vondran said firmly. "Where hands do not touch without consent, eyes can do no harm. Besides, Morghail is one of the best guides we have and he is also familiar with the Hadra. You are not a Wanderer. You have only sheltered with us for a while and I have no say over you. With Amairi it is different. She has taken the oath from me and as leader here I have some responsibility." Then, turning to me, he said, "Of course I cannot oblige you to do anything against your will Amairi, but you accepted me as leader when you took that oath so now you must listen to what I have to say. After that, you can make your own choice.

"There are many dangers between here and the coast, the greatest of these being the Drylands and the Muinyairin. The

Wanderers have old agreements with the Muinyairin and so can pass safely. Other travelers may not be so lucky. Some of their bones lie scattered on that dry and bristly landscape. Also Zelindar is not so easy to find. There are no signs along the way. The Kourmairi of the coast are very protective of the Hadra and as likely to send you in the wrong direction if they think you look suspicious. Also for you Amairi, traveling this way will all be new and you may need more support and protection than one person can provide.

"Nastal here has far more passion and courage than she has wisdom or experience. She can light the torch, but I would not yet trust her to carry it very far. For all those reasons I think you should take other Wanderers with you. It would be much safer. I would like to see you come back here alive. Also I want a report from you on how the Hadra are preparing for this war that will likely engulf them soon if we cannot find some way to stop it. We are going to be camped here for a while at this Gathering Ground by the Burnt Hills, hoping to meet with other Wanderers for an exchange of goods. Now think it over carefully and let me know what you decide."

I threw up my hands. "Enough words, Vondran. There is no need for all that. What you say is true. I, for one, would feel safer and more comfortable with a Wanderer escort." As I spoke I did not dare look in Nastal's direction, fearing to meet anger in her eyes.

"But it was to be my trip!" she burst out. "Why did you have to interfere and spoil it, Vondran? What business was it of yours? You are no different from my father."

"If I am no different from him then perhaps he is not such a bad man after all. Nastal, it is your trip only if you go alone and are not a Wanderer. Once you ask another to go with you, especially a new Wanderer, it becomes my business. When Amairi has been a Wanderer a little longer and done some more traveling about, I will not need to be so protective."

Still not looking at her, I said sternly, "Nastal, if you want me to come you must give some thought to what I need and let me have some choice in the matter. Otherwise I will not go."

I was taking a risk. She might tell me not to come. By now I was very curious to see this Hadra city, almost as curious as she was. And also I very much wanted to travel with Nastal and share this adventure. But I knew Vondran was right; I was not experienced enough and Nastal was too hasty, too wild and impetuous. She looked down at the ground and scuffed her feet angrily in the dirt. Much to my surprise, when she finally looked up at me there were tears in her eyes. "I wanted to be one who was there when you needed something. I wanted to be the one who protected you," she said softly, "Not those men."

I did not laugh or remind her that I was older and had survived many hard things on my own or mention that some of those Wanderers escorting us might well be women. I was touched by her love. No one had ever loved me in that way before and it was certainly exciting. Yet it also had its other darker side. It made me uneasy, as if she had an invisible little cord tied around my wrist and could tug on it at any moment.

In the end only Morghail, Comanth and Undaru came with us. As Morghail stayed clear of my bed, not even flirting with me, and the other two seemed to have a growing interest in each other, that part of the trip was peaceful enough. For me, all of it was new and exciting. There were many things along the way that I had never seen before. But I will not speak of it here as I have written elsewhere a separate, detailed account of that trip that I will attach to this journal.

Jolaina

When I could collect myself again, I slipped off my horse and began circling the field by keeping to the edge of the woods. My little horse wove easily through the trees where a larger animal might have balked. My plan was to come into the field from the back where the trees were closer to the camp and there was less chance of being seen from the road.

I was more than a quarter of the way around the field, and had just begun to think I would succeed when they were on me. I never heard a sound. All my training availed me nothing against the two of them. All in an instant they had a hand over my mouth and my injured arm twisted up in back of me so that I sagged against my captors with a groan of pain.

"Why are you creeping up on a Wanderer camp?" one of them whispered harshly in my ear. "We have been following you since you left the road. What kind of mischief do you intend here?"

I mumbled against the hand and he lifted it slightly. "The truth," he hissed in my ear. "We need no lies. These are dangerous times. The truth now!" Then he jerked my arm for emphasis.

"Please let go of me," I gasped. "I took an arrow in the shoulder. The wound is festering and very painful."

"A woman," he said in surprise and released me immediately.

I sank to the ground, tears of pain streaming down my face. "Are you Wanderers?" I asked in a choked whisper.

"Of course we are Wanderers. What else would we be? We are the sentries this night for the camp. What do you want here? Anyone with honest business in a Wanderer camp rides in openly."

"I was afraid you were the guard. I am a hunted fugitive and cannot ride openly anywhere. I am seeking my brother Douven to ask him to go on an urgent errand. Terrible things are happening. I need him to go to the Hadra of Zelindar with a message from me."

"Jolaina?" The other one said softly. I was surprised by the sound of the voice to learn that this one was a woman. "You must be Jolaina. The guards are beside themselves with fury that you slipped through their hands. They are telling terrible stories of you and seeking you everywhere. They have already been here twice to question Douven and will no doubt be back. I think they are watching the camp."

"Do not say my name aloud here again. Call me Otta. That is what Douven called me when he was little. I have no doubt the guards are watching the camp; that is why I came creeping in through the woods."

"Sit there a moment, do not move," the one who held me said. Though he was still speaking sternly, there was a little more kindness in his voice. He released my arm and stepped away for a moment to talk in whispers to the woman. When they came back they motioned me up on my horse. "Come with us and be silent," the woman said. "My name is Shamu and this is my son, Ablon."

It shamed me, but I had to ask for help in mounting my horse. The pain in my shoulder was too great for me to use my hand and I had almost no strength left in my legs. The man, Ablon, took the reins of my horse and Shamu followed on her horse. In this way, helpless and half dead, I was escorted into the Wanderer camp.

We went no further than the edge of the woods. There was a smaller circle of wagons there and another fire. It was situated so that one could enter without being seen from the road. Ablon stopped my horse and Shamu said, "I will go find Vondran and Douven. Douven must identify you so we are sure this is no trick and Vondran will say what we are to do with you. Do not move from here or make a sound or speak to anyone till I come back with them."

"Remember to call me Otta, then Douven will know," I whispered desperately. "It is much too dangerous to say my real name aloud here."

I was nodding on my horse's back, almost gone out of consciousness from pain and fatigue, when suddenly Douven touched my arm. I startled from my newly-learned habit of fear. Then tears sprang to my eyes at the sight of his beloved face. "Oh Sister, what has happened to you?" he gasped. With a groan of relief I slid into his arms.

Between them, Douven and Ablon half carried me to the fire circle. I saw Shamu there talking to a tall man with long, tangled red hair and a red beard. As my two helpers lowered me down, Shamu and the man quickly came to my side. Almost immediately a little crowd of Wanderers gathered around us. "Sit down, all of you," the red-haired man said sharply. "If we have watchers we do not want them to know anything out of the ordinary is happening here." Then to me he added, "Good evening Otta, Welcome to our Wanderer camp. I am Vondran-The-Red, what passes for leader among these Wanderers. I hear you have led the guards on quite a wild chase. You are the talk of Garmishair. Every traveler coming into this camp tells tales of you. Now tell us your story yourself. What brings you here among us in the dead of night?"

"Wait, Vondran, let her lie down on a mat. I think she is badly wounded," Shamu remonstrated.

"No," I said quickly. "If I lie down, I may pass out. I need to tell my story now, while I still have the strength, and then be gone from here. They will be back soon to look for me."

"If you are going to do anything at all you must eat. You look half-starved." With that she went to a pot at the fire and brought me back a steaming bowl of food. And so, with Douven sitting next to me, lending me the support of his arm and helping me eat, I told Vondran my story from the moment Dharlan had awakened me. Then, over Shamu's objections, Vondran asked me many sharp questions about the different factions in Maktesh and what they might be planning. He also got from me as much information as I had about the other Zarns. After that some of the other Wanderers questioned me. When they were done, Vondran said, "What a shame you were not here a few days earlier. A small party of Wanderers has just left for Zelindar. They could have taken your message."

I shook my head vehemently. "No! No one else! Douven is the only one I would trust to deliver that message."

"Ah well," Vondran said with a shrug. "As it must be. Perhaps he will catch up with them on the way." Then he turned to my brother. "So, Douven, are you willing to go on this mission?"

"Of course!" Douven was instantly on his feet.

"Then you had best leave tonight for we have only a little time. Take Ablon to be your guide and have him choose two or three others to go with you. You will need their help dealing with the Muinyairin of the Drylands and then in contacting the Hadra who are not always so welcoming to strange men."

"Not Ablon," Shamu interrupted. "I will need his help in getting Otta to the refuge and trying to heal her. She will die soon if that wound is not tended to."

"Larameer and Rhondil then," Vondran said with some impatience. "They are some of the best among us. Go tell them quickly Shamu and let them choose the others." Then he turned back to Douven. "And you, make yourself ready while your sister writes her message. Then either commit it to memory or be ready to chew it up and swallow it if you are taken. Take our fastest horses and be gone from here as quickly as you can. There is little time." He stood up and looked down at me, shaking his head. "So, the pieces are falling into place in the great game. This time the Wanderers will have to play a part."

I gave him a sharp look. "I thought Wanderers did not mix in the affairs of house-bound mortals."

"You mean the Ganja? Sometimes, for the sake of peace, we bend the rules and try to tip the scales. This is such a moment. Much is at stake here, perhaps even the survival of the Hadra. They are the future for that part of the world. As long as they are a power on the coast there is a chance for some freedom there. If they go under, Zarn rule will hold everything in its grip.

"And the Hadra — though they appear so strong and bold

they are really a very fragile flower, just beginning to bloom. If they are destroyed they will not come again on this earth and all the hope they bring dies with them. The Zarns know that. That is why they band together this time. The Wanderers have a high stake in this. Our very way of life may be threatened. But we must play in such a way that we do not show our hand."

Then he shook his head, saying, "We already knew there was talk of war against the Hadra. We did not know there was also a plot afoot against the Zarna's life. Write your message Otta. The game waits on your move."

Shamu had been rummaging around in a wooden box fastened to the back of one of the wagons. She handed me pen and ink and one sheet of yellowed, water-stained paper. With a shaky hand I wrote, *To the Zarna of the Hadra, in this dangerous time of war it is imperative for your people and mine that we meet immediately. Since I am too weak from a wound to come to you I must insist that you come to me with ten to twenty of your best and most trusted warriors. An invasion of Zelindar is being planned. The Zarna is being held captive to force her hand in the matter of war against the Hadra and the coast. It is my brother Douven who carries this note. He will tell you who I am, answer any questions you may have and lead you here.*

When I was done, Douven came to kneel by me. He gently put his arms around me and kissed my cheek. "What a strange way to meet again, Sister. May the Goddess heal you and the Cerroi keep you safe till I come back."

"May speed and luck ride with you Douven. I am sorry to send you into such danger, but I had nowhere else to turn."

"I am honored to be the chosen messenger. At least on a horse I am as fast as any man." Then he stood up and was gone into the night.

As soon as he left, Shamu tried to help me out of my shirt. It was glued to my shoulder and back with dried blood and pus. With the help of others she cut it away and began applying hot compresses. When I started to cry out she shoved a rolled up rag in my mouth. "Bite on that for silence. I am sorry for the pain but I have no choice." I managed to keep my silence while tears ran down my face and sweat poured from my body.

The moment Shamu was done they laid me down gently on a mat, covered me and sat talking about me over my head, planning where they would take me and how. When I objected Shamu said sharply, "Hush, we know better than you do right now what you need. At this moment you are helpless as a new baby and half out of your mind with fever." After several plans were proposed and rejected it was decided that they would take me by wagon to the top of the hill above the camp, a place they called " 'Dragon's Head.' "

I immediately protested in a hoarse whisper which was the best I could manage, "I must keep moving or they will find me. Any road a wagon can go by the guards can follow."

"It is one of our secret places. We hide the entrance to that road. Only a Wanderer who knows the signs can find it."

"I would not feel safe being still somewhere."

"And you will soon be dead if you are not still long enough to heal. Rest easy, warrior. We have been at this business for quite a while. In a land where violence rules, the Wanderers have survived a long time by their wits. Never fear, we will keep you safe and cure you and make sure you are ready to meet your fate at the appointed time."

Noya

I have had no chance to write here for a while. If I do not do it now, I fear the sweep of events will soon make writing impossible. As it is, I am not writing in the early morning as I did before, but late at night, by lamp light, hoping that at this hour no one will interrupt my work. So much has happened since I last sat down at these pages. Things seem to be moving faster and faster, falling into place or perhaps falling apart. I think I am beginning, though only dimly, to see my part in the pattern.

For safety, my first act as Councilor was to advise that we clear the Zildorn of its treasures and store them away in the great cave chambers beneath it — all the books and accounts contained in the archives, and all the tapestries and paintings and statues in the building. Also that we hide there whatever in the city is fine or old or irreplaceable, especially the *Mother and Daughter* sculpture that has stood in the central circle since it was first made so many years ago by Kara the Potter and her helpers, as well as the image of the *Great Mother* that sat in front of the Zildorn at the very top of Third Hill.

There was considerable muttering and grumbling about doing all this work, but after all, I had been chosen Councilor for a reason. I also saw to it that a store of seeds was set aside there as well as a stash of dried food, clothes, clean water and whatever else we would need if we were attacked. Then the entrance was made secret from the eyes of curious visitors.

After that the city seemed to me bare and sad, robbed of its ornaments. We still had flowering trees and shrubs and banks of flowers for the adornment of our streets, but I particularly missed the *Mother and Daughter* that I had said good-morning to every day of my life. We did a final ritual before the image of the Goddess, washing her feet, wreathing her with flowers and praying for a peaceful outcome to our troubles before we also hid her away. I wondered if she would remember us there in the dark. When all that had been taken care of I went about the city with a heavy heart, not at all sure what came next in this strange dance with war. Unknown to me, events were already rushing toward us.

The day after all the hiding was done, a small group of riders appeared. I was very glad they had not come sooner and found us at our secret work. Pathell brought them to me in the Zildorn: Amairi, a Shokarn woman turned Wanderer;

Nastal, a young Kourmairi, who I assumed by her looks and gestures to be Amairi's lover; and three Wanderer men, one of whom, Morghail, I already knew.

The two women were looking all about them in amazement as if they had just walked into paradise. I wanted to tell them it had all been much more beautiful a few days earlier. Instead I kept my silence on it and let Pathell lead them away again. She was to be their guide in the city. They would probably follow her about for a while like love-struck children, looking at all the wonders of Zelindar. I had seen that look before and even been the object of it, but right now my mind was on other things. I found myself wishing they had chosen some better time for their visit.

Later Morghail returned and we talked at some length. For privacy we sat next to each other on one of the little window seats set in the carved arches of the great library windows. Those windows looked out over the city and the bay. The sight of the empty shelves in the Zildorn made my heart ache, but aside from that the scene was so tranquil, so ordinary, it was hard to believe a war was on its way. "Is this war real, Morghail? Sitting here, looking out at the peaceful beauty of Zelindar, it hardly seems possible."

"Believe it, Noya. The war clouds are gathering fast. If we cannot find a way to change the course of things, Zelindar will be one of its main targets along with the Kourmairi city of Mishghall. After that the Zarns will try to destroy any settlements they find along the coast.

"I acted as the guide for Amairi and her companion, but mostly I wanted to come and talk to you, now that you are saddled with being Councilor in these troubled times. Vondran wanted me to tell you that the Wanderers are in the game this time. When the Zarns fight only each other we can stand back and watch without taking sides. This is different. We will not let the Hadra go down, not if we can help it. Of course we still have to be careful of how openly we show our hand."

Then he spoke with some admiration of the woman

Amairi. "She is an interesting mix of things, a Shokarn Highborn who fled her husband's violence and became a Wanderer. Before she was married she ran, single-handed, a large estate for her parents. From what I hear she was efficient, fair and kind, an uncommon combination for a Shokarn, especially for an estate owner since that power often lends itself to terrible excesses and abuses. You would do well to cultivate her company, Noya, instead of avoiding her. She walks in two worlds and might be very useful to you in the future."

"It surprises me to hear you speak of people in that way, Morghail, as if they were merely useful tools, to use or discard as we please."

"Hadra, let me speak plainly — if you want to save yourself and your city, you had best use whatever tool comes to hand and not quibble over the niceties of philosophy. Besides, I do not think this woman will lend herself to anything unwillingly. That kindly, gentle manner hides a strong, determined will."

I laughed suddenly at his passionate seriousness. "And what of the Cerroi, Wanderer? What does the Cerroi say of using people in this way?"

"For the Cerroi, for the balance of things, the Hadra are needed in this part of the world and must not be allowed to perish. That is what the Cerroi says on the matter."

"You think it could come to that?"

He nodded and his face looked stern. "Be warned; that is what the Zarns want. That is what they are planning, your utter, complete, and final destruction. They are only waiting for the Zarna of Maktesh to line up with them. Then they will be ready to make their move."

"Will she do that?"

"Not willingly, no. But I hear she has been taken under guard to the summer palace a month early. Her personal advisor is at this moment a hunted fugitive accused of all sorts of unspeakable things. I suppose they hope to bend Aranella's will with Jolaina's tortured body in the usual manner of men in power. But so far, word is that Jolaina has somehow managed to evade their clutches at every turn. The wheels are turning and the game is moving faster, but I suspect they will want to catch Jolaina or kill her before they are really ready to move. Loose, she is a danger to them. Aranella is a new thing in the world, a popular Zarn or rather Zarna, much loved among ordinary folk, and Jolaina is her representative. While Jolaina is still free they are not really safe in tightening the noose and bringing their plot to fruition. Now forget your pride and go befriend Amairi. She is from Maktesh and has some knowledge of that world out there."

"Who knows, I might even befriend her for her own sake. She seems to me worth knowing, for her courage if nothing else."

During those next few days I took Morghail's advice, spending some time with Amairi each morning, showing her the city and answering endless questions. We were both right, Morghail and I; she was worth knowing and she might be useful. How had Morghail said it? *A loving heart, a gentle spirit and an iron will.* She made interesting company.

Jolaina

I lay in the wagon, hearing the muffled murmur of voices and what sounded like rocks, logs and branches being hauled across the road. I was very curious as to how they were concealing the entrance of this road, but I did not have the energy to prop myself up, much less the strength to clamber down from the wagon to see. Sooner than I would have expected, Shamu climbed back into the seat in front of me. A moment later Ablon joined us, mounted on his horse. We set off with Ablon leading the way and Shamu driving the wagon. She

clicked softly to the horses and we were moving again. This
time the horses' hooves must have been muffled and the
harness oiled for we went almost soundlessly. Indeed the
night-singers — the crickets and nightbirds and frogs — made
a loud enough noise to cover our slight sounds. I soon dozed
again.

When I woke next it was the faint gray of dawn and we
were just coming to a halt in front of a little shelter. This hut
was no bigger than a single room, built of red stones right up
against a fire-red outcrop of rock. Ablon jumped off quickly to
give me a hand. Shamu came on the other side. Between them
they helped me down. They would have carried me in, but I
shook my head. "First I have to look around and see where I
am."

"We are at the very top of Dragon's Head, the Fire Hill
that rises above the Wanderer camp. At the bottom of the hill
in this direction is another camp, a secret one, not a place
where we meet and trade with the Ganja, but a secret refuge
for us. Indeed, few Ganja have ever been there, though that
is where you will meet with the Hadra if they consent
to come . . ."

"They will come! They have to come!" I interrupted
fiercely.

Shamu nodded and went on, "If you walk on that little
path around the base of this rock outcrop you come, in a few
steps, to a place where you can look down and see the camp
we left last night. From the top of the rock you can look out
in all directions and see both camps and all the roads. You will
be safe here. From down below our little shelter looks just like
a part of the rock."

"Show me the camp we left." I was so weak I could hardly
stand, even with their help, yet I had to see. I needed to orient
myself. Shamu nodded to Ablon and they helped me around
the corner of that great knob of flame-colored rock. There was
hardly room for three of us on the narrow path. The tree tops

77

dropped away below us in dizzying patterns of swaying green. At the bottom I could see the broad expanse of field with its circles of wagons and beyond it the Zarn's highroad.

Aranella! Oh how I wanted to be on that road, going the other way. Yet here I was, high in this mountain aerie, helpless in the hands of strangers. "Enough now," Shamu said with gentle insistence. "Come lie down and let me see to your wound." I was about to comply when I saw dots moving at the far edge of the road, dots moving fast. Those dots soon materialized into guards, riding hard. As we watched, some of them turned and rode into the Wanderer camp while the rest of them rode on without slowing down. Ablon sucked in his breath, but Shamu said in a firm, calm voice, "Vondran will handle them as he always does." To me she added, "Good thing we got you out of there last night and did not wait for morning."

"All those men, looking for one wounded muirlla," I said in disgust. Suddenly I was filled with bitterness. I turned my back on the view and let them lead me away.

The little shelter itself was sturdily made of stone chinked with clay and straw; a single, modest-sized room with a curtain hung up for privacy. They lowered me onto a pallet made of planks covered with a mat and raised on rocks. Then Shamu went to a crock to fill a cup and shook some yellow powder into it. "Drink this," she ordered, thrusting the cup into my hands.

The taste was so bitter I scrunched up my face and was about to spit it out. Shamu quickly clapped her hand over my mouth. "Drink it all. It will fight this infection that is raging in your body. You do not have to like it, you only have to drink it. As my mother says, 'The bitterer the brew, the better the cure.' That is yellow tharsa, a potent plant, very rare and hard to find, not to be wasted. It will also help you sleep. Right now sleep is what you need more than anything else, sleep and rest."

Agitated, I struggled to sit up again. "No! No! I cannot

sleep long. I have to ride to the summer palace to take word to Aranella that . . ."

She pushed me down gently. "There is nothing that you have to do right now, Jolaina, except try to live through these next few days. In fact, there is nothing that you *can* do. You have already done all you can for Aranella and Nhuriani. At great risk to your own life you have set the wheels in motion to free them. You have done your part. Now all will proceed by the will of the Cerroi. It is out of your hands and in the hands of others. At this moment, sick as you are, you could not even sit on a horse unaided, much less take a hard, long ride as a hunted fugitive. If the guards did not kill you first, the fever surely would. Dead you are no use to Aranella or anyone else, except maybe Khundorn and his men.

"You must believe me, Otta. You would undoubtedly die if you left here now. And that man would be glad to display your body in the streets or perhaps parade your head on the end of a pike. Rest now, Jolaina, and do not try any foolishness. Rest and gather your strength for what is yet to come. Rest, sleep, sleep, sleep, sleep . . ."

There was an insistent voice in my head shouting, *Get up quickly! Go now while you still can! Get up! Get up!* and another one droning on and on, *Rest . . . Sleep . . . Rest . . . Sleep* . . . As this little war was going on inside my head, Shamu's voice began fading away to a murmur. Finally my mind released me, my will flowed out of my limbs like water and sleep laid its heavy hand on me, silencing all voices.

For the next few days I only woke occasionally and stayed awake only long enough for Shamu to feed me, help me relieve myself, change the compress on my wound and drug me again. I no longer struggled or argued. The drug or the fever or the exhaustion had done its work. I was helpless and had no will. If guards had suddenly kicked in the door I would have died where I lay, not having the strength to rise and flee or fight.

After a while I began to stay up for longer periods of time. Finally I was strong enough to go outside and sit in the sun on a long, low bench in front of the shelter. From there I could see down into the secret encampment. Wanderers were drifting in and setting up camp for the travelers. They, at least, seemed to believe the Hadra were coming. I was beginning to have my doubts, but Shamu teased me gently, saying, "Of course they will come. Who could resist such a commanding note from the advisor to the Zarna?"

Ablon I seldom saw as he was often up top keeping watch for us, or off on some mysterious errand. Shamu was also busy, tending the little terraced gardens that kept us fed or working with her healing herbs and tinctures, keeping the shelter well supplied. But sometimes she would bring her loom outside, sit by me and tell me stories of the Wanderers and of her life among them.

"As Vondran says, most of the Wanderers have some dreadful tales to tell of what they are fleeing or escaping. I am one of the lucky ones. I was born a Wanderer. My parents were both Wanderers and so were my grandparents, at least on my mother's side of the tree. I have no horrors to share. On the contrary, mine is a very different problem. Life on the road does not appeal that much to me anymore. But life in a Kourmairi village as a Kourmairi wife, that would surely be like death to me. Never could I live with a settled man and his ideas of what a wife should be. I would like to stay still in one place, yet I could not settle with the Kourmairi. I have learned too much independence from living among the Wanderers. Strange as that may sound, I could only settle with another Wanderer. I wish there was still a Wanderer encampment near Zelindar. Someone told me there used to be one in the old days. I think I could go and make my life there, living between those worlds of Hadra and Kourmairi and Wanderer. Perhaps that would suit my nature best of all."

I saw the look of yearning in her eyes and wondered, *Is everyone always hungry for what they do not or cannot have?* "How is it that the Zarns have allowed the Wanderers so much freedom? How is it that the guards do not kill and torture you as they do with the rest of us? I hear the Zarns even have an old pact with the Wanderers."

"You hear right, though none of us knows how far back the pact goes or who first made it. As it is now, the Zarns do not dare really harm us. We are the river of trade that flows from one Zarn city to another, as well as across Garmishair into Yarmald and back, going all up and down along the coast. That makes us very valuable to the Zarns and they have learned over the years to let the Wanderers be. Wanderers are tricky. It does not do to push us. Sometimes, if pressured enough, we will acquiesce and agree to do something against our will. But soon, though we may smile and say yes and do as we are told, things begin to go awry. In fact things happen that have just the opposite result from the one wanted by the Ganja without the Wanderers appearing to have anything to do with it.

"As to the pact, the story about it goes like this: once the guards killed some young Wanderers because they could not get the information they wanted from them, killed a man, a woman and a baby. The other Wanderers came on this dreadful scene just as the guards were finishing their bloody work but it was already too late to save the young family. The Wanderers burned their dead at a Wanderer gathering place and marked the spot with a huge pile of rocks. After that they vanished from public view for a year. All the Wanderers were gone from their gathering places. Their caravans disappeared from the roads. The word had gone out as if by magic and they did no trade in any part of Garmishair or Yarmald.

"Of course the merchants tried to get up their own caravans to move goods, but it was no use. If they were going between Zarn cities they were attacked by the Thieves Guild. If they tried to cross the Drylands to reach Yarmald they were raided by the fierce Muinyairin. As for going up and down the coast, the roads quickly became impassable with rock slides and mud slides and giant trees across the way. This went on for a whole year. As you can imagine, the Zarns were not happy about this turn of things. After all, their vast wealth rests on what they siphon off from trade. Those poor fools of guardsmen. Of course they were killed for their part in this. If they could have been brought back to life they would, no doubt, have been killed ten times over and probably tortured as well.

"After the year was up, the Wanderers reappeared at all their gathering places and held a commemorative service for the young people who had been killed. In fact, we still remember them every year at our Fall Gather. After that, trade resumed. There were never any formal agreements made between the Zarns and the Wanderers; no papers were signed, no words spoken. But the message was clear and the lesson well learned. Now the guards never kill us or abuse our women. Sometimes, when they come into our camps looking for their own, they may be rude and rough, but no more than is tolerable. They have their line and we have ours. We do not mix in the affairs of Zarns and they leave us alone to live our lives."

"But that is changing..."

"Yes, that is changing. Now tell me about yourself and how you came to be here."

And so I told Shamu of my own life. I spoke a little about my time on the farm before I met Aranella, but mostly I told stories from after she came into my life. I talked on and on about Maktesh and the court and the changes we had been trying to implement before Aranella was made a captive and I myself became a fugitive by the orders of Khundorn and his people.

Shamu was an attentive listener. She leaned forward intently and asked many questions. In the end she encouraged me to write it all down. She even found me ink and pen and some strange rough paper in one of the many secret little niches in the rocks. "Like most Wanderers I cannot read, but it is important that we know your story. Some of us can understand written words and those can read to others around the fire. Besides, I hear the Hadra collect such accounts for their archives in the great Zildorn at Zelindar. Yours might be valuable to them."

I saw the look of hunger on her face when she said she could not read and I offered to teach her in payment for my care or at least to make a start in that direction. Shamu shook her head. "Not now, there is not the time, we would be too quickly interrupted. Maybe later Jolaina, when all this is over. Meanwhile write down your part of it."

Well now I have done what she told me to and I hope she will be pleased. And what else is there to do here? For the moment I am prisoner to my healing and the writing at least gives me some occupation. As advisor to the Zarna I had always kept an account of the day's happenings to look at later and so was often able to correct someone else's fallacy from my own notes. I had never thought to write of my own experiences, but with Shamu's encouragement I have written this account of my flight and escape, working a little longer each day as I gain strength. Next, if I have the time, I will write of my first encounter with Aranella.

Amairi

Oh Zelindar! What an amazing place! I had never seen anything like it. We reached it in the late afternoon of a gray stormy day, arriving wet and weary. Just as we came within sight of the city the slanting sun broke through the cloud cover to light up the white stone buildings that dotted the green hillsides and the great white palace that crowned the third hill. That first sight of it touched my heart in ways I could not begin to explain. I could almost believe we had come to the boundaries of a magic world. *Not magic,* Noya tells me with some impatience, *not magic, for every rock and log has been put there by women's hands, free women who chose to do that work, not slaves or servants who were forced to it by fear or hunger.* But I am leaping far ahead of myself here. Besides there *is* a little magic at work here. The Hadra use their powers, their kersh, to lift and move heavy objects into place and what is that power if not magic?

Zelindar is built on three hills between the Escuro River — which we had to swim our horses across because it had risen from the storm — and an inlet of the sea that is visible from almost any part of the city, and is, at this moment, covered with whitecaps. The city is full of flowering trees and fountains and terraced gardens with many benches for looking out at its glorious views. Some of its streets are so steep and narrow that the Hadra do not allow horses on them; others are broad avenues where a whole procession could easily pass.

We were escorted into the city by sentries. Women and children rushed out to greet us, laughing and talking excitedly. One of them, Pathell, offered to take us to the Zildorn — that is what they call the palace I had seen — to meet with Noya, the Councilor of Zelindar. Though it was only an offer, I understood that it would be wise to comply.

It was amazing how young and unassuming Noya was for one who had so much power. She was also very beautiful. Her wide gray eyes stared back at me with an animal intensity as if she could look right into my soul. And indeed, I suppose she could, for I hear they have the power to read minds.

She greeted us politely enough, saying gravely, "Welcome to Zelindar. May our home be your home. Goddess bless the travelers." Then she asked a little about each of us, except Morghail whom she already knew. Yet even as she talked she seemed distant and distracted. Clearly her mind was not on visiting so we soon went off with Pathell to see the marvels of the city.

I went about looking at everything with wonder and delight, but sometimes I found myself watching Nastal even more than the scene around me. She bubbled over like a child with her joy at what she saw. In her expression, there was none of that sullen wariness to which I had grown accustomed.

Suddenly I saw her as she would have been if she had grown up a Hadra with the blessing of their powers, instead of a Kourmairi with her love of women being the curse in her life. I understood now why she grasped at me and held me so tight. I was the first woman she had been allowed to love openly and also the first who had ever returned her love. How could she be sure there would ever be such a treasure again? But here among women who loved each other freely and walked unafraid in their streets, she seemed like a different person.

That night, when we lay together in the back room of Pathell's house, she whispered intently, "When this is over, if we survive, I want to come back here. I want to live near the Hadra or with them. They tell me these powers are something they are born with, but surely there is something they can teach me or show me or share with me. This is how I want to live. Will you come with me? Please Amairi, promise you will come with me?"

The words "if we survive" stabbed at my heart and a sudden chill ran up my back. Why would someone so young even think such a thing? "What do you mean, if we survive?" I asked sharply.

"With this coming war, who knows how it will touch our lives or what will happen. Will you promise to come back here with me when the time comes?"

It surprised me that Nastal thought this war would touch her young life, though of course there was much talk of it in Zelindar. I was reminded of the grasping greed with which Horvath had spoken of this city. Nastal was so eager, so vulnerable; I could not bring myself to tell her *no*. Yet neither could I tell her *yes* with a free heart. And so I murmured some endearment into her hair and pressed her tight against me. That seemed to suffice, at least for the moment. I understood suddenly how the Hadra skill of reading minds could be a double-sided gift; honesty can sometimes be a very troubling thing.

I thought she was asleep and was just dozing off myself when I heard her voice start up. Speaking softly, almost in a whisper, she said, "I never told you the whole story of my wedding. It was not simply that I did not want to marry. There was much more. I had been lovers with a few different girls when I was younger, always very careful and very secret, but we were playing really, nothing serious. Then Riyani's family came to live in the village; they had some cousins there. For the first time I fell in love. We were together only a few times when we grew careless and were discovered.

"Her family sent her away. My father beat me almost to death. Then he agreed to marry me to Thorgan who had been lusting after me. His family, who were landless, were only too glad to marry their son into my family in exchange for a small plot of ground. When he came to our house I refused, crying and pleading with my father. Thorgan said he knew how to persuade me. When my father left the room Thorgan tied me down and raped me. First he shoved a rag in my mouth for silence. Before he took out the gag he slapped me twice across the face and said, 'Remember this if you ever think to refuse me anything again.'

"I did remember! Only too well! The next morning, before they had me in the confinement of those wedding clothes, I said I wanted to take some flowers to the feasting house. My sisters went with me, to keep watch over me I suppose, but I insisted on going in alone. I managed to set fire to the thatch of the roof with a candle and escaped in the confusion, riding off on a horse belonging to my intended. Desperation had given me courage. I did not care if they killed me for it, I had even accepted my death, but I was not going to marry that man and bind my life to his. Now you see why I can never go home again."

Suddenly she was shaking and sobbing in my arms, all her

86

suppressed grief pouring out in a wild flood of tears. I held her a long while, letting her cry herself out, murmuring in her ear and stroking her hair and back until she finally dropped into a troubled, restless sleep. After that I lay awake myself for quite some time, thinking of her story, seeing how we were bonded by our common past as well as by our bodies.

The next morning, in spite of my lack of sleep, I woke early, eager to see more of the city. Much to my surprise Noya made herself available to be my guide, at least for part of the time. Nastal had gone off riding with Pathell and some of the other Hadra and I was glad to be free of her intense attention, at least for a while. I find myself liking Noya more and more. Her honesty and directness are refreshing. In fact, I find myself liking all the Hadra. They all have that quality of directness, so freeing after the subterfuge and dishonesty of speech in Maktesh. How amazing to hear words that are intended to convey the truth rather than some calculating and convoluted falsehood. They are fine women. When I think of all the ugly things said about them in Maktesh I could cry. But then, I suppose, that is how one must speak of an enemy. It is much harder to kill people if you admire them and praise their virtues.

Noya was even blunt about why she was spending time with me. "Morghail said I should cultivate your friendship, that you might be useful to us." Before I could take offense she added with a charming smile, "But I told him a woman of such courage would also be worth knowing for her own sake." With that she slipped her arm through mine and we walked about the city, asking and answering each other's questions and enjoying each other's company.

Other Hadra greeted us with ease. Being Councilor did not seem to set Noya apart from the rest of them or make her feared. I wanted to know about everything. It amazed me to see a city with no great wealth and no poverty. How could I, who had grown up in a Zarn's city, have imagined a place where there was no power to coerce, no slaves or masters, only equals? All the work here is done by willing hands or at least it is not forced. Things are planned and built and organized and held together by agreement, by the will of many and not the power of the sword. Blessed Goddess, that such a thing is possible!

Not that they are perfect, these Hadra. They are loud, boisterous, and opinionated. Their curtness and directness is sometimes hurtful and would certainly have been considered rude elsewhere, especially in Maktesh where women are mostly silent. No wonder Nastal feels right at home here. I have even heard public arguments on the streets with raised voices and what looked to me like threatening gestures. Yet no blow was ever exchanged, anger dissipated quickly and the quarrelers might even be laughing or hugging each other the next moment. It seems that little is hidden or subtle here, yet under all that openness I feel some strong, silent, secret flow of life that I can neither see nor hear, some great underground river that connects them all together.

Everywhere I look I see things of use that are carved and decorated by women's hands, all done for pleasure, not for show. There is a wondrous combination of skill and love in everything the Hadra make. Horvath used to speak with such hungry greed of the treasures of Zelindar, yet in truth I think it is actually the city itself that is the real treasure. Its beauty is like a living web that binds together all the women who live here now with all who have ever lived here in the past and had some part in the making of it. The city shines like a jewel, a lovely living thing. And yet there seems to be nothing here for men to covet and fight over.

For four days now Noya has gone about with me in the morning and then left me on my own in the afternoon. On the third day she told me with much grief in her voice about all the things missing from the library and the archives and how the Hadra had hidden away all the treasures that had been in the Zildorn, though these were still not treasures such as men could cart off for loot. How I longed to see those books and accounts and pictures and statues. I hoped they were well and safely hidden.

Jolaina

This part is written especially for Shamu as she has begged me to set down on paper how Aranella first came into my life and what followed afterward.

I will never forget the first moment I set eyes on Aranella. And she has said the same of me. I was still a Kourmairi farm girl at the time, working in my father's fields. My father often said he had two worthless sons and a girl who was worth two boys. It was not what he would have chosen; it was what he had. It hurt me when he spoke of my younger brother that way. Douven was kind and loving and my good friend, but he had been born with a twisted leg. In his disappointment my father often spoke harshly to him and treated him unkindly.

I knew my father's words hurt Douven so I tried to soften the blow whenever I could, for I was bound to him by bonds of love and pity that went to my very core. Yet we were as different as could be, Douven and I. I had our father's dark skin and some might say his stubborn hard-headedness as well. Douven was fairer like my mother. He blushed easily and cried easily. My father said he cried like a girl, but since I was a girl and hardly ever cried, I thought he cried like a boy.

My older brother Korzil I will speak of here as little as possible. There was no love between us. He had decided at an early age to be a drunk. He was always a bully, only the drinking made it worse. I learned early to stand up for myself against him, with the fury of my fists if nothing else. Douven never could, so I had to protect him as well.

Well, I have gone far astray from my story. I was trying to explain why I, the only girl in the family, was out plowing the field instead of with my mother in the kitchen. I was twelve or thirteen at the time, big and strong for my age. Though I had just budded new breasts I had taken off my shirt and bound it around my waist as I was all alone there in the field. The heat was fierce, sweat was running down my body, and I was not yet used to keeping myself covered. I had also bound up my skirt to keep it out of my way.

Just as I was finishing the plowing, I heard cries from the village of "Shokarn! Shokarn!" I was certainly in no rush to go look at the Shokarn who usually only came to collect taxes and bully our village. After doing my work at my own pace I undid the plow, fastened up the harness and was headed back through the orchard. Mounted on Vlon's broad back and loudly singing some country song, I was suddenly confronted by three figures on horseback, two richly dressed men and a splendidly attired young woman of near my age.

Not expecting to meet anyone on the way I was still barebreasted. It seemed foolish, now that it was already too late, to struggle my sweaty body into my shirt in a flurry of embarrassment. The men were clearly Shokarn. I made the required bow, no more than was necessary, but my eyes were all for this amazing young woman, this extraordinary apparition. Her gold-blond hair stood out around her head, shimmering like the sun, and her eyes were as blue as the blue velvet dress she was wearing or as blue as the sky above us. She was pointing her finger straight at me, saying imperiously in a loud, commanding voice, "That one! That is the one I want!"

She wanted me! For what? A slave? A servant? A sacrifice? Whatever it was, I was ready to go with her. Though I had been trained all my life to hate and fear the Shokarn, still I thought she was the most beautiful thing I had ever seen. Later she was to tell me how deeply I had impressed her too at first meeting, she who had been raised to hold all the Kourmairi in contempt. She talked of how she had seen me coming through the fruit trees that were in a froth of pink and white blooms, riding on a huge gray horse, naked to the waist, skin dark as narlwood and gleaming with sweat, head thrown back, singing. All that was later. At that moment I saw myself as a sweaty, dirty, half-dressed farm girl being claimed by this glorious apparition. I bowed again, this time to her. "Lady, do you want me for a servant? I am yours for whatever you need." For that brief, thoughtless moment I would willingly have given myself over into servitude. Fortunately for me that was not her intention.

"No," she said impatiently. "I have more than enough servants and slaves. I want a companion, an equal, someone who will speak her mind freely and tell me what she thinks. I can find no one like that in all Maktesh. The Kourmairi there are all too terrified of the Shokarn and the Shokarn women are too used to the habits of subservience, subterfuge and cunning. They fawn rather than speaking straight out. They could not say an honest word if their lives depended on it. I am bored with them all and have decided to travel about looking for what I want."

I did not tell her then that it is not possible to *buy* an equal. I did not even understand it myself at that time. But after my first moment of utter submission some of my defiant spirit returned. I looked her straight in the eye and said, "Be sure that is what you want, Lady, for that may well be what you get. I have always been known for speaking my mind."

I might not have been so outspoken at that time if I had realized I was speaking so boldly to the Zarna herself. Thank the Goddess I did not know or out of my Kourmairi training I might have flung myself down on the ground before her and so spoiled my chances. One of her companions, a thin hard-faced man with dark burning eyes, started to ride at me with his sword raised. "Insolent whelp! Do you realize who you are speaking to?"

Instantly she put out her hand to stop him. "Wait Manyier! Let her be. Not another word. She is just what I want. She is perfect. Who would imagine that I could find such a treasure in this little out-of-the-way dirt-village. What is your name, girl?"

"Jolaina, my Lady."

"Do not 'my Lady' me. Call me Aranella." I could see Manyier scowling at that. She paid him no notice and went on, "If you are willing to come back with me to Maktesh and be my companion there, then put on your shirt and lead us to your family's home. We must settle the terms with them."

I nodded and bowed again in silence, afraid to say one more word out of all the tumultuous explosion of feelings churning inside. Not in my wildest dreams could I have imagined such a thing and I still did not really know who she was. The man who had tried to silence me, Manyier, kept watch on my every movement as if he thought I might be some dangerous wild creature, intent on harming his charge. He even tried to place himself protectively between me and Aranella. It both amused and annoyed me, but in the end it mattered little. Over his objections Aranella insisted on riding next to me. She seemed to have no fear of him or me or anything at all for that matter.

When we got to the house my mother was all atremble with awe and anxiety. My father groveled and fawned in abject servility before the Shokarn. None the less, he bargained a good price for me, saying I was his only real help and crying the sad story of his two worthless sons. They finally sent me out of the house before the sum was settled on. When I stepped out into our little farm yard, it was crowded with a whole company of guards, churning up the mud with their horses' hooves and surrounded by a fringe of frightened, curious villagers.

It was the other one, a shrewd, older, dignified-looking man named Bardaith who did the bargaining for my purchase. When he came out of our house, he was shaking his head with a look of disgust. My mother followed him, her face wet with tears. She had packed a little bundle of my things and hugged me tightly, sobbing, "Good-bye Daughter, may it go well with you. I shall miss you every day."

After a moment or so, I wrenched myself free of her embrace. Turning my back on her, I went to hug Douven good-bye and said in his ear, "I will try to send you word as soon as I reach Maktesh." Of course neither of us knew how to read or write a single word at that time, nor did our parents, but the Headman of our village did.

Douven himself looked close to tears. My father only asked me if I had finished the plowing. I nodded. Then he said I should do whatever I was told and not bring dishonor to his name. I answered coldly that he had sold me and what I did now was no longer any of his concern. With those words I mounted the black mare Bardaith brought forward for me. Then I rode out of the farmyard with Aranella and Bardaith and Manyier and that company of guards without once looking back. In my mind that part of my life was over and done with.

Once on the road I soon discovered who I rode with, but by then Aranella and I had talked and laughed and even stopped to relieve ourselves together, so I was not as awed as I might have been. I think she meant to keep it a secret until we reached Maktesh and was angry at Bardaith for telling me.

We slept that night in a grand inn that was three times the size of my father's barn. For the first time in my life I slept in a feather bed. Aranella had new clothes laid out for me as soon as I had bathed, a dark green riding habit that was very fine though it pinched slightly at the waist, and high soft boots of red leather. She wanted me to give away my old clothes or burn them; I said I wanted them washed and returned to me. "I need to keep them to remember where I came from. Who knows, perhaps I shall have some use for them again." This was my first act of defiance in my new life, the first time I spoke to Aranella out of my own will, though certainly not the last.

When Manyier saw me dressed in good clothes his attitude toward me seemed to undergo a change. He no longer regarded me with such suspicion or tried to herd me away from Aranella. Bardaith winked at me. He seemed to be amused by the whole thing. "Well, I see you have turned out to be human after all. Sometimes it is surprising how little it takes to make that change."

My hand grows weary now and my arm aches. I will read this part to Shamu when she comes. The rest will get written later.

Noya

Our next visitors were not so leisurely, nor were they there to see the beauties of our city. I was resting for a moment on a bench at the edge of one of our terraced gardens when a young Wanderer came charging up, looking for me. He was calling out, "Where is the Zarna of Zelindar?" Several Hadra laughed at that. Then someone pointed in my direction and he came riding up a street where horses are forbidden, even though Pathell and our sentries and his Wanderer companions were all shouting at him to stop. When Pathell finally halted his horse with mind-speech he slid off and limped toward me at a run.

"Are you Zarna here? My name is Douven, and I am Jolaina's brother. My sister is advisor to the Zarna Aranella who is in desperate trouble. My sister herself is wounded and hunted. She sent me here for help. We must not say her name again aloud. Call her Otta. I am to find the Zarna of the Hadra and give this message to her and to no one else." His words came all in a rush without any pause for breath and his face was flushed with exertion.

Trying not to smile at his desperate earnestness, I answered, "Well Douven, I am not a Zarna, but I am Noya, Councilor to Zelindar. We have no Zarnas here. Councilor will have to do as that is what we have. Now what do you need with me? What is so urgent that you ride recklessly up our narrow streets?"

Drawn by the commotion, Morghail suddenly appeared at my side and asked with surprise. "Douven, what are you doing here?"

"My sister sent me to . . ."

Morghail gave a quick shake of his head and tapped me on my arm, saying, "Perhaps some more private place would be better for this business."

I beckoned Pathell. Together with Morghail and Douven we went to the large back room of the house I shared with Vranith, a place I often used for private talks. Vranith gave me a strange look as we passed through as if she did not approve of my company. Then she shrugged and went out, saying nothing as she left.

Douven dropped into a chair. Groaning with exhaustion, he handed me the message he carried. "I cannot read, though I can probably answer any questions you may have. My sister did not come herself because she has been wounded with an arrow. She may die of the fever. You must hurry back with me as her life hangs in the balance."

With amazement I read, *To the Zarna of the Hadra, in this dangerous time of war it is imperative for your people and mine that we meet immediately. Since I am too weak from a wound to come to you, I must insist that you to come to me with ten to twenty of your best and most trusted warriors.* I read on, amazed at the tone. Though there was no signature at the end, this was clearly a demand, not a request, a demand from someone accustomed to having power. Hadra are not commanded, not even by each other. "What makes you so sure I am going with you?" I asked sharply.

Douven blushed and blurted out, "Because you must! It is of vital importance or she would not have sent me."

With that Morghail spoke up suddenly, "You have not asked my advice, Noya, but I will give it anyhow. This is your chance to find out what is happening from someone who has been at the center of things. In the end, you will probably defend Zelindar better by going out and meeting what is coming than by hiding here."

I handed Pathell the note and she scanned it quickly. "Pathell?" I asked.

"He is right," she answered instantly.

"Then we should call a Council meeting. I am Councilor here. I cannot simply ride off with no word."

"No time," Douven said desperately. "If you do not come right now it may be too late."

Pathell was nodding in agreement. "They did not choose you Councilor to sit on your backside, Noya. Garlian said it, they chose you for your fire. Let Garlian take your place here for a while."

"But she was going to go to . . ."

"No time," she said quickly, echoing Douven.

With a nod I stood up. "As it must be," I said softly. I would not ask Vranith's feelings in the matter. I already knew what she would say. I also knew what I had to do. With a sense of fate moving me, I went quickly to gather my things while Pathell went to gather ten or more of our best "warriors" and make preparations for food and horses. She promised to send Garlian to me. Morghail went off to get the Wanderers ready to leave.

And so, well before nightfall, I found myself riding out of Zelindar in a company of Hadra and Wanderers, going to find my own piece of this strange war that was being forced upon us. All this was a new experience for me. I had lived in Zelindar all of my life and only traveled a little up and down the coast. Now I was riding into Garmishair to meet with this war that was not yet a war, but could be a war at any moment if we did not make the right decisions.

Jolaina

Many times I have had cause to look back on that day that changed my life forever. I never found out how much Bardaith paid my father on the Zarn's behalf to buy me for Aranella and she would not tell me. But it must have been quite a sum for when I finally went home a year later for a visit, my father had made a large addition on our little house, built a bigger barn, doubled our herd and added several fields to our farm holdings — all this with the help of his two "useless sons". Proudly he showed me everything and seemed very pleased with himself. I looked at it all and boldly made suggestions. My mother followed us about, wringing her hands and watching me with a puzzled look on her face as if I were some stranger. Finally she asked, "Are the Shokarn women in Maktesh all so forward and outspoken? Is it the style there?"

"No, Mother," I answered with some impatience. "The Shokarn women are all tame little lap dogs, ruled by their men. That was why Aranella had to come so far to find a companion who could be her equal."

"You have changed much, Daughter, since you left home."

"Not really, I have just become more myself." I could feel anger rising up the back of my neck.

"I hear talk, whispers, rumors that you are more than a companion, that you . . . that sometimes . . . that maybe . . ." My mother was actually stammering and blushing.

"That I am her muirlla, her puntyar, her sexual slave, is that what you are struggling to ask? Well, what did you expect? She came to buy a toy and you sold her one. It is a little late now to get all in a flutter about it." My mother gasped in shock and turned away. She asked me no more questions. What a sharp cruel tongue I had at that time. I might as well have slapped her. Now, of course, I have lived to regret my unkind words. My poor mother, she died a year later of the winter cough. She probably went to her grave thinking I had been sold into sexual slavery. I never had the chance to tell her how happy I was and how that day had transformed my life, in every way for the better.

None of that mattered to my father, one way or the other. He had what he wanted, his barn and his cows. And now, of course, he is married again, this time to a pretty young wife who has given him two more sons, twin boys, both with straight legs. How strange. I suppose Aniya and those boys are also my heirs, heirs to this sudden wealth that my sale brought into the family. Since it was so much to my advantage, what was the source of my harsh anger toward my family? I suppose it was that my father did not really care. As long as the price was right he would have sold me into sexual slavery or anything else for that matter. He never once asked me if I wanted to go. My happiness was no part of the bargain he made and my poor timid mother just let it happen.

That visit was a strained homecoming. The house did not seem like my home any longer. Even with the new addition it felt small and cramped. When we all sat down together for a meal, my bitter tongue was like poison. I saw how it hurt my mother. Yet I could not stop myself and so I pretended not to care. When I walked about in the village, people looked at me with a combination of awe, contempt and pity that I found unbearable. Whispering, staring, pointing or suddenly turning their backs, they made it clear that I was no longer one of them. Perhaps I never had been.

The only person in that house I could really talk to was my brother Douven. One morning we walked together up to our favorite childhood place, a little spring at the edge of the woods. Others thought it to be haunted. That suited us well enough since it meant that no one else ever came there. Poor

Douven, he told me the house had become unbearable. Now that I was gone my father freely heaped abuse on him at the slightest provocation and Korzil joined in with relish. Shortly after I left again, I heard that Douven had taken one of the new horses and gone off to ride for a while with the Wanderers. In my heart I wished him as much joy in his life as I had found in mine and wondered if we should ever meet again. But for a while that morning we shared our lives, much as we had as children. He told me everything that had happened since I left. Then I told him of my life in Maktesh while he listened wide-eyed, full of awe and curiosity and eager questions.

"Oh Douven, how can I convey in words what this amazing first year in the city was like? How can I tell you in this short time of all the new things I have tasted and seen and heard and felt? The beauty and vastness of the palace; the grandeur of the city itself, its immense size; the crowds thronging in the streets where there is never silence, even in the dead of night; the richness and lavishness; the astounding display of wealth. I was the little country girl going about with my eyes wide and my mouth hanging open, trying to see it all. And always there were more wonders to be found.

"But there is another side, though at first I was too dazzled by all that splendor to notice. The poverty there is as great as the wealth; people begging on the street, people starving, whole districts of filthy back alleys where people live out their lives in utter despair and many of their children die young. I have no great love for this village, yet I know we would never allow such poverty here in our midst. It would be considered a disgrace to our good name. Those who meet with misfortune here are sheltered among family and neighbors. There, in Maktesh, it is no shame among people of wealth to pass by others lying in the street. And yet we are the ones thought to be crude and uneducated.

"When I complain to Aranella she says, 'Stay with me, Jolaina. Be patient. I will make it different. You will see, I promise. But only with you can I do this. Without you I can do nothing.' I love her so much, I am so happy at her side that I try to trust in her words. But will I really be able to change anything in that ancient city where evils have gone on so long? Does Aranella herself really have the will?

"I am the outsider there, the dirt-child. Her poor frail mother, I am too much for her, too large, too loud, too dark, too bold. She hardly knows how to speak to me at all. And from the start, her father clearly had no love for me. The feeling was certainly mutual, though after a time we have come to have a grudging respect for each other, forced on us by our mutual love for Aranella. For his part, the Zarn did not know how to deal with this dark woman-child in his household, a Kourmairi who was neither slave nor servant, who was rough and outspoken and had no habit of subservience, who went about the palace freely, under no orders but Aranella's.

"It is Aranella's will that has kept me safe. If not for her, I might have met my death ten times over this first year for my insolence. Though I have lived in the magic circle of her protection, still I have seen many cruelties and know well enough what could have befallen me without it. Perhaps my bold outspokenness is nothing but a cover for my fear. I know what has happened to others there and my knees turn to jelly at the thought that it could happen to me.

"I think Bardaith and Manyier must have taken it upon themselves to watch over me, or perhaps Aranella had told them to, though when I asked she shook her head. Either way I was glad. It gave me a little sense of safety in that strange place when I met one or the other of them in the hall or on the stairs or even on the street too often for coincidence and felt their observing eyes on me.

"As to the Zarn, everything you have ever heard and more is true. He is a cruel tyrant, as bad as any of the stories told by the Kourmairi in horrified whispers. The things I have witnessed would make a strong man weep or loose his sleep or even his meal. The stories of tortures, beatings, beheadings, hand-cuttings — they are all true, Douven. And I only know a little of what really happens there. That city is ruled by fear. I move through it all as if I have a charmed life, but it does not make me deaf or blind to what goes on there.

"When Aranella remonstrates with her father, he says, 'If you are going to rule you must learn to be hard. There is no other way.' And he is training her to rule. That is how he has finally come to tolerate me. He can see his daughter needs a strong independent voice and ear, beholden to none of the power factions that buzz and hum about the palace. Cruel as the Zarn is with others, he loves his daughter, I will say that for the man. He loves, respects and in some strange way fears Aranella as if she holds a different kind of power. He even lets her speak freely, the only person in Maktesh who has that privilege.

"Over and over Aranella has said to me, 'I will not rule that way. Under my hand it will all be different.' But even Aranella has the habit of power. At one time she had her maid lashed for forgetting to mend her favorite gown. The girl's little brother had just fallen from a tree and broken his leg. For that moment Zeeli's mind was not on her work. When I protested angrily to Aranella, she answered me in her haughtiest manner, 'But how else is she to learn?'

"Incensed, I shouted at her, 'You see! You are no different from your father! Cruelty runs in your blood.'

"At that her beautiful face suddenly flushed an angry, ugly red. She raised her hand as if to slap me, saying furiously, 'I could have you lashed for your insolence.'

"I looked her straight in the eye and said coldly, 'Yes, you could. And after that you had better have me killed or sent back to my village for I would never speak to you again or do anything at your bidding. You brought me here to be your equal. If that is not possible I would rather be a farm girl, plowing my father's fields, than to live here, dressed in these fancy clothes, and to be treated as your father treats his people.'

"Aranella raised her hand higher and I stood staring straight into her face. This was the moment when everything would be decided. I held my breath and there was a circle of silence around us. Slowly she lowered her hand. 'You are right Jolaina, and that is why I need you here. But it is so hard to change. I have been trained to indulge my anger. What other examples do I have of power? And I mean to have power here, even if it is a very different kind of power. But please do not leave me, do not go back. There is no one else I can talk to. And that is as close as I can come to begging. Please do not make me ask again.'

"She did not apologize to Zeeli, but she gave her an old gown she had outgrown and had her brother brought to the palace while he healed, to be in the care of the court physician. Personally I would rather have the horse doctor myself than that fool, but Zeeli was immensely grateful for the caring as if simple kindness were an undeserved and unexpected miracle."

Re-reading this I am suddenly filled with nostalgia for that simple peaceful morning by the spring, sharing my life with Douven. So much has happened in the eight years since. In spite of all I had seen I think I was still an innocent back then. That did not last much longer . . .

Amairi

Around noon of our fourth day in Zelindar I was amazed to see Douven come galloping into the city in a desperate hurry. When I saw Noya and Morghail consulting with him, I felt the hair on the back of my neck go up. Before anyone told me anything at all, I knew that somehow this concerned the coming war and that things of great import were happening. Soon I heard that Morghail, Rhondil and Larameer, along with several Hadra, Noya and Pathell among them, planned to ride back at full speed with Douven. Noya told me that Nastal and I could follow later at our leisure with other Wanderers.

I shook my head. Though Nastal might have been glad to stay in the city, I told Noya I would go with them when they left. At that her face hardened. She answered quite bluntly, "I doubt if you can keep up the pace. We cannot slow down for you."

But I knew it was time to leave. I had a premonition that I had some part to play in what was to come. No matter what the difficulty, I could not allow myself to get left behind. My parents always said I could "smell the wind." I may not have Hadra powers, but I do have some sort of power of my own. It draws me into the future, lets me see a little of what may happen there. Freed from Horvath's grasp, I could feel it growing stronger and clearer with each day. "You need not fear for me, Noya," I found myself saying boldly to her. "I need to go now. I will keep up with you well enough."

Noya acquiesced grudgingly. "See that you do, Amairi. Make no complaints. If you fall behind it is on your head, not mine." She spoke sharply, but I saw Morghail give her the nod that decided it.

Now that is a subtle one, that Morghail. I wish I could see what goes on in that man's head. As soon as I think I know him, he shows yet another side. Sharing his bed for that time has given me no access at all to his mind. He often makes me wish for the Hadra power of reading thoughts. All the same, I was glad he signaled for me to go and so softened Noya's resistance.

As we rode at a mad pace out of the city, my thoughts went tumbling through my head in a wild mix of fear and excitement. We were already on the road before I heard the whole story. Mostly it was Morghail who filled in the pieces, telling me that Zarna Aranella had been caught in Khundorn's snares and Jolaina was a hunted fugitive who had barely escaped with her life. She must have sought shelter in the Wanderer camp only a day or so after we left. I remembered how I had once thought to warn those two women of danger, though nothing had been clear to me at the time. Would it have changed the course of events if I had been daring enough to follow my impulse? Ah well, *As it must be,* as I had so often heard the Hadra say.

Even hearing Morghail's account I still did not fully understand the scope of things. I only knew I had to go with Noya and the others. My inner wind had told me it was time to leave. *Now, not later,* that familiar cold voice said in my head. I did not yet know how I would be needed, only that I would be.

I knew a little of this Khundorn from having met him at some of those dreadful parties Horvath had forced me to attend. When we finally stopped to rest, I told Noya all that I had observed of the man, none of it good. Most of the men I had met at those parties I remember as being sly but charming, men with courtly manners and smooth talk to cover their ugly doings. Not Khundorn! He did not even pretend to charm. He struck me as hard, calculating and brutal. Ruthless is probably the best description. A big, harsh, bony-faced man, he looked at everything with the cold, hooded eyes of a bird-of-death. There was an aura of power about him as if power was something he was constantly weighing and gathering.

Though Khundorn showed utter contempt for men like Horvath who were always trying to ingratiate themselves with someone higher up, he seemed to have no hesitation about using such men for his own purposes. He could bow and kiss a lady's hand and do all the things a gentleman of that class is supposed to do, yet there was no warmth in him. He never tried to hide the coldness. He never let you forget it. It was always there in his eyes, in the measuring calculation with which he watched everyone and everything in the room.

I feared for Aranella's life. She could expect no mercy from Khundorn. If he did not kill her now he would kill her soon. He would have to. A living Zarna would always be a threat to his power, even as his prisoner. I was not surprised he had made himself leader of the warring factions. If I were a gambler like my once-husband, I would certainly have bet my money on Khundorn to come out on top of the heap in that final scramble.

Jolaina

I never again went back to visit my family. There was no love or welcome for me there, not in that house or in that village. I missed Douven and felt some guilt for abandoning him, but my new life was too full to look back with regrets. Shortly after I came back to Maktesh the Zarn's lady had a baby, another girl that she named Nhuriani. Not long afterward the mother came down with birth-fever and the doctor declared there were to be no more children. That baby had been the last hope for a male heir. The Zarna closed her heart to the child and turned her face away, saying, "My womb is cursed, this child is a curse. Let others care for her."

Now I understood why the Zarn had been grooming Aranella for power. It was not so much that he loved the idea of a woman on the throne, especially since his wife fussed and worried incessantly, saying, "How can you do such a thing Husband? Whatever will become of her? She will not be a proper woman and she can never really be a man. She will be something that has never existed before in Maktesh." But there was no one else and he wanted to keep the power in the family. The brother, Ralyn, two years younger than Aranella, was a gentle idiot, certainly not fit to rule. Aranella, however, was very fond of him.

Her father was an amazing mixture of pride in his daughter and meanness to others, a man I came to admire grudgingly even as I loathed him. Shortly after Nhuri's birth I overheard a heated argument between Aranella and her father about Ralyn. The Zarn was saying, "But there must be no opportunity for anyone to use him against you, especially the eastern faction who want to wrest the power from this family and set up Khundorn instead."

"But you cannot Father! You must not! Promise me that!" I heard Aranella cry.

Less than a week later Ralyn was dead, accidentally drowned in a shallow pond. If I had any innocence left it was gone then. After that I always tried to watch my back. The man-servant who had been Ralyn's attendant was quickly put to death for his carelessness. Of course there were whispers and rumors and gossip, but a Zarn is accountable to no one.

For a month or so after that, Aranella would not speak to her father. She would not even look at him. It was during that time that Nhuri came into our care and bonded with her older sister in a way she never had with her own mother. All Aranella's grief and guilt over her brother's death she poured into the baby's care. It was almost as if Nhuri were our own child. Later we came to see her as a magic child, a miracle who had been put into our hands. Dharlan, who had been Aranella's nursemaid, joined us in caring for the baby. We had rooms made up for them next to our own.

After a while of this silence from his daughter the old Zarn sought me out, saying, "We do what we have to do. Sometimes, when we have no choice, we do things that break our hearts. Tell her I love her. Tell her that for me, Jolaina. Perhaps she will listen to you." It was the first time he had ever paid me much mind. Now, in his pain, he was actually begging me to make the peace.

At first Aranella refused to listen to me. "How could he do that after I begged him not to? How could he? No! I will never forgive him. Never!" Finally she softened, seeing the terrible grief in her father's face. Much as she hated the things he did, Aranella loved this harsh, cruel, brutal old man. In fact she was far more like him than she was like her gentle mother who seemed almost too fragile for this world.

Though Aranella tried hard to make me her equal she was still the one who gave the orders. It was with great seriousness that she undertook my education, wanting me to learn everything there was to learn, everything she knew and more: to read, write, do sums, study the history of Garmishair and especially of Maktesh, sew a fine seam, design an embroidery, dance, ride well, dress appropriately for court. There was seldom an idle moment in the day. There was also a whole other side of things she wanted me to learn, all the skills of combat and physical mastery. "You never know what will be needed," she was fond of saying whenever I questioned her on any of this.

Actually, of all I learned in those first few years, it was the skills of armed and unarmed combat I most enjoyed. I was far better at sword play and wrestling than I was at fancy stitchery. At first Jalmoth, the Sword Master, refused to teach me in spite of Aranella's insistence. "Not fitting for a woman to learn such things," he kept saying. "Besides her presence will disrupt the yard." Finally the Zarn had to intercede.

Feared and respected by everyone, Jalmoth was a big ugly bear of a man who had the strength of four and kept iron discipline in his yard. Though he taught me sword play and was a fair teacher and a good one, he never let me forget that I was not wanted there. Rhenfel, who taught unarmed combat, was a little friendlier. He even had a few words of praise as I took my bruises in silence and, in his words, learned faster than anyone he had ever taught. Sometimes I would pretend that my opponent was my father or my older brother Korzil. That would give me added strength when I most needed it. In the beginning the boys jeered at me. After a while, as I bested them one by one, the insults stopped and were replaced by grudging admiration though never by camaraderie.

In time Bardaith and Manyier went from being my guardians to being my teachers. Bardaith taught me how to read and write and how to do sums. Manyier taught me games of strategy and chance like pargamont and changchi. He said such games were good for teaching logic and developing mental abilities as well as for patience and observation. He also taught both of us how to read maps and chart the stars though I was far more interested and better at it than Aranella. Altogether I was a good student, bright and eager. Saddled with the hard work of the farm, I had never had the chance to develop my mind and certainly never any time for games no matter how "beneficial" they might be.

Sometimes, when Manyier set out a game of pargamont, we would try to lure Bardaith into it if he was not too busy with his duties as advisor to the Zarn. Then we would even beg Dharlan to join us. She would protest all the way that she had no time for such frivolity. But once she sat down and put her eagle eye on the game, she usually won. I think it bent Manyier's pride a little for a woman to be "too clever" as he used to say, but it made Bardaith laugh. I am not sure if this was a proper education for young ladies, but I loved the easy fun and camaraderie while it lasted. Lessons were in the old nursery, a sunny, cozy space away from the rest of the house and if Dharlan was there, Nhuri was there too, gurgling and laughing and watching everything in her bright-eyed way.

One afternoon, a few months after Ralyn's death, the Zarn paid a surprise visit to our school room. We had worked hard all morning on sums and reading, but at that moment we were playing a noisy game of changchi, all of us assembled there, even Dharlan. It felt as if we had been caught at some childish mischief. Manyier blushed, Dharlan had a fit of coughing and

Bardaith began explaining very seriously the virtues of the game for the education of the young. I thought I saw a little smile quivering at the corner of the Zarn's mouth. Then he gave a roar of laughter. "Well, well, so this is what you do when I think you are all hard at work?"

Aranella started to protest but Manyier interrupted her. "Sire, is it really true then? Are you really training Aranella to be Zarn?"

I stopped breathing, expecting the guards to be called any moment. No one ever questioned the Zarn. In spite of an edge of threat in his voice, he answered quietly. "Of course it is true. I have been telling you that for months. That is why she needs a thorough education — including card playing. She must know everything about everything."

"But it is not proper for a woman to rule over men. It is not fitting and people will not stand for it."

The Zarn changed in an instant. Face red with rage, he shouted at Manyier, "This one is worth two men any day. Besides I have no sons. What would you have me do? Declare Bardaith my heir?"

"Begging your pardon Sire, there is not enough money in the royal treasury to persuade me to be Zarn. I will be Aranella's advisor as I have been yours and I only hope she will take my advice better than you have."

Now I found myself trembling and in a sweat at the same time. This time I was sure the guards would be called and both men dragged off, never to be seen again. But perhaps the Zarn was reluctant to do this in front of his daughter. Instead he grabbed Manyier by the arm and shook him. "You will teach my daughter everything she needs to know with no more arguments. Is that understood?"

Manyier actually found the courage or the madness to answer again. "It is wrong for a woman to rule over men," he said stubbornly. With a curse the Zarn pulled him to his feet and this time he did shout for the guards. Then he dragged Manyier out into the hall with Bardaith following after them.

After that I could no longer understand the sense of the words. I only knew they were loud and angry. Hardly daring to breathe we three stared at each other in horror as we heard the guards running down the hall. Aranella had gone very white and her eyes were wide. Dharlan had her hands pressed over her heart and seemed to be praying under her breath. In a few minutes Bardaith came back in and said, "No more lessons for today." Aranella opened her mouth as if to ask something and he added quickly, "And no questions."

We thought we would never see Manyier again and were afraid to ask. Much to our surprise he reappeared in the school room at the end of the week, subdued and wary but seemingly uninjured except for a little bruising on his face. He did not tell us where he had been or what had happened to him and we did not ask. Our lessons with him resumed and sometimes we even played a few games of pargamont, but the old easy camaraderie was gone.

Noya

Nastal and Amairi insisted on riding with us, or rather Amairi insisted. Nastal, it seems, is ready to accompany her anywhere. Nastal looks tough enough for the trip. After all, she was a Kourmairi farm girl, raised on hardship before she joined the Wanderers. But Amairi was a Shokarn Highborn. She is new to life on the road. I urged her to come later at her leisure with some of the other Wanderers, but she shook her head vehemently. With her jaw set in a stubborn line, she told me, "I will not be pampered like a Highborn lady. I left that life behind me when I left my husband's house. I believe I have my part to play in these great events. I need to be there now, not later."

Looking her right in the eye I said, "You will have to ride

hard to keep up with us, Amairi. We are going to go as fast as our horses will allow, and will stop only for their needs. It will be a very rough ride; we cannot allow you to slow us down."

With that she raised her head and looked straight back at me with her piercing blue eyes. For the first time I saw the Shokarn arrogance in her, the iron will that Morghail had spoken of behind her sweetness. "Do not be afraid for me," she said firmly. "Never fear, I will keep up well enough. I promise not to delay you."

I caught a meaningful look from Morghail and nodded my consent. "Very well, then," I said curtly. Later I had cause to wonder if Amairi really had any idea what she had so rashly promised.

As for the Hadra who came with us I chose six, Pathell chose three and Garlian chose three. In a way though, they all really chose themselves, for we certainly did not command anyone to accompany us on this dangerous venture. We only picked from those who spoke to go. I chose women who had been close to me all my life. I also chose for those qualities that might be needed by us all: Danil for her great skill with horses; Nairin for her knowledge of plants and herbs and healing; Koshar for her toughness and determination; Mitru for her ability as a guide and pathfinder; Zanti for her extraordinary empathic powers; and lastly Tenari, because she had been my closest childhood friend.

Garlian, along with half the city of Zelindar, came to see us off. She made us all a little speech about "strength and vision and courage in the hard times to come." Then, after kissing me on both cheeks, she said for my ears alone, "Go child, I will take care of everything here and sit at your place in Council till you return. You have been summoned. Things are moving now beyond our sight or control. It is important that you go. I can think of no one more capable to do this. After all, are you not the Zarna of the Hadra?" With those last words she gave me a wicked grin and pinched my arm. I did not remind her then of the much-needed rest that she was losing. Apparently this coming war afforded little time for such luxuries.

It hurt when Vranith wished me safe journey with only the curtest of farewells, a cold kiss and barely a touch. With my heart aching, I answered her in mind-speech from my side of that invisible wall between us, calling out in a silent plea, *Vranith, let us part with love. We may never see each other again.* But I felt her shutting me out and there was no time for mending things at that moment. She had turned away before I was even mounted on my horse, Morning.

I watched her go, wishing I could have shared my fears with her and found some comfort there, but that was not to be. Then Morning whinnied and tossed her head. Shifting from foot to foot, she was impatient to be moving. I put my face down against her neck, breathing in her sweet scent. There was more comfort to be had there than in Vranith's cold kiss and colder touch.

When we were all assembled, Douven was amazed to see how the Hadra rode with no saddles or bridles. "We use mind-speech and consent with our horses," Danil told him. "It works as well as any bridle, far better in fact. When this madness is over we could teach you. Even those without Hadra powers have a little mind-speech with creatures if they leave themselves open to it."

I was surprised to hear Danil make such an offer to a man and pleased to see Douven nodding his consent. He was looking from one to the other of us in amazement. "So the stories of you are true," he said with awe.

"Some of them are," I answered with a wide grin. "Some of them I certainly would not lay claim to."

That was the first and last time on our trip that I had a chance to smile. Douven set the pace. I felt his worry like a whip on my back, driving us on. We rode well past dark that night and only called a halt because Danil insisted on doing so for the sake of the horses.

When we finally stopped I could clearly feel Amairi's pain and discomfort with my Hadra empathy. It had to be even harder for Zanti who was the most sensitive of us. I saw her pacing about, holding her head, and I quickly made myself a strong inner shield to shut out Amairi's feelings. After all, Amairi had insisted on coming. Let it be on her head. I could not afford to pamper her. I will say this for the woman, she never complained, not one word, not even with Nastal and Nairin hovering over her, trying to make her comfortable. Even at that fierce pace she had not tried to hold us back. Grudgingly, I almost found myself admiring her. Then some little bit of pity crept into my heart. I knew the next day and the day after that would be harder still.

Amairi

Oh how our foolish, arrogant words come back to eat us alive! I was good to my promise. I rode with them all the way. I kept up, not falling off or hanging back. But my body certainly suffered. Except for Horvath's beatings, I have never experienced such pain. When I got on or off the horse, I had to bite my lip not to groan aloud. Even sitting down or rising was a terrible effort.

There was part of me that registered the pain, that inwardly groaned and complained and wished myself in some easier place. Another part of me was delirious with joy at the freedom of this new life and my ability to be part of it. I was traveling with the Hadra and the Wanderers. No longer was I a prisoner in my husband's house, bored to distraction, feeling trapped and useless as I tried to give orders to servants who already knew far better than I did what to do. Instead I would soon be meeting with Douven's sister, the fabled Jolaina. Following our own paths, we had both fled Maktesh to save our lives. And now those paths are about to cross. Riding hard, sleeping under the stars, I feel myself to be part of the flow of great events, and Goddess knows I might even be of some use in this rapidly unfolding drama.

Jolaina

While I have the chance I am writing this very last part of my story for Shamu. Soon enough there will be no more time to dwell on the past. For right now, while I wait for the Zarna of Zelindar to appear, it gives me something to do with this fever of restless energy that has been eating me up.

I have become impatient beyond reason with all this lying about. Vondran has sent word that I am forbidden to come down until they are here. He says it is safer that way. I think the truth of it is that he does not want me pacing about like a caged animal in his camp. With Aranella still Khundorn's prisoner, every minute that goes by without freeing her is a torture for me. I will try to distract myself with this writing if I can.

To set the record straight about that early time there is something I need to say here at the beginning. All that talk of sexual slavery was nothing but a cruel sham to hurt the parents who had sold me without once asking my will in the matter. Aranella was as ignorant of the pleasures of the body as I was. Everything I was to know of sex we discovered together, exploring with each other. We were each one another's most devoted pupil and most caring teacher. But that is a whole other story for another time, full of pleasures and secrets.

As my body developed from all that work in the combat yard, I grew broader and stronger. Working out with a sword or with my hands and feet, I wore old cast-off pants and a loose tunic. Soon I found I could not stand the confinement of skirts and tight bodices. I began actively complaining to

Aranella. With Zeeli's help, she had costumes designed for me that were as graceful as any lady's, but were made with straight waists and split skirts sewn in two parts like trouser legs. They were not so confining, yet they did not look like men's clothing either. They were something in between, both comfortable and elegant. As I went striding about in my striking new clothes, I could see the envious and hostile stares. The people of Maktesh had almost gotten accustomed to my dark face, but that did not mean they loved me, especially when I defied their sense of decency in some way.

When Aranella saw how well those new clothes did on me, she insisted on having some made for herself as well, even over her mother's pained objections. Her father laughed and thought it very fine. Not so her poor mother. She was afraid for her forceful daughter and afraid of her as well, afraid of the example she would give her little sister and afraid of what would become of Aranella herself. I suppose she had never really reconciled herself to the thought of her oldest daughter becoming a Zarn.

Four years after Nhuri's birth the Zarn's Lady died. She had been sickly all that time, never really regaining her health and slowly wasting away. After that the Zarn turned into an old man. Right before our eyes he seemed to lose all his will to live. Perhaps he had loved his wife after all in his own harsh, gruff way. As quickly as was decent he had Aranella crowned as Zarna in a huge, pompous ceremony that rivaled any Zarn's. Then he officially stepped down from the throne. The Khundorn faction grumbled and complained about a woman in power, but not too loudly. After all, what could they do?

Aranella was twenty-one at the time and I was almost nineteen — not only *women* in power, but *very young women* at that. Soon after that the old Zarn himself died as if he had willed it, having taken care of everything before he went.

And in spite of what Manyier had said, people loved Aranella. She was like a breath of fresh air in their lives. She appeared in public on every possible occasion, wanting to consolidate her power. Everywhere she went she had me on one side of her and Nhuri on the other. People cheered for her. And why not? She was beautiful, she was charming, she was gracious and she actually spoke to them — something very new for a Zarn.

As soon as Aranella was crowned, Manyier went to Eezore to live with his brother and help educate his sons. I think the sight of a woman Zarn was too much for him. Not so with Bardaith. He was always there in the background, advising, smoothing the way, keeping us safe. I think Aranella was his charge just as Nhuri was ours, not out of duty or obligation and certainly not for pay, but because that was what he had chosen in his life. He saw to it that there were always guards, men-at-arms strategically placed everywhere we went, unobtrusively watching over our safety. He often told us, "Pay attention any time you are in public. Even in the midst of a smiling crowd, danger can be lurking. It only takes one madman or one angry one for your life to be in danger." I had the sense of Dharlan watching over us too, keeping her eyes and ears open for danger or trouble. If only I had been smart enough to listen.

Aranella was not always as confident as she appeared. Sometimes she cried herself to sleep in my arms, weeping from fear or exhaustion. "Oh Jolaina, why did I let him talk me into it. I am not strong enough for this." I would hold her and stroke her hair and murmur words of comfort in her ear. Then the next morning, griefs forgotten, she would be bright and cheerful and full of energy, and we would make our plans for the new day.

Well, now we have had six years of making changes, making enemies and finding loyal friends. I had heard the muttering and grumbling often enough: how the skirts had taken over the governing of the city; how women had made a chaos of everything, turning all established order upside-down. "Soon the Kourmairi will rule over the Shokarn," some said, blaming me, the dark-skinned peasant-child among them, blaming me because it was easier than blaming their beloved Zarna. They spoke as if the old Zarn would not have tolerated such things, as if this were all a conspiracy against his memory, conveniently forgetting that he had trained his daughter to be Zarna and had accepted and encouraged me as her advisor.

But others, especially the younger ones, flocked to us, full of enthusiasm for what we were attempting. And the people on the street loved us, shouting and cheering whenever we passed. It was this that had made me deaf to Dharlan's warnings, contemptuous even. What arrogance! And in truth what had we really accomplished in those six years? Not nearly as much as I had hoped for. Far less in fact. It is so easy when you have no power to picture how you would manage if you did, so easy to have great dreams and lofty ambitions, to imagine all the bold, brave, kind and daring things you would accomplish. It is very different when you suddenly have the reins of power thrust into your hands. Then you see constraints and barriers and limitations and warnings where before you saw none. And you must begin to placate and balance and compromise with things you had never even noticed.

My greatest hope, my real ambition, was to end slavery in Maktesh in my lifetime. Though I had tried to harden myself to survive everyday in the streets of the city, still the sight of slaves was always painful to me. I had not even told Aranella yet of my plans. She may have wanted to rule differently, but she was still a Shokarn. I know she had worked hard to ensure that slaves were treated with kindness and fairness, yet I am not sure that in her Shokarn mind she could ever imagine a world without slaves. She blocked me when I tried to speak of it. "Too much and too soon," she would say quickly. I had not even told Dharlan though she had once been a slave herself; she was too close to Aranella. And I had certainly not told Bardaith. There was no one I could safely talk to on the matter.

Meanwhile we had done many small things so that the city was a gentler and pleasanter place to live. Maktesh was no longer ruled by terror. Hand cuttings were forbidden, tortures and beatings were rare, there were few executions and masters were called to account for the treatment of their slaves and servants. Being a muirlla no longer meant your death. There were many small courts set up to hear and deal with the complaints of ordinary people against their Upper-caste overlords. That made us very popular, at least with the common folk. No one had ever listened to them before.

We even made some changes in the Zarn's Council. It was enlarged and split into two parts. There was the Zarna's Council, a small circle of advisers that she chose herself, and the larger City Council made up of representatives of the Uppercaste chosen by lot from among themselves and having some independence from the palace, a thing we occasionally had cause to regret.

People actually spoke more kindly to each other in the streets. You could hear the difference in their voices. And still it had all seemed much too slow to me, tedious even, a little gain here or there and then a little setback. Yet when I talked to the Wanderers who were the eyes and ears of that part of the world they told me they were very aware of the changes.

Sometimes I had felt like an acrobat doing tricks or fancy dancing on a high rope over a pool full of fangfish while everyone watched, waiting breathlessly for me to fall and get eaten alive. I was afraid if we moved too fast we might anger and frighten the Highborn and so set off some lethal civil strife that would wipe out all our gains and make things worse than before or perhaps even provoke in invasion from one of the other Zarn cities — an unthinkable disaster. On the other hand, if we moved too slowly to alleviate the pain and poverty of ordinary people this might cause an uprising from below by those whose hopes we had raised and so provoke civil strife from the other side of the road. Of course I found myself criticized from both sides for whatever I did.

Though I often felt discouraged I know I could fill a volume or two with all we did and all we tried to do. Perhaps I will write of that when I return to Maktesh since all my notes are there — if I have the luck to live long enough to get back there on my own account and not in chains or on the point of a pike. Meanwhile, here we are at the end of our six years with the Zarna of Maktesh a prisoner and myself a hunted fugitive. And now, if we cannot thwart Khundorn's plans, none of this will even matter. Everything we have worked so hard for will be destroyed. When I think of that I grow tired of waiting for the Zarna of the Hadra, so impatient I can no longer sit still. We have so little time to plan and so much to do if Aranella is to be saved.

Well, I am done with the writing. At least for the moment the past has caught with the present. Now I am going to put all this away. Then I will go out to look down one more time into the Wanderer camp and see if anything is happening there. Surely they will come today.

Noya

For the last part of the ride Morghail was our guide, taking us on narrow twisting roads with many forks and turns, most of them invisible to the ordinary traveller. Even with my sharp Hadra senses I could not have found the way again, though Mitru assured me she was keeping close watch on it all and could retrace our steps if necessary. So this was how the Wanderers kept their private places out of public view and could vanish like smoke when they needed to.

We came in late at night. Most of the Wanderer camp was asleep, except for the sentries and two others — a young man named Ablon who immediately leapt on his horse and vanished into the night, and a woman of middle years named Mhirashu, who greeted us warmly. She held out her hands to me, saying, "Greetings, you must be Noya, the new Councilor for Zelindar. Welcome to our camp. There is warm water by the fire for washing and a pot of steaming hot tea, as well as some trail bread still warm from the grill."

I nodded wearily. She was so gracious she might have been welcoming us to a grand house instead of a grassy field much trampled by horses' hooves. I took tea and a few pieces of bread and went to stand by the fire. Nastal had gone to help Amairi from her horse and lay her down. Though she still made no complaint, she groaned with relief. Nairin said a few words in private to Mhirashu who then put together some compresses of wet tea leaves and went to help Nairin with Amairi's care. Douven followed Mhirashu about, asking anxiously, "Where is my sister? Is she well? Is she alive? Why is she not here to greet us?" To all of Mhirashu's calm reassurances he responded with yet another question.

I found myself gathering Douven's anxiety and becoming anxious myself until Mhirashu said firmly, "Douven, listen to me, she is well, she knows you are here and you will see her tomorrow. Now it is time to sleep. I will answer no more questions until morning light." After that Douven limped over to the fire and poured himself a cup of tea. With a groan he sank down next to me and stretched out his legs. The man was so quick and graceful on a horse. It hurt to see how much trouble he had walking. I could feel the pain it cost him. When I thought no one was listening, I leaned toward him and said softly, "I do not wish to give offense, Douven, but the Hadra have ways . . . your leg could probably be healed if . . ."

"I was born this way. I am used to it," he said curtly. But I saw the pain that flashed across his face and felt the bitterness.

"Nonetheless, it could be healed," I persisted.

"Well, no offense taken Hadra. Maybe I will think on it

later, when this is over, if we all live through it. For now this crooked leg does me well enough."

Needing to get away from the pain that was bleeding out of him, I gave him a nod and got up to go rub down my horse. Morning nickered softly and rubbed her head against me while I thanked her for taking me on that hard ride. Before she went off to graze with the others, I gave her a little treat of grain from my pack. Then I lay down in my sleep roll and fell out of this world. Tomorrow could take care of itself.

Jolaina

So the waiting is finally over. Ablon has just ridden up to tell me the Hadra are in camp. It is too late to go down now. He will come back for me in the morning. After he left I went out and stood for a long time looking down at the lights below, my thoughts flowing back and forth between the past I have written of here and whatever is rushing at me from the future. Almost too weary to stand, I have now gone back inside to gather my things and jot down these last few words. Who knows when I will have the time or the desire to write again. This little stone hut has been my prison as well as my place of healing and my refuge. I am very grateful for it. I am also very glad that this is the last time I will have to sleep between its walls.

Noya

I woke early. In spite of Mhirashu's assurances I shared some of Douven's fears. What if, after this long hard ride, we were not to be met? What if something had happened to this brave, bold woman? I had been disappointed and even a little worried not to find Jolaina waiting for us in camp the night before. When I went to find Mirashu and question her, she just laughed at me. "Try to be patient, Hadra, and find something useful to do."

The Wanderers had provided some tents for our use. I went alone to one of them and was sitting on the ground with the morning sun pouring in at a slant on maps and notes spread out before me, trying hard to understand what was happening in Garmishair and what it might mean for the future and survival of Yarmald.

Jolaina

Just as it was turning light Ablon returned. He had brought a horse for me. I followed him back down to the camp riding on my own. This was the first time I had been on a horse's back since the Wanderers had taken me up to Dragon's Head in a wagon, helpless and close to death. It was so good to be riding again. I could feel my strength coming back though I still had to fight moments of weakness and dizziness.

Now that the Zarna of the Hadra had finally arrived, I wanted to see her before being seen and so I told Shamu I would introduce myself. Though I knew I was being unfair, I was angry at being forced to wait so long and now wanted some advantage in the matter. Mirashu showed me the way and I went on silent feet, slipping as quietly as I could up to the entrance of the tent.

Goddess, she looked so young! I had expected — no, hoped for — someone older, more seasoned, more experienced. I was young and Aranella was young. I was looking for someone to give guidance, to be wise, to know what to do in this matter.

In short, I was looking for someone to save us and this Zarna did not look to be the one.

She was seated on the ground, reading maps. At that moment she looked like a serious child, with her toys laid out before her. Then she heard me or perhaps sensed my presence and looked up. When her intent gray eyes fastened on mine, I saw this was no child. I shivered. Different — that was my first feeling when I looked into her face — different at the core, different from the rest of us in the world, the Hadra difference, I suppose. It was in the eyes, in the glance, though I could not say for sure what that difference consisted of. Some kind of certainty I suppose, some way of being in the world, the knowledge of having powers.

Noya

I heard no step, but I sensed her presence and looked up. She was standing at the entrance of the tent, watching me. My Hadra senses must have been asleep to let someone come up on me that way, or my mind too occupied, or else she was very skilled at deep silence. She was a big woman, broad shouldered as well as tall and very dark skinned. There was pain in her face, a drawn tightness, but also fierceness and determination. When my eyes met hers something leapt up in my heart, a sudden fire burned along my nerves. I was actually blushing. To cover my confusion I said quickly, "I was lost in my maps and did not hear you."

"So I noticed," she answered with a nod of her head and an ironic little smile. "May I come in?"

"Of course."

She ducked under the tent flap, stepped up next to me and pointed to the map. "Those troops are assembling there, not there as it is marked on the map. I am Jolaina, advisor to the Zarna of Maktesh and you must be Noya, the Zarna of the Hadra." Her eyes that had been so full of pain were suddenly full of mocking amusement as she looked down at me sitting in the dirt.

Jolaina

I thought her startlingly beautiful which was certainly an unexpected turn. Her skin was dark, darker than any Shokarn, though not as dark as mine. She wore her wavy, black hair loosely drawn back in a partial braid and bound with a bright sash. Her face was elegantly shaped, as if by a sculptor's hand. She looked me up and down appraisingly. I looked back and when our eyes met something lit up between us. It was like the flare of torchlight or like the sudden reflection of sun on dark water. My heart gave a lurch. I knew she felt it too. For just an instant she lost her cool composure.

Noya

I scrambled to my feet and held out my hand. When our hands clasped that fire ran along my nerves again. "Yes I am Noya, but I am no Zarna," I answered sharply. "A Zarna rules by accident of birth. I am Councilor of Zelindar, a leader freely chosen by free women. And so you are Jolaina, the writer of that imperious message. When you were not here last night I feared something might have happened to you. Now, what is of such importance that you have summoned us all to this meeting?" I talked fast and with some pretense of authority to hide my feelings. It would not have taken Hadra mind-

124

reading to sense the sudden rush of emotions I was feeling in the presence of this woman.

"We thought it best for me to stay hidden till you were here. Ablon rode up last night to tell me you had come, but by then it was very late."

"Please sit down. This is all the hospitality I have to offer," I said with a nod. Tenari was passing by the tent so I called out for her to bring us some tea.

Jolaina sat, but there was an impatience in her as if she might spring up at any moment. She leaned forward and said urgently, "What I have to tell you concerns us all. I would have come myself to meet with you, but I caught an arrow in the shoulder while escaping and have been in hiding with the Wanderers, recovering from a near-fatal fever."

With cup in hand, I sat and listened to her story, trying to remind myself to pay full attention to her words and not fall into a reverie looking at her face. When she spoke of Midsummer Day and how the Zarna would be publicly forced to capitulate and declare herself for war, her words had my full attention. "But we must stop them!" I burst out. "This must not be allowed to happen!"

"Exactly. That is why I sent for you. Working together, perhaps we can change the course of things. The Zarns are not the only power in this world."

I shivered with the impact and meaning of her words. "But Aranella will by guarded by troops of armed guards and the Hadra cannot use weapons in that way. How can we do this?"

"That is what we must discover."

Jolaina

I was stunned. I had not felt like this since I first met Aranella. In fact, aside from Aranella, I had never looked at another woman in that way. This sudden attraction frightened me. It also made me angry. At the same time it drew me irresistibly. I know she felt it too. It bent all our words strangely.

When we introduced ourselves she told me curtly that she was a Councilor, not a Zarna. Then I said, more sharply then I meant to, "It took so long I was not sure you were coming."

"It is a long way from here to the coast. We came as fast as the horses were able. Your brother saw to that."

She ordered tea for us both. I sat opposite her, clinging to my warm cup for some sense of safety in this storm of feelings and trying, at the same time, to speak coherently of all that had happened up to the writing of that note. We talked of war and danger and alliances and possibilities, things of crucial importance. But all the while I found myself distracted and had to keep remembering not to stare at her. Later, when we went to strategize with the others and make our plans, I could hardly keep my eyes from her face.

Amairi

So this was the famed Jolaina. No wonder Khundorn wanted her dead or in chains. Power flowed out from her, power and force and urgency, at least as much power as Khundorn himself exuded, but of a very different sort. I will never forget my first sight of her. She was standing in front of Noya's tent, gesturing with her hands and talking excitedly. "We will find a way. We must! There is no choice and we have very little time." I was instantly magnetized by her presence and stopped to stare, any thought of manners forgotten. I was not the only one watching. Several others had gathered to gawk, but Jolaina's attention was not on us; it was all on Noya.

Jolaina was not beautiful, not as such things are judged in Maktesh. For one thing, of course, she was much too dark for Shokarn standards. Yet she had beauty in her face, and pride, and pain, and passion. I found myself captured by her force and knew in that instant that I would gladly follow wherever she led, even into trouble, even into terrible danger. And I do not follow easily. Without even thinking of what I was doing I stepped forward and said, "I offer to help in any way I can. Whatever you need we will find a way."

She turned and looked at me in surprise as if I had suddenly dropped from a tree. Since I had just that morning scrubbed the last of the stain from my hands and face, she was no doubt taken aback by my Shokarn whiteness in that Wanderer camp as well as by the boldness of my words. I reached out my hand. "Once I was Elvaraine of Maktesh, but I had to flee to escape my husband's violence. Now I am Amairi the Wanderer, at your service."

I saw her eyes flicker with only a moment of hesitation. Then she clasped my hand and said warmly, "So Amairi, here we meet, two fugitives from Maktesh whose lives have gone through sudden drastic changes. The circle of fate that the Wanderers call the Cerroi must have brought us together for some purpose. You are a brave woman; I accept your offer. Come with us. We are about to meet with the others and decide how to do this thing. We must have Aranella and Nhuri safely out of Khundorn's hands and away from there before Midsummer Day is over." Then she swept forward like the prow of a great ship with the rest of us in tow, following her wake.

Sitting at the meeting that day, it did not take the Hadra skill of mind-reading to feel the simmer of attraction between Noya and Jolaina, nor did it take the talent of a fortune teller to read future danger there. The air between them seemed to crackle with small, constant lightning. I am sure I was not the only one who felt it.

Noya

Jolaina and myself and the rest of the Hadra went to meet
with Vondran, Mhirashu, Shamu, Morghail and several of the
other Wanderers, as well as Ochan, Toki and some others from
the Thieves Guild that Vondran had summoned. We gathered
up Amairi on the way, a new unfamiliar Amairi, back in her
own white skin. Though she looked pale and weary and was
still exuding pain, Morghail had requested that she be present
at our meeting. Nastal came uninvited and sat protectively
close to her. As we began to make our plans together I
thought, *Khundorn will not have such an easy time of it after
all.* Midsummer Day promised to be memorable and, Goddess
willing, it might be a turning point in this strange shadow
war.

Though the rest of us talked and argued and planned, I
sensed it was really the Wanderer leader, Vondran, who held
the reins in his hands. He was the one who had an overview
of where all the pieces should fit into the pattern and how best
to get them there. Morghail was often at his shoulder,
whispering in his ear. I, for one, was grateful. Though I was
nominally the Hadra leader, I knew little or nothing of the
world out there and was only too glad to do whatever part fell
to my lot.

Jolaina, even ill as she had been, was a strong, forceful
speaker, her voice full of power and conviction. In spite of all
the dangers that hummed around us I could not help admiring
her. Feeling the heat of desire rise in my body and rush
through my blood I found myself blushing. Though I tried
hard to shield my feelings from Hadra mind-touch I am sure
some of it leaked out into the gathering. The thought made
me blush all the more.

That night, when many were either sleeping or gathered
by the fire, I found myself drawn to go to Jolaina's tent on

some feeble pretext. I could see her candle burning there. She welcomed me in as if she had been expecting me. I started to ask some question about strategy as she was lowering and fastening the tent flap. She turned and looked me in the eye. "Why make pretenses, Hadra? We both know why you are here and why I kept a candle burning, waiting for you. Leave those lying words in that other world. We have no need of them here, and no time. We have been doing a dance around each other all day, from the very first moment we met. I know we are both pledged elsewhere. I have even asked about you. But we meet here in the midst of troubled times, not even knowing if we will ever meet again with those we love. And the Goddess has thrown us together, life in the shadow of death."

I slipped out of my cloak and held out my arms to her, saying, "Yes, the Goddess has brought us together and we meet under her eyes." Very deliberately, looking me right in the eye, Jolaina walked step by step across that tent and into my arms. Urgency flowed through me. I crushed her against my body. Instantly her mouth was on mine, fierce and insistent and familiar and totally strange. I felt myself taken down into another place where there were no Zarns or worries, where there were only passions and bodies and the Goddess flaring up like fire between us.

We sank down on her mat, pulling off clothes until we were body against body, flesh against flesh. I could feel her hands on me, hard and rough with need, and her own body under my hands and mouth, meeting my force with willing force.

This was not a Hadra. Though I could read her thoughts, I could send nothing back. There was only silence where there would have been connection and inner speech. Yet something in that strangeness made the passion all the more intense, as if I had to fling myself forward and leap vast distances to touch that other person. Some different connection was made between us on some other level, throwing off sparks like a fire. It was like nothing I had ever known before.

Jolaina

Late that night Noya came to look for me on some slight pretext. Sensing that she would, I had left the candle burning. Some part of me felt danger at the core and was shouting warnings. Yet I could no more have turned her away or shut off my own feeling than I could have turned a river back to its source. It was like being sucked under by the current. I even felt some anger at being forced or pulled by something much larger than myself, as if I had become a plaything of the Goddess. For a moment I thought of resisting, but when Noya held out her arms, I walked into them without an instant of hesitation. The moment she touched me, I was lost.

Different, so different, such a strange flow of power, lightning brushing up and down my body and my whole body quivering, reaching out eagerly for more. Yet there was fear mixing with desire, fear of that strangeness and that difference. It was as if her finger tips had eyes and her mouth had fingers and she was drawing up power from some mysterious source. I had heard the Hadra called not quite human and more than human. If Noya was any example, maybe it was both. Wild creatures who have never been domesticated may have such power, but not ordinary humans who have grown up under the yoke of compulsion. Not even Aranella had that kind of inner freedom. And Noya could even read my mind, hear my thoughts. I could not shut her out or enter her mind in turn.

Hearing my inner speech, she answered softly, "I could shield and block out your thoughts, Jolaina, but then I would block out so much else of you, nuances of feeling and response. I would rather not do that." Roughly I put my mouth over hers to shut off the words and was instantly pulled into that wild, dark place that is beyond words, or below words, that in fact has nothing to do with words. Yes, not quite human. Some knife edge of danger cut through me. It was like making love with a cat or a hawk or some other free creature or perhaps with the Goddess Herself. I shut my mind and turned myself over to whatever had called us together.

Noya

Later I thought guiltily of Vranith. There was already trouble brewing between us. I had not expected it to take the form of another woman. And yet I could no more help myself than I could help being burned by fire if I held my hand in the flame. I could indeed have believed in Jolaina's sorcery at that moment. Still I would not have condemned her to death for it — only to bed. In the next few days I was drawn back over and over to the sweet heat of that pleasure and soon gave up any pretense of struggling against it.

Jolaina

As the time flew past we did everything that needed doing, but in memory it is all a blur. The one thing I remember clearly is the feeling of Noya's lips on mine, her flesh against my flesh. But my passion was so mixed with guilt there was as much torment in it as pleasure. The Wanderers knew and gave us knowing glances, but Aranella was like a living ghost between us.

Amairi

That week was a series of meetings with many comings and goings. Wanderers and Thieves Guild and Hadra and Kourmairi and Muinyairin and even some Shokarn appeared and disappeared. Plans were constantly being discussed and preparations made. I did whatever was asked of me, whatever was needed while the wind in my head said, *Wait ... Not yet ... Soon ...* Meanwhile I bided my time and made friends with those of the Hadra that I did not already know.

Finally, we were on the road again, moving with a sense of urgency toward the last camp before the Parade Ground and Midsummer Day. We stayed in that camp only long enough to organize ourselves. Most of the wagons left a day or so before the rest of us. Shamu and Ablon and Mhirashu and several other Wanderers went to set up their booths at choice places and cook the food they would sell at the gathering. Then, in the dark of night, we set off with Vondran in the lead, Rhondil and Larameer far in front to act as our eyes and Morghail bringing up the rear to watch behind us. The Hadra, in stolen guard uniforms, would be following at dawn, with Jolaina as Captain, but really led by Mitru who happened to know that part of the world quite well. *Soon, it will happen,* the wind in my head told me, *Soon you will be needed.*

Noya

Midsummer Day was rushing at us and we could not be late for that appointment. There had been so much to organize and set in motion and now we were on the move. At that moment Garlian and the Council and even Zelindar itself seemed very far away, in another country or another world.

And yet everything I did was done to keep my city and my sisters and the beloved coast of Yarmald free from harm.

Our meeting place with the Thieves Guild was to be our last camp site before the Midsummer Day gathering. The Wanderers who knew the land so well had arranged all this, or rather Vondran had. He seemed to have taken over responsibility for this part of the enterprise as well. When we rode in, the little clearing in the woods appeared empty of people, though there were already tents and wagons and two cookfires burning. At Vondran's whistled signal, many Wanderers and some folk from the Thieves Guild appeared to melt back out of the woods and suddenly it was a busy camp again.

I recognized Toki and Ochan. They brought two more 'thieves' to meet with us as well as a young woman named Veridas. This Veridas was provocatively dressed in something red that barely covered her shapely young body. Somehow she managed to appear bold and bashful at the same time, a sort of calculated innocence, ducking her head and pretending to be too shy to greet me while at the same time looking sideways at me, flirting with her large dark eyes that were heavily ringed with dark eye paint. She was no doubt assessing my usefulness. This one would be something to watch. I had to resist clutching my money pouch tight against my side. Looking at her I thought to myself, *No doubt we are all going to be using each other in these next few days.*

The Thieves Guild had procured guard uniforms for all of the Hadra and for a few of the Wanderers as well. Even more surprising, they had gained proper guardsman's tack for our horses since of course we had no saddles or bridles. I was wildly curious as to how they had done all this, but I knew better than to ask. With the Thieves Guild you can accept their gifts or refuse them; you do not ask questions. They had also brought us some paste and powder, the kind used by Shokarn ladies who want to appear even whiter than they are by nature or sometimes used by Kourmairi house servants who want to seem more like their masters.

With much nervous hilarity we tried on our disguises. Jolaina, being so dark, looked blotchy under her concealing paint and I had to stifle my laughter. I suppose I did not look so very grand myself. In fact, I felt strange and awkward in the uniform of the guards. Veridas made so many suggestive jokes to Ochan and Toki about how the uniforms had been procured that I assumed she had had a hand in obtaining them, probably by the use of her body. She spoke loudly for the benefit of our ears, yet each time I looked at her she glanced away.

There were only two captain's uniforms. Morghail insisted one should be Amairi's for later use. He had some plans for making her our spy among the Shokarn. Jolaina said I should wear the other as I was the leader of the Hadra, but I deferred to her with a mock bow. "No, it is yours Jolaina. I speak Shokarn with the accent of a coastal Kourmairi or, worse yet, a Hadra. I would betray us the moment I opened my mouth. In voice you can pass for one of them. You have lived among them long enough and better know their ways. Besides you have a deeper voice. You have only to remember not to smear your face paint and pray there is no rain."

Later, after we had eaten our rough meal of boiled potatoes, onions, and cabbage, I purposely placed myself next to Ochan and Toki and said in what I hoped was a casual way, "I thought there would be more folk from the Thieves Guild here among us today."

Ochan grinned at me knowingly. "Not to worry, Hadra. We are already there at the parade ground in large numbers, finding our places between the cracks, ready for tomorrow's doings. The Thieves Guild would not have missed this gathering for the world. The high and mighty are going to have the surprise of their lives and the poor are going to be a little richer for it."

Being raised in that Hadra culture of absolute honesty, some part of me did not approve of the Thieves Guild or perhaps even of the Wanderers, but I was learning to take advantage of what was offered. I had heard enough warnings that we would not survive unless we set aside some of our scruples.

As if he had read my feelings, Toki said bitterly, "Later, when you think of the Thieves Guild and are tempted to speak of us with contempt, remember what we did for you and the part we played in tomorrow's happenings." I nodded, seeing the pride and anger and hurt in Toki's face. I resisted saying what I was thinking, that they were not just doing this for others. They would have plenty of advantage from the chaos of that day and would make a good sum for themselves. But it was not mine to worry whether some guardsman or some fine lady from the Zarns' cities lost their purses in the melee. The safety of my city and of the whole coast of Yarmald was enough for me to worry on.

Suddenly, thinking of what we were facing the next day, I felt overwhelmed and far from home and way beyond my abilities. At that instant I was flooded with loneliness for Zelindar — the sight of those familiar and beloved streets, the sound and smell of the ocean, the voices of Hadra strolling through their city. Even the sound of Jallin's voice or Linyate's would have been most welcome. I would have given everything in my purse for Garlian to fold me in her arms at that moment and tell me all was going to be well.

Hastily mumbling some excuse, I broke off my talk with Toki and slipped away to look for my Hadra sisters. Almost instantly I crossed paths with Tenari and Zanti. It was as if they were answering my silent call. Without a word spoken they both put their arms around me and held me tight. We stood that way for a while in the fading light until Zanti said softly, "Noya, I think you have need of the Goddess. Perhaps we all have need of the Goddess in this strange place so far from home."

I was worried for Douven, afraid of what would happen if he entered into the fray at the Parade Grounds. On horseback he was as swift and agile as anyone except perhaps the Hadra themselves, but on the ground he could not move fast enough to escape from harm. I tried to think of a way to give voice to my concern without giving offense and could never find the words. Then, on our last evening together in camp, I blurted out all my fears.

Douven gave me a look that froze me into silence. "Otta, you are no longer the big sister with the self-appointed task of keeping little Douven out of harm's way. You left home a long time ago and made your own life to suit yourself. I have made mine to suit me and have lived many years without your protection, following my own advice, making my own decisions, and taking my own risks. That does not change now just because we meet again.

"If you want to worry for me that is your burden to carry, not mine. Think how I feel, seeing you go back into such danger with an unhealed wound and a price on your head. I might rather see you safe somewhere, sitting by the hearth in a little cottage, stitching. But that is not to be and I would not think to tell you how to live your life so I could be free from worry.

"I took your message to Zelindar, but that does not mean I will take your orders. In the turning of the Cerroi we each have our own paths to follow and they both lead into danger. Whatever you do on Midsummer Day I wish you luck and you should wish me the same." Then, not waiting for my answer, he turned and hobbled away as fast as he was able. Without once looking back he disappeared among the horses. His words were like a blow. I had never heard Douven say so much at once or speak with such passion. For the rest of his time in camp he avoided me and so those were the last words between us before he left for the Parade Grounds with the Wanderers.

Noya

Dusk is a good time for calling in the sacred. With no words Tenari and Zanti helped me make an altar on a large stump at the edge of the woods, a little distance from the camp. Each of us added some small treasure from our pouches and something we had gathered from the woods around us. In the center I set the little Goddess that Vranith had made for me before we took to quarreling. No bigger than my thumb, she was beautifully carved out of bone and polished to a deep luster.

While the other two went to gather the rest of the Hadra I lit a candle stub from my pouch. Then I sat quietly by the altar, falling into a sort of trance or reverie. To my surprise, I found myself missing Vranith. Not the Vranith who had parted from me so coldly, but the Vranith I had known since childhood, the laughing girl with the magic hands who used to say, "When I am grown I will make a hearth Goddess for every house in Zelindar." I thought of her great skill and the passion we had shared and all the wonderful familiarity of her ways. Yet even as I missed her I could feel Jolaina's presence hovering about me with the unknown Aranella watching jealously over her shoulder.

When the other Hadra joined me, I got to my feet and we made a quiet circle around the altar, just barely touching fingertips. None of us had any wish to chant or drum or dance in usual Hadra style. After a long silence Pathell asked, "Noya, you called this circle, do you want to speak?" I shook my head. She said in her usual direct manner, "Goddess, please guide us tomorrow and help us do more good than harm in this matter." The other Hadra echoed her words.

At the end of our little ceremony, I said, "As it must be," the way the Witches in the past had taught the Hadra to do. Then I raised my palms, turning myself over to the will of the Mother. The rest did the same and we all stood together that way in silence for a moment. When we parted I felt a deep calm come over me, a sense of peace and purpose.

Later, when we had all conferred together for the last time, I was so weary I had to bite my lip to stay awake, fearing I might doze off sitting up, perhaps in the middle of a sentence. But that night my calm left me and so did my tiredness. I tossed about, unable to sleep, afraid we had forgotten something crucial and our plans would all go awry. When I finally slept, I dreamt wild, chaotic dreams full of screams and shouts and fire and horses running. In those dreams I was the hunted fugitive as Jolaina had been.

Jolaina

Midsummer Day! I woke to birdsong and jumped to my feet in haste. It was barely light; streaks of paler and darker gray banded the sky. The moment I opened my eyes my stomach clenched with fear. The waiting was finally over. The day we had all been preparing for was suddenly upon us. I had done everything I could to bring us to this place. Now I hoped that we were equal to the task. There was much to gain and much to lose, all riding on this moment.

Some of my companions were already staggering to their feet. When I went to rouse the others, I was amazed to find Noya still asleep. Looking down at her, my heart felt ripped apart with tenderness and loss. She was so deep in sleep I had to shake her several times before she responded. Her eyes, when they finally opened and met mine, were full of longing and in the next instant, sudden pain. Then her expression changed again and she leapt to her feet. Gripping my hand between hers, she said in a fierce, determined way, "This is the day we free the Zarna and change the course of history, you and I." She pulled my hand to her mouth and brushed my fingers with a quick kiss. Then she turned and was gone, calling to the other Hadra and gathering them together while I stared after her, shivering with uninvited and powerful desire.

Quickly we whitened our faces and put on our guard uniforms, the ones the Thieves Guild had stolen for us. For me there was something solemn in this. It was not a sham anymore, it was a ritual of sorts. Some day soon I would wear this uniform of red and gold for Aranella. It would be the truth then, not a disguise. As I buttoned the last buttons, I made a pledge to myself and to the Goddess, *No matter what obstacles lie before us we will get Aranella and Nhuri to safety this day.* The others, as they dressed, were equally serious. There was none of the nervous clowning of the day before.

Almost immediately after we were on the road, a company of guards rode by us in the other direction. They said they were looking for the witch, Jolaina. I spoke up boldly, telling them they would have to be very clever or very lucky to catch up with that one. Meanwhile I was shivering inside. How strange to be so hated and feared and despised. What had I ever done to deserve that? I wondered what it would be like to have the powers that went with the name. Watching them ride off, my feelings ran from rage to tears to laughter.

Noya

Jolaina woke me with a none too gentle shake. I was amazed that I had slept at all and somewhat embarrassed to have needed waking. Seeing her bending over me, meeting her hungry gaze, I felt my whole body flush with desire. I wanted nothing more than to pull her down on top of me, plunge my hands under her garments and begin kissing her all over. With all the force of will I could summon I got to my feet and turned away, instantly throwing myself into the day, this day that we had all been waiting for and riding toward.

This morning we had the camp to ourselves. The Wanderers and those from the Thieves Guild had already left in the night, taking Amairi and Nastal with them. They planned to position themselves about, selling food from their wagons, keeping watch and being ready for whatever came.

This time we were silent and serious as we lightened our hands and faces and dressed in our guard uniforms. There was no laughing or teasing as there had been before. When I caught sight of Jolaina in her uniform, her air of power and authority was oddly disturbing. A little shiver of excitement ran down my back.

The Wanderers had already doused and buried the fires and taken the wagons. We had nothing left to do but pack our bedrolls, then saddle and bridle our horses with this new and unfamiliar gear. I had to apologize several times to Morning for the strange contraption I was putting on her, but I arranged the bridle so it only looked as if there were a bit in her mouth. Then, single file, we rode down the little lane, following Jolaina.

Almost as soon as we reached the cobbled highroad we crossed paths with a small troop of guards riding in the opposite direction. The Captains saluted one another, Jolaina looking quite smart in her uniform. In her deepest voice she said, "I thought this was the way to the Parade Grounds."

"You are no more than an hour's ride away and have only to follow this road. We are in search of the witch Jolaina. We heard rumors of her in this direction."

"Well, unless you are very lucky or very clever, rumors are

surely all you will ever find of that one. We have been searching for her too. First we hear a report of her in one direction and then in another. By the time we arrive, she is nowhere to be found and soon we are chasing rumors again. The local folk are very frightened and beg us to catch her. These men of mine are all well trained, but sometimes I feel as if we are chasing shadows or a ghost rather than a flesh and blood woman. Who knows, perhaps she uses her powers to change shapes, becoming an animal or a bird at will. We are on our way to the great meeting to make sure she does no mischief there."

"I doubt if she would dare to do anything there. There will be too many guards about. I hear the Zarna will be there today to cede Maktesh to Khundorn. Better for a man to rule in these times of trouble."

Jolaina nodded. "Yes, yes, much better and Khundorn surely is the right man for the work. Well, take care, Captain, and keep your wits about you. You can never be too careful when there is a powerful witch on the loose."

I had to bite the inside of my cheek and fasten my eyes on the uniform in front of me to keep my laughter from bursting out. All around me, I could feel the quivering of silent Hadra laughter, especially from Koshar. A terrible great cough was rising in my throat. I choked it down, afraid I would explode with it before the guards were out of hearing and so be our undoing.

Without another word, Jolaina led us off at a brisk trot. When we could no longer be heard by the guard she turned and said mockingly to the rest of us, "Yes, she changes her shape, you fools, and today she has become a Captain of the guards. Take care, tomorrow she may become a snake or a hound or a bird-of-death." Underneath the banter I could sense Jolaina's bitterness and pain at being the target of so much hatred. I shook my head, wondering how this all would end. Even if Aranella won back her rightful place in Maktesh would these same men ever be loyal to her again and loyal to Jolaina as well? Loyal to this woman they had hunted as a witch? With a shiver I thought, Midsummer Day may be only the beginning of this story, not the end.

Section II:
Midsummer

Part I:
Midsummer Day

Aranella

They say they want me to write my part of Midsummer Day and what followed after, but what about all that came before? What of my first meeting with Jolaina, and my years of training to be Zarna, and my captivity in Khundorn's hands — what of all that? Is that not also part of the story?

Ah well, I suppose that is a whole book in itself. Besides, why should I want to write anything at all for the Hadra after what Noya has done? Well, I will do only this little piece for them. Maybe, later, I will write the rest of it for myself and for the records of Maktesh. Certainly the Zarna's words on the matter should be recorded. However, for the purposes of this account, I will start with that moment on the platform, but only after others have written all that led up to it.

Aranella, Zarna of Maktesh

Amairi

Midsummer Day and we were almost at our destination. As we had started out in darkness, it was still early morning when we drew near. The road came to the top of a small rise and there were the Parade Grounds spread out before us. That vast meadow, flat as a table top, was bordered on the north by the winding blue gleam of the Scarn River and on the south by the straight dark line of the great Zarn highway. Vondran signaled us to stop and wait while Larameer and Rhondil rode back to join us.

I was very glad we were on a small farm-track, empty of other travelers. I was about to re-enter the world I had left so precipitously. Suddenly, unexpectedly, I was very frightened. Perhaps terrified would be a more accurate word. Vondran seemed to sense my feelings. He reached out to put a steadying hand on my arm, saying, "You are a different person, Amairi. They cannot swallow you up again. You are a Wanderer now. Besides, no one would recognize you, not even your own mother." I nodded, trying hard to subdue my fear and wondering if Horvath would be there or Nhageel. It did not help that Nastal was hovering around me, putting out waves of anxiety on my behalf.

Then I thought of Jolaina's courage, Jolaina who was riding back into the jaws of death when there was a price on her head and so many had tried to kill her. Taking a deep breath, I straightened my back and my resolve. After all, no one had dragged me here. I had insisted on coming out of my own persistent stubbornness. Now I had to be ready to take my part in whatever happened.

Even at that early hour the meadow was a bustle of activity. In the distance the carriages of the Shokarn Highborn as well as the carts and wagons of ordinary folk were cluttering the highroad and flowing into the grounds in a steady stream from the east. Great quantities of guards were rushing about in all directions like brightly colored ants. Even from that far away I could see the different city colors: the red and gold of Maktesh; the black and gold of Eezore; the blue and gold of Pellor; and the green and gold of Nhor. All the Zarns were represented there, even the Zarna. *So,* I thought with a shiver, *they are really going to try to do this thing and we are really going to try to stop them.* My heart was pounding loudly in my chest.

Now that I had seen Zelindar for myself, I much better understood what a wonder the Zarns were trying to destroy. It made my heart ache when I thought of those streets where women walked so freely, those beautiful buildings and parks and gardens, the great Zildorn at the top of the hill. All that would be gone, utterly crushed and destroyed if Khundorn and his followers had their way. There was indeed treasure there, but not the sort that men could put in their sacks and haul away. I tried not to picture bloody bodies lying in those streets.

After a quick consultation among the Wanderers, we started down. Rhondil and Larameer were leading us to the Wanderer wagons and soon, ahead of us, I could see our red, yellow and orange banners flying. Stobah was riding next to me and I said fearfully to her, "I have never seen so many armed men. How will we ever be able to slip through them to rescue Aranella?"

"Phaaa," she said contemptuously. "We are the little ones, the silverlings, the minnows of the Escuro river. The bigger the net, the easier to slip through. All those men will only get in each other's way. They will not have a single voice to command them."

"Khundorn will try."

"And so will others. In the confusion we will follow our own course. Stay alert and watch for opportunities. You know their ways and speak their language and you have a guard uniform you can put on. You will find your place in the web of things. We must not allow this to happen today, too much hangs in the balance. All of Yarmald hangs in the balance." I had the feeling she was saying more to me than her words, yet I could not quite grasp the meaning under them.

In spite of the grim reason for this day's gathering it had the look of a grand festival. City flags were flying everywhere as well as town and village flags. Banners rippled colorfully in the wind over the stands and booths and wagons. Every guard troop seemed to have its own banner. We rode in through noisy herds of sheep and cows, no doubt all there to be killed for the three day feast. Flocks of fowl scattered before us, squawking loudly. There were huge fires at the edge of the field with enormous spits and what appeared to be slaughtering pens nearby. All manner of rough men were at that work and a multitude of women were bustling about in filthy aprons, pounding down dough, chopping vegetables for the steaming pots and tending the fires. Vondran and the other Wanderers called out greetings to these folk as we passed and were heartily greeted in turn. I had a sense of the Wanderers being part of some vast underground river of life, taking its own course, well hidden from the Highborn.

When we came to our own wagons I could see they were set up like a small market, each wagon having been turned into a booth. Goods and gossip were already flowing freely and some performers were practicing their acts. Veridas was dancing wildly on a high platform. Her red dress, the color of fire, was rippling out on the wind of her motion and her feet were moving faster than the eye could follow. She had drawn quite a crowd, mostly men. There were many guards among them. No doubt the Thieves Guild were diligently working their trade among the pouches and pockets assembled there while their owners were watching open-mouthed, absorbed in their own lustful fantasies. And of course Veridas made sure there was plenty to watch. She created a tempting display with quick, seemingly accidental glimpses of bare breast or thigh.

After leaving our horses at the Wanderer encampment, a group of us made our way from the edges to the center of the field. Everything there became much more formal. A huge stand for seating had been erected. It was covered with velvet fabric and soft, bright cushions, flanked on either side by mounds of flowers. Family places were marked by the banners of the Great Houses. It was empty still, but when it was full it would hold thousands. Opposite it was a raised platform with several ornate seats or chairs. At the back of the platform, with steps going up to it, was an elaborate red and gold throne, the seat of power of the Zarns of Maktesh.

I had only seen that throne once before. That was when the Zarna had been crowned just before her father's death. It had also been the last time I was with my parents before my marriage to Horvath cut me off from them. Flooded with memories, I stood gaping so openly that a passing shepherd leaned toward me and said with a sneer, "Khundorn may think to sit his skinny arse on that throne before the day is out, but much may happen between now and then. This day is likely to be full of surprises for him."

Stobah grabbed my arm and said sharply, "Come along, Amairi. Do not draw attention to yourself by staring that way. You endanger us all."

I shut my mouth and let her draw me away, well aware of the look of sly interest on the man's face. At the same moment I heard a guard saying angrily to him, "Get these animals out of here right now, man, and take them to the edge of the field. This place is for people, not for animals."

The shepherd mumbled quick apologies, saying, "So sorry sir. My sheep ran off and I have been hard at work trying to gather them together again." He called his dog and made a great show of effort. Somehow I did not think there was a word of truth in what he said. The guard, meanwhile, had already turned his displeasure on us. He shouted harshly, "Finish your business here here and be gone. By noon this place must be cleared for gentle-folk, Highborn and guards. Such as you must keep to the side."

Stobah was bobbing her head and wringing her hands. "Yes sir, thank you sir, to be sure sir."

I turned to stare at the man, bristling with anger and indignation. As Lady Elvaraine he never would have dared to speak to me that way. Morghail came up on the other side and gripped my arm, whispering in my ear with a hiss, "Amairi, take your Highborn indignation and stuff it in your pocket. This is not the time or place. Wanderers do not win by answering back. We win by winning — by using our wits. Perhaps it is time for you to put on your guard uniform and go about spying out what useful information you can discover for us. Soon I will do the same." I nodded and let out the breath I had been holding in a little hiss of anger.

When the guard was out of hearing Stobah said through her teeth, "Arrogant fool, by tonight he will be singing a very different tune."

Jolaina

The moment we rode into the vast confusion of the field I began looking about hopefully for Aranella's great red and gold coach. Of course I knew it unlikely that she would be there yet. As I wove this way and that, the Hadra followed where I led, but I felt nervous and awkward leading my little troop. I was more used to advising than commanding, not sure

150

if my captain's uniform made me in truth a captain or only a sham of one.

Finally, at Noya's request, we stopped to confer. I quickly discovered that I was just one captain among many and could only lead if others agreed to follow. Pathell was the real strategist, not Noya and certainly not me. Pathell was the one who mapped our moves. The Hadra might be a contentious lot and argue among themselves but, as I soon discovered, they had a quick way of coming to decisions, using nods and glances as much as words. Much as I admired these bold brave women, sometimes their mind-talk left me feeling angry and frustrated, the outsider in their midst.

I was about to slip away when Pathell fixed me with a stern look. "Jolaina, do not think to play the hero or the fool in this enterprise. When the time comes, let the Hadra be the ones to surround Aranella and protect her with our bodies. You and Danil and maybe one or two others keep hold of the horses and ride in to get us . . ." Before she could finish her words I saw a guard riding toward us in haste. I felt a rush of alarm, afraid we might be unmasked already, but Zanti, seeing my look, said quickly, "It is only Morghail." More of Hadra powers no doubt. How else could she have known at such a distance who that was in a guard uniform?

Morghail trotted up and bowed to me, saying in a semi-mocking way, "Captain, I have come to report on everyone's location and hear your plans. It seems I am to be the courier who carries messages and conveys plans."

"Ask Pathell," I said waspishly. "She is the real captain here. She has just been informing us all of our places."

For her part, Pathell made no response to my sarcasm. While she and Morghail exchanged information, I stared into the far distance at the road that was disgorging more and more wagons and carriages onto the field, wondering if Aranella's carriage would also be coming from that direction. Soon she would be there, soon . . .

151

Amairi

Before I changed into my guard uniform, I told Nastal she must stay with the Wanderers. She argued with me, refusing to leave my side and asking in a frightened voice, "But who will keep you safe, Amairi? Who cares for you as I do?"

I was insistent however, telling her I could not do my work with her watching over me. Then Morghail added his firm voice to mine. "Amairi has an important task and you are hindering her. Make yourself useful here and do not cause trouble. There will be enough to deal with for one day without your adding to it. Go ask Mirashu what needs to be done." Nastal flushed in anger and looked away, but did not try to follow me anymore.

As soon as it seemed safe to do so, I slipped into the front of Mhirashu's enclosed wagon, going in as a Wanderer woman and coming out the opposite end as a guard in a smart new uniform of red and gold. Anyone watching would probably think some exchange had been made of sex for coins and the guardsman was going off well satisfied. With no word to the others, only an arrogant stare, I mounted a horse that had been left ready for me and rode off into the vast confusion of the field.

For a while I reveled in my new sense of freedom, with no one watching over me. Then, at a loss for what to do next, I wandered around the entire encampment, checking to see where the Wanderers and the Thieves Guild had placed themselves, where the guards were strongest, who was watching whom; trying to gather any information that might be useful to us later.

I soon spotted Jolaina waiting at a strategic spot with some of her troop and several horses, and I was glad to see Noya and the others close to the platform. I even saw a few guards that I knew from Maktesh and recognized a few fine folk in the tiers of seats that were beginning to fill, people I had met at those hateful parties. They, of course, did not know me. To them I was just some nameless guard, not the abused wife of their supposed friend.

Then, just as I was passing the back of the platform again and sneaking one more look at the throne, I sucked in my breath in surprise. There was Horvath, in a captain's uniform, riding in with a whole troop of men from the estate, farm-boys in the uniforms of guards, men that I knew, some since childhood. Nhageel must have gathered these men and loaned them to Horvath. We passed quite close, he and I, but of course he did not recognize me and neither did any of the men.

I got a quick grip on my fear and found I was rather enjoying my invisibility. Horvath merely gave me a slight nod as he passed, one Captain to another and I nodded back, biting my lip not to laugh in his face. I vowed to myself to keep an eye on him. He meant no good for Aranella, of that I was sure.

Noya

Having left my horse with Jolaina, I made my way over to the raised platform in the middle of the field along with several other Hadra in guard uniforms. I felt somewhat uneasy as it was surrounded by a large company of real guards, all wearing the red and gold of Maktesh. But we must have looked convincing enough. No one tried to block our way. Using Zanti's empath powers to keep touch with each other, we worked our way in among them without too much difficulty until we were halted by sheer numbers. The opposite stands were rapidly filling with people who were obviously rich and important. The seat in the middle of the bottom tier was set apart and far grander than any of the others. From the talk of the guards, I gathered it was to be Khundorn's place of honor. Listening to these men who were obliged to do his bidding, I did not think they had much love for the man.

There was tension in the air as before a storm. I could feel the hair rising on my arms and the back of my neck, then a shiver ran down my back. Shortly after we found our places, the arrival of the royal coach was heralded by a loud fanfare of drums and trumpets. The coach, ornately decorated in red and gold, was surrounded by still more guards. I heard Tenari say in my head, *Now it begins.*

When the coach stopped, the way parted and a beautiful young woman in a long, dark blue gown stepped down. She was accompanied by an obviously terrified girl-child and a tall, hawk-faced man. I assumed this man to be the Khundorn of Amairi's description. He escorted them up the steps to the throne, seating the woman on it and the child next to her on one of the ornate chairs. They were followed by an older, plain-looking woman of proud bearing. Dressed in black as if for a funeral, she quietly seated herself behind Aranella. I could feel waves of anger coming from this woman. Her eyes watched Khundorn with a look of relentless hatred. Observing her I thought, *If eyes could grow blades that man would be dead on the spot.*

Khundorn stepped back and waited for silence, standing very tall and grand. When all was quiet he made a deep bow and a wide sweep of his arm, saying loudly, "My Lady Aranella, Zarna of Maktesh and all surrounding lands from the Rhonathrin Mountains to the sea." At his words the fine folk in the stands rose and bowed deeply. Then, to my amazement, the common folk began to shout and stamp and applaud, calling out her name and making a thunderous noise. I saw Khundorn flush a deep, angry red as he raised his hands again for silence. When the noise had subsided he said in a resounding voice, "The Lady Aranella favors us with her

154

words today. Give her the respect of your absolute silence and attention." Then he bowed again and went across to sit in his grandly appointed place on the lowest tier of the stands. Guards quickly stationed themselves on either side of him.

I saw Khundorn nod; then Aranella rose as if on strings and stepped forward with her sister at her side. There was a fixed, dead look on her face. Her eyes were empty and her body moved as if it belonged to someone else.

Jolaina

Aranella's beautiful face was all wan and drawn with pain. I would have done anything to have spared her that pain. She seemed to have aged ten years since I had last seen her. Her bright hair was even covered with a dark shawl. Her jaw was clenched, her eyes hard and cold. Though she was surrounded on every side with hostile forces, she clutched Nhuri against her as if somehow she could shelter the child's life with her own body.

I wanted to be the one to stand beside Aranella, the one to rescue her. It was hard to see others there in my place after all the work I had done to free her. I had agreed with Pathell that it was better to do it that way as the Hadra could guard and shield her with their own bodies if necessary, and I was too easy to wound or kill. Now I was not so sure. I had to bite my lip not to call out, *Have courage Aranella, I am here.*

Amairi

I quickly pushed forward to a spot where I could watch both the stand of seats and the platform. No sooner was I in my place than I heard the sound of drums and trumpets and saw the grand red and gold carriage of the Zarna drive up. Then Aranella herself stepped down, flanked by guards and aided by Khundorn. Poor Aranella, my heart went out to her. She seemed so small and slight, fragile almost. She looked like a child, with Khundorn at her side, hulking over her, waiting impatiently to pick her bones. The man appeared more like a bird-of-death than ever. I wondered if Aranella had been tortured. She was all gray and weary, looking very different from those times I had seen her in Maktesh with her bright smile and her golden hair shining in the sun. Of course those had been joyous celebrations. For Aranella, this was probably more like a funeral. She even had a dark shawl over her head. Her sister, Nhuriani, was at her side. The child clutched the Zarna's hand in a tight grip and kept glancing around fearfully. When Aranella began to speak in that flat, lifeless voice it cut to my heart. What had they done to her to make her willing to stand there before everyone and speak their lying words?

Aranella

I felt like a dead thing, pressing Nhuri against me for warmth and a little glimmer of life, knowing this might be the last time we ever saw each other alive in this world. Khundorn had just led me up to the raised platform, presented me to the assembled crowd, and seated me on the throne. Then he walked grandly across the way with a company of guards and seated himself in the place of honor at the bottom of the stands. The common people had cheered for me, something unheard of for a Zarn, and Khundorn had flushed with anger. They trusted me; I think they even loved me. And there I was, about to betray them, about to turn them over to Khundorn's

156

power because I could not bear to see my sister tortured, had not the courage to be the cause of her terrible pain and her death.

Even seated I kept Nhuri close. I felt her tremble against me; heard Dharlan in back of me muttering encouragements; saw Khundorn lean forward, gloating; was aware of the Highborn in the stands waiting with bored expectancy for me to speak. In despair I glanced about one last time, but there was no sign anywhere of Jolaina. She had said she would be there and I had foolishly clung to that hope. Now I had to accept that all was lost. At least I could console myself that she had not been killed by the guards nor was she Khundorn's prisoner. If he had her he would surely have taken the greatest pleasure in letting me know by parading her body before everyone, whether dead or alive.

For just that one moment I was sharply conscious of the heat of the day, the cloudless blue sky, the dust, the noise of the animals, the bright colors. Then I saw Khundorn give me a slight nod. It was time. I rose and took a deep breath, feeling like a moving corpse, pulled into life by strings in another's hands. With the taste of bile in my mouth, I was just about to name him as Zarn in my place. I waited for total silence, then in a lifeless voice began the speech that had been forced on me and rehearsed so many times. "It is with deep regret that I come here before you today to make this announcement. Due to my fragile health and the seriousness of this coming war I have decided to step down from the throne of Maktesh in favor of..." Before I could say that detested name my ugly little speech was interrupted by one of the guards standing near me. It was a woman's voice that said loudly, "Otta! Otta is here! Otta!"

At the sound of that name life suddenly came flooding back into my body and my spirit returned. I could feel blood coursing through my veins again. My heart was pounding from excitement. I was no longer afraid. I remember thinking,

What does it matter anyhow? Sooner or later he will have to kill me and Nhuri too. Let death come quickly if it must. Better to die as I have lived, being free and speaking my mind. At least I will not be the one to bring him to power. Let the Goddess herself decide what happens next. Then words came thundering out of me without any need for thought, words full of power and conviction. "No! I will never name that man as my successor! Never! He may kill me for it, but at least I will have this one moment to speak the truth . . ."

Noya

I could see the look of gloating expectation on Khundorn's face as he leaned forward, eager to hear himself elevated to Zarn by Aranella's own words. Unable to push myself through the crush to whisper in the Zarna's ear, I called out desperately, "Otta! Otta! Otta is here."

She must have heard me. Instantly her body stiffened. She lifted her head, threw back her shoulders and raised her hands. Then, in a voice like thunder, a voice that must have carried all the way to the farthest cook fires, she shouted, "Lies! All lies! Lies forced on me by Khundorn, that worm of a man. He made me lie by threatening to torture and kill my sister, Nhuriani. He wanted me to name him Zarn today so he could drag you, the people of Maktesh, into this disastrous war against the Hadra. But I will not speak his lies; I will speak my own truth before you all. I will never name that man to be my successor! Never! Instead I name him traitor! That man Khundorn is a liar! He is a torturer, a killer, and a traitor!" With her arm stretched out she was pointing her finger straight at him.

Khundorn had leapt to his feet, pointing back and shouting, "Kill her! Kill her! Kill her!" over and over again.

With a cry Aranella threw back her head and screamed, "Kill him!" All her fear and fury came bursting out in those two words. Khundorn had only the chance to shout once more before I saw the flash of a knife and a sudden flower of red blossomed at his throat. In mid-cry his expression changed from rage to amazement to horror as he toppled forward.

Amairi

I saw Noya say something to Aranella and everything changed. Suddenly the Zarna was shouting, "Lies! Lies! Those were all lies they made me tell!" The color came rushing back into her face. She threw back the dark shawl that had covered her head and drew herself up so that she was standing straight and proud with her bright hair blazing in the sun. This was no longer a broken child before us, mouthing another's words. This was the Zarna of Maktesh in all her power, eyes flashing, arms raised. Her words echoed across the grounds and instantly everything erupted into motion. Carts and wagons filled the space between the platform and the stands so quickly they seemed to have dropped from the sky. Cows, pigs, sheep, chickens and horses were running loose. Guardsmen were rushing about, barking out orders and unable to get through.

I saw Khundorn rise, shouting wildly, "Kill her! Kill her!" and pointing at Aranella. She whirled in that direction, pointed back at him and called out fiercely, "Kill him! That man is the cause of all our troubles." Then a quick knife flashed in the noon sun. I never saw the one who wielded it.

That hand was too skilled and fast. Khundorn's look of fury quickly changed to horror as he fell. With no grief at all I watched the man die. The guards could not even rush to apprehend his killer. Too much was happening too fast and the way was blocked in every direction.

Aranella

What happened next was that the whole world suddenly erupted! Everything turned upside down and inside out. Khundorn leapt to his feet with a shout, pointing at me, then instantly fell forward in a gush of blood. There were shouts, screams, explosions, bursts of dust, fire, smoke, animals howling and bleating, wagons rumbling in, guards roaring orders, horses running. Then I heard Jolaina calling, "Aranella, Aranella, this way." The guard who had called out "Otta," and was really a woman, pushed me quickly into Jolaina's arms. Jolaina had me mounted on a horse in an instant. I saw Nhuri mounted next to me in front of another guard who was also probably not a guard and heard Dharlan's voice behind me. Then we were galloping away through the chaos with a mob of guards who were not really guards all around us, rapidly following some madwoman in a red tunic who kept veering wildly this way and that across the field.

Noya

In the next instant everything was happening at once. Women were screaming and men were shouting. The space was suddenly crowded with wagons and people. Guards were bellowing for the way to be cleared while farmers were shouting at their animals and at each other. Added to this uproar were screams and shouts from the stands, "My necklace is gone! My earrings! My money!" The Thieves Guild at work already! Though I had been expecting it, the scope of the chaos still caught me by surprise.

For just one moment there appeared to be a shepherd orchestrating this turmoil. Then two wagons were hauled into the middle of the bedlam, one pulled by the other and driven by someone who looked much like Douven. The driver cut the horses lose and was speeding away on one of them when there was a giant explosion. The wagons burst into pieces, wheels and boards flying in every direction, totally obstructing the way. Instantly the stands disappeared as dust and smoke blocked the view and the shouts and screams grew louder. All of this happened almost faster then the eye could follow.

I was looking about for a way out for us when I heard Jolaina's voice close by. She and Veridas and several others suddenly materialized out of the smoke at the edge of the platform. They had come with our horses. Some of the guards, seeing what was happening, tried to grab us or block our way. Using my body as a shield for her, I pushed Aranella into Jolaina's arms. Then I leapt from the platform onto Morning's back.

I saw the flash of a knife as Jolaina slit Aranella's skirt to enable her to ride and in the next instant she had her up on a horse. Aranella kept shouting, "Dharlan, save Dharlan, do not leave her in their hands." But Koshar already had the older woman mounted in front of her. I saw Pathell on horseback with Nhuri in her arms. All around me Hadra were mounting hastily. Veridas kept calling out impatiently, "This way! Quickly! This way! Follow me!" The noise and chaos seemed to be getting louder by the minute: shouts, screams, curses, explosions, people and horses running, dogs barking, orders being shouted, other orders countering them and then more explosions. The Wanderers and the Thieves Guild had certainly done their work well!

Veridas and Danil were leading. Somehow they kept finding us a way through though we could not take a straight course. We had to zig-zag around countless obstacles. In mind contact with the other Hadra, I tried to keep Jolaina and Aranella at the center of our fast moving pack, as well as Pathell for she had Nhuri mounted in front of her. Finally Jolaina grew impatient with these maneuvers. "Let me go at the front," she shouted to me. "If any guards block our way I will be only too glad to bloody my sword with them."

"And cause us no end of trouble that way. Stay at the center and keep Aranella safe. Bloody swords will not help us now. At this moment I am leader here and you must honor my word, Jolaina." I tried hard to sound commanding. In reality I was breathless and confused, feeling far more like a follower than a leader as I tried to keep Veridas' red dress in sight on our wild veering course. I felt Danil drawing many of the riderless horses along with us by mind contact. Koshar, riding next to me, said to Dharlan, "Can you ride alone, Lady?" When Dharlan nodded, Koshar passed her the reins and flung herself onto one of the free horses. I saw Dharlan go white with fear, but when I asked, "Can you do this?" she answered tersely, "I have ridden since childhood. I will follow wherever you lead to stay with Nhuri and Aranella."

Aranella

A way through that jumble kept opening miraculously before us. It was all I could do to hold on to my horse. I needed to put my full attention there. For so long I had struggled alone just to keep my wits about me and life in my body, trying with all my strength to resist the hostile pressure designed to crush my spirit. Now I was beyond exhaustion. Helpless in this rush of motion, I surrendered myself to the flow of events. As long as Jolaina was riding near me I felt safe. She had promised to rescue me. I felt sure she would get us away to safety. The rest of our escape from the Parade Grounds is only a blur in my memory.

Amairi

That part of the show was over. Khundorn was dead. Now he could never be named Zarn. The Hadra were riding away in haste, taking Aranella, Nhuri, and Dharlan with them. For that moment at least there was no organized move to stop them. Having felt useless for most of that day, I was determined to keep up with them and help guard their backs. But wild explosions and fallen wagons and all manner of other sudden barriers soon cut me off from them. Veridas was leading, mounted on a nimble little spotted pony that skillfully wove its way through the chaos. Occasionally I would catch a glimpse of her red dress and aim my horse in that direction; then I would lose her again in the dust and smoke and swirling confusion.

Jolaina

I could hardly believe it; Aranella free and riding beside me! And Khundorn dead! My heart was pounding wildly from joy and excitement and fear. There was no safety yet. It was all much more dangerous than before. I was terrified of losing Aranella in that wild turmoil of dust, smoke and violent motion. We could easily become separated from the others and even from each other. And we might at any moment be captured.

I wanted to go faster, to break through the circle of horses that surrounded us and gallop toward the river. It felt as if we were being led in circles and we would never get free of the Parade Grounds. When I tried riding to the front and out of that moving enclosure of Hadra horses, Noya ordered me to stay where they had put me, saying sharply, "At this moment I am leader here. You must honor my word, Jolaina. This is the best way to keep Aranella safe. We are using our bodies to shield her."

Clearly I had no choice. Yet I felt trapped and helpless. I was sure we would be stopped by guards as we wove our way across the field. Suddenly we had to veer around an obstacle and almost came to a halt. For a moment we were headed back the way we had just come. Then it happened, exactly as I feared. When the smoke thinned there was a troop of guards riding straight at us. The Captain was shouting Aranella's name.

Noya

Suddenly our way was blocked altogether by a jumble of overturned wagons. We came to a halt, nearly running into each other. Once again we had to change directions. Momentarily we turned back toward the platform. The air was so thick with dust and smoke it was impossible to see far ahead. I kept hearing frustrated shouts of pursuit from all directions and was afraid we were headed right into enemy hands. Then Danil shouted, "Turn! Turn now!"

Before we had the chance to turn the smoke lifted and I saw a guard troop right in front of us, heading straight in our direction. Waving his sword triumphantly, the Captain was shouting, "Halt! Give us the Zarna!" There seemed no way we could avoid this dangerous confrontation. In the next instant I heard the thunder of hoof beats in back of us. Suddenly one lone guard dashed between us, blocking the Captain's way.

Amairi

I was feeling even more useless than before, having lost all my people and wondering one more time why I was there. Then the smoke cleared momentarily. In that instant I could see Veridas and Danil and all the rest of them. They had changed direction and were riding straight at me with the Zarna in the middle. Next, there was a loud shout from the opposite direction. When I turned to look, I saw Horvath rushing toward them, followed by his whole troop of guards. He was heading right toward the Zarna. Seeing Aranella in front of him, a look of malicious triumph crossed his face. "Halt this moment and give us the Zarna!" he shouted, brandishing his sword.

Jolaina

Now I thought we were surely lost for one lone man could never stop that sizable troop of guards. I was not even sure if he meant to save us or join them when suddenly he called out, "Stop, Horvath, put down your sword. You must not harm the Zarna!" With amazement I realized that it was Amairi's voice I was hearing over the turmoil.

Without a moment's hesitation I rode between them, blocking Horvath's way. In my own voice I called out loudly, "Horvath, put down your sword. Husband, it would not do you well to harm the Zarna." All my life I will remember with pleasure the look of shocked amazement on the man's face. Noya had spoken before of my courage. This time it was not courage. It was utter recklessness. I had thrown myself into the gap as if I were as invincible as a Hadra.

"Elvaraine, what are you doing here?" Horvath shouted at me furiously, reining in his horse. "What is this madness? Out of the way before we lose her!"

Ignoring him, I took off my captain's cap as I called out to the men, "Yorant, Argus, Gorinth, it is I, Elvaraine of Maktesh. I command you to let your Zarna pass safely. It would be a terrible thing to have her blood on your hands." They had stopped and were milling around in confusion. I needed to command their attention. "Listen to me, all of you," I yelled, waving my arms wildly. "I have known you most of your lives. You have always trusted me. Listen to me now!"

Horvath also looked confused and frightened, but he raised his sword again, trying to appear bold. "Out of the way now, woman, or I will cut you down with no further warning! That is my final word!"

When he started to ride at me with that intention, Gorinth rushed him and knocked away his sword so that it went flying through the air and landed harmlessly in the dirt. Then Yorant gave a roar of anger, leapt from his horse, pulled Horvath down and bore him to the ground. There was no struggle. Horvath is not a small man or a weak one, but Yorant is like a moving mountain. It was like having an ox fall on him. Suddenly Horvath was lying empty-handed in the dust, mouth open in surprise while Yorant was rising to his feet again, dusting off his pants and picking up the fallen sword to put in his belt.

Noya

It all happened too fast for me to follow. When the dust had finally cleared, the man Amairi had called Horvath was lying empty-handed on the ground. One of his men was just re-mounting while the rest of them gathered around. By some sudden transformation they no longer seemed to be *his* men. Much to my amazement, there was Amairi at the center of it all, appearing to be very much in command. "Leave him and follow me!" she ordered the men. "We must make sure the Zarna gets away safely." Then to us she shouted, "Go quickly and I will guard your backs." In an instant she was gone, leaving her once-husband standing in the dust without his sword, shaking his fist after her and shouting curses.

I turned for a last sight of Amairi, splendid in her red and gold captain's uniform, sitting proudly on her horse as she rode off at the head of her newly acquired troop of guards. Then Veridas spun her pony about to ride off in the other direction, followed by the Zarna and her unlikely escort. Horvath scrambled out of our way as we all swung about and swept past him, riding hard after Veridas.

Amairi

These newly acquired troops of mine were not trained guards. They were more like peasant soldiers, armed and sent off to fight for something they did not understand. They knew nothing of such matters. It had been easy enough to get them to switch sides at my command. In fact, they seemed overjoyed to be following me instead of Horvath. After joining forces we made it our work to ride about encountering troops of guards and sending them off in the wrong direction in hasty pursuit of the Zarna.

I had never before in my life told so many lies or taken so much pleasure in lying. Perhaps I was no longer fit to be a Wanderer since Wanderers were supposed to tell the truth. My men were like little boys on some sort of wild mad holiday, playing a giant game with me, tricking their betters. They would joke and laugh uproariously each time another troop of guards went dashing off the wrong way, saying, "Well done, Lady Elvaraine, well done, no danger from them now."

These grown-up farm boys, many of near my age, were on a lark, an adventure. I fear if it had been a different adventure with a slightly different leader they would have been looting and raping and burning with just as much pleasure and just as little thought. For myself, I was in a turmoil of feelings. When I remembered Horvath's angry face I would feel a tremor of fear at what I had done. Then I would want to laugh aloud at his look of shock and surprise when he heard my voice. Next I would feel a swell of pleasure at the thought of him lying helpless in the dust, vengeance for all the pain and grief he had caused me in our time together. And to think I had told Vondran I had no taste for vengeance.

After a while of misdirecting the guards I circled back with my men to see what was happening at the stands. There the last of the Highborn were streaming off their tiers of seats. Having lost all semblance of their Uppercaste manners, they were shoving and shouting in a most undignified way, scattering the embroidered cushions and tearing the velvet to rags in their panicked flight. Even the bright, fallen flowers were quickly trampled into the dirt under their running feet. Soon the carriages of the Highborn were bumping along in haste with their coachmen shouting imperiously to make way for this important person or that one as they crowded onto the Zarns' highway along with the carts and wagons of the poorer people. Khundorn's body had already been carried off. The spot was marked by a splash of bright blood on a pale yellow cushion.

No one seemed to pay us any heed. All around us fires were being put out, animals herded together, wagons righted, spilled goods gathered up. The field was deeply trampled, scattered with clothes and food and various belongings. Those who were hurriedly gathering it all up, probably not always the original owners, were filling sacks and pockets and bags. They did not even glance in our direction. Shokarn troops from the four Zarn cities were being called to order by their Captains and preparing to march out. I was just wondering if I would ever find the Wanderer camp, even with the careful directions Vondran had given me, when Morghail appeared at my side in that sudden way he had. "Greetings Lady, I see you have been hard at work creating chaos, very effectively I might add."

"You have been watching me?"

"At moments I was able to observe a little of your work when I was not too busy making my own mischief and you were not too fast for the human eye to follow. And who are these fine men that you are leading about?"

"This is my former husband's troop that I freed from him, men from my family's estate, farm boys that I have known all my life. They seemed glad enough to leave him and follow me. We have been causing a grand confusion together. Yorant, Argus, Gorinth, meet Morghail, my comrade of the road."

And so I, the renegade Shokarn lady, introduced Morghail the Wanderer to these farmboys turned guardsmen who were now my followers. Morghail reached out and clasped hands with some of them across their horses' necks. "Even if you wear the uniform of the guards you cannot be altogether bad if you follow this woman," he said with a grin. Then he turned to me and went on in a very different tone, "Time for us to

169

be gone from here, Amairi. It may seem safe enough right now, but at any moment the wind could blow the other way and with no warning. Some of those troops are still loyal to Khundorn and they might decide to stop and question us. I would rather leave on my own than flee across the river with guards on my tail."

"My men? I cannot leave them."

"Yes, they had best come with us for the moment. It may not be healthy for them here either." Then his tone changed again and he shook his head with a wry grin on his face. "Well, this story is not yet over, there are new chapters being written as we speak. At least Khundorn is dead and I did not have to kill him myself. That is one big advantage of this day."

"Whose hand cut his throat?"

"Ah, only the Goddess and the killer know for sure. I have no regrets for that man's death, but I promise you the hand was not mine."

"Morghail, would you have done it? Could you have killed him?"

"Ah, yours to ask and mine to know, Lady. No need to speak of that now, Amairi. Just follow me out of this place and keep a good eye on these men of yours."

Riding out of the Parade Grounds, I found myself weary beyond exhaustion. I had done it, that thing I had so strangely foreseen. I was no longer needed in that way. Ever since I had fled from Horvath, I had been running one way or the other, pushing myself day after day beyond the limits of my endurance. Now that this piece of work was finished and Aranella safe and my part over, I would have been glad to lie down in the trampled dust, cover myself with one of the rags of clothing lying about and sleep for a week. Of course that was not to be. We had one last push to make before there was any safety to be had. I groaned inadvertently and Morghail looked at me with concern. "Are you alright, Amairi? Can you go on?"

"Of course," I said more sharply than I intended.

"Do you want to ride my horse with me?"

"Too dangerous. Besides, it would look foolish for a Captain to be riding in a guardsman's lap."

Odd to remember that we had once been lovers, this man and I. That seemed to have happened in another life or to another person. After that exchange I felt a little stronger, but I noticed that Yorant and Argus rode up on either side to keep watch over me. That simple kindness and the look of concern on their rough faces almost brought tears to my eyes. Glancing around I was suddenly very glad to be riding away from there. I had just noticed bodies in the field lying among the litter, human bodies as well as animal ones. I had seen enough for one day. With grim humor I thought, *This will surely be a Midsummer Day to remember in the years to come.*

Once we reached the edge of the great clearing Rhondil and Larameer joined us and conferred briefly with Morghail. They were to ride with us for a while and act as our scouts and guides. Fearing pursuit, I kept looking back nervously. Finally we turned north and the sounds and smells and smoke of Midsummer Day faded behind us. When we came to the Scarn River we rode our horses across, afraid the bridges might be watched. Soon after that Rhondil found us a road into the woods.

For a while we went in near total silence while Larameer rode back to see if we were being followed. After he returned to say there was no one on our trail I lost some of my wariness and rode more freely, listening to the men around me joking and bragging and sharing stories of the day. All that changed however when I rode up next to Argus and asked, "What is the news of my parents, Argus? And how is the estate faring? And why were you all riding with Horvath this day?"

I knew at once from the look on his face that the news was not good. He shook his head and looked away, spluttering, "Not me, I do not speak well. Better to ask another."

"But you are the one I asked. Tell me Argus, I insist on it. You speak as well as any man and I need to know."

"Lady it hurts to tell you. I wish I could spare you this. Your parents both took sick and died within a week of each other a month or so back."

Both dead! Both my parents gone while I was wandering about like a beggar and indulging myself by bedding strangers. I held back a storm of grief and guilt to ask again, "And the land, how goes it with the land? Are the crops all planted? Are the people well?"

"Lady, I mean no disrespect, but you have asked and someone should tell you. I suppose it must be me since no one else seems willing to speak. In your brother's hands it all goes from bad to worse. He has no head for such things. Neither do his friends. And his best friend is the bottle which is no friend at all. So now I have told you everything."

"Not by half; I need to hear it all." And so, for the rest of the way, I questioned Argus about my parents' death and pressed him for details about the condition of the estate, all the while holding a tight rein on my own grief. It was all bad, as hard for me to listen as it was hard for him to tell. The only bright spot in the telling was that my brother had another child, a boy, born a month before my parents' death and named for my father.

Once we reached camp I gave way to my own weariness and have no memory at all. Some kind person or persons must have helped me off my horse, laid me down and covered me over for I was already asleep.

Part II:
Aranella's Story

Aranella

Under the seeming chaos of that camp there was some core of order. A big red-haired man named Vondran was apparently the leader of the Wanderers. The others also accepted him as leader though he seemed more prone to making suggestions than to giving orders. It was amazing to watch all these people hard at work with no one in power over them to give commands. Ethran and Mhirashu had undertaken the organization of the camp itself with an easy practiced efficiency, assessing what was already there, directing what needed to be set up and saying where things should be put or moved as they appeared. Shamu, Ablon and Douven quickly set to getting us all fed — a miracle of sorts. Yurith took charge of Nhuri and soon had her laughing gaily. Shamu gave me some clothes to wear, clothes far more suited for a rough camp than the stiff formal dress forced on me for Khundorn's intended coronation. I was only too glad to be rid of that dress. But when I declared myself ready to throw it in the fire and started in that direction, Veridas rushed up to collect it lovingly in her arms, saying with a mocking little bow, "Lady, if you are done with this I can make good use of it."

Time felt to me strangely bent or twisted. I would be totally absorbed, watching everything around me in the camp with interest, when suddenly the thought would go through me again, *Khundorn! Dead! The man is dead and all that is over now!* Then my head would instantly be filled with scenes from the Parade Grounds and the Summer Palace and the terrible ride from Maktesh as a captive. I would see Khundorn's face again, leering at me. Though I knew he was dead — had seen him die right before my eyes — still it sent cold shivers up my back to remember the power he had held over my life. If I did not forcefully close my mind to it, I could still feel his hand on my arm and hear his harsh threatening whisper in my ear. He had almost had his way. We had come so close. If not for Jolaina . . .

Nhuri and I were treated with kindness and concern in that camp but certainly not with the sort of deference that as Zarna I had come to expect. They seemed very glad to have us safely there among them, all except one Wanderer woman named Stobah who looked me up and down with open contempt, wrinkling her nose as if she smelled bad fish on the table. "All that fuss over such a stick of a girl," she said to Mhirashu, purposely speaking loud enough for me to hear. "A Zarna does not look so different from the rest of us except that she is pale as a slug. She has two legs, two eyes and a nose, just like ordinary folk, and probably other things as well." With those last words she made a rude gesture between her legs.

174

"Hush," Mhirashu said sharply. "Have some kindness, Stobah. She has just come through a terrible ordeal." Though she spoke sternly there was a little smile crinkling the corners of her eyes.

"Kindness maybe, but do not ask me for politeness. I have never been known for my manners and I am not about to start now just because there is a Zarna here. And do not ask me to be bowing and scraping to her; my back is too stiff; I am too old. We have rescued her; now she must accept us as we are."

After that Mhirashu drew me away to help chop some vegetables for the pot as if I were really part of the camp. I worked next to Old Nairth and she gossiped in my ear, leaning close and telling me the names of the Wanderers around us and some little morsels of information about each one. In turn she asked me questions about Maktesh and the life there.

Busy as I was for that while, I never lost my sense of Jolaina watching me from her place by the fire and the feeling of connection between us, a cord that ran from heart to heart. And no matter how much other noise there was I always listened for the sound of Nhuri's clear, high voice that rang like a bell for me. The terrible chill of fear that I had lived with for so long was slowly beginning to thaw.

Jolaina

Every time I look at Aranella I feel a great rush of joy, an immense relief quickly followed by the sharp bite of guilt. *I have to tell her. I have to tell her soon, but not now, not yet. Goddess, let her enjoy this gift of freedom for a while after all she has endured.* I am so thankful she does not have that double-edged Hadra gift of mind-speech. I feel Noya at the dark edge of things, watching, and I feel her pain. What a wasp nest I have stepped into! Nothing is simple and everything has a sting to it.

I want to sit by Aranella, touch her, hold her, stroke her hair, her back, fold her in my arms, listen to her words, hear everything that has happened since I saw her last, but there is time enough for that later. After a little while of clinging close to her I have had to let her go into the life of the camp. Now, from a distance, I enjoy watching her as she moves about with grace and ease among these people who are so different from what she is accustomed to. And the pleasure of hearing Nhuri laugh again, such a simple thing and worth more than jewels. It warms my heart to see my brother Douven making friends with her in his kindly way. Perhaps he can be the older brother she never really had. For this moment at least she can be a child, though who knows what lies in wait for her in her dreams at night, or for that matter, what lies waiting in her future. The magic child, so full of innocence and knowledge, what did they do to her in those months of captivity? Goddess only knows, in this coming struggle for power, what she will grow up to be.

Douven and I met, as if by accident, in the middle of the camp. We both said at the same time, "I am sorry for my hasty words . . ." Then we instantly fell to laughing and ended by hugging each other. He had a bandage across his forehead, having come through his wild adventures with nothing more than a cut from a flying board.

Later, when I tried to do my part, helping with the camp, Shamu drew me away by the hand and pushed me down to sit by the fire. "Stop now," she ordered with kindly sternness. "You are barely healed and you have strained everything in these last few days. Pain radiates out from your shoulder like the smoldering heat from a sick fire. Let me put a little salve on it and rub away some of that soreness. Then I will get your journal and you can sit here by the fire and write of everything that has happened."

Shamu was right of course. As her hands were kneading my sore flesh, I found myself groaning aloud with relief. I had grown so accustomed to pain it had become my constant companion. I hardly noticed it anymore.

So now I sit here, writing about the incredible events of Midsummer Day and all that went before it. At the same time I am watching Ablon turn mountains of grain cakes on a giant grill while nearby Larameer and Rhondill raise tents as if by magic. I am also keeping an eye on Aranella and Nhuri and Noya and Douven and all these other people that I am learning to love.

Aranella

We camped that night, Nhuri and I, with the most extraordinary collection of people. There were a number of Hadra and among them their Zarna, Noya. There were guards who were really Hadra, and guards who were really farmers. There was an assortment of Wanderers, among them a Highborn Shokarn woman turned Wanderer turned guard Captain who looked vaguely familiar. She had apparently appeared at just the right moment to save our lives and rescue us from a troop of enemy guards belonging to her brother or perhaps her once-husband, guards who had now come over to our side. All very confusing and really quite amusing now that we were safely out of enemy hands. There were even some people from the Thieves Guild as well as a shepherd named Gairith who was probably not really a shepherd and his dog, Gotha. These were not at all the sort of folk I ever had occasion to meet before and as deposed Zarna I suppose I added my own little bit of spice to this strange soup.

In spite of all the differences among us we had this much in common: we were hungry, sweaty, weary, smelly, excited and very pleased with ourselves. Except Amairi, the woman who had saved us from the guards. That was because she had fallen asleep on her horse. Vondran and Morghail between them gently lifted her off and laid down to rest. She hardly stirred and continued to sleep through all the noise.

The talk was loud and lively as each one had some tale to tell of Midsummer Day, sometimes even interrupting another's story in their eagerness to tell their own. Only Noya remained silent, sitting in the shadows, saying little and seeming to watch everything. Once in a while I would catch her eye on me, then she would glance away again quickly.

Jolaina sat next to me, her body pressed against mine, her arm around my shoulder or my waist. Each time I looked at her, she met my glance with a smile and a deep look of her own. She seemed to take pleasure in saying my name as often as possible. No need among these folk to hide our love or pretend it was something less than it really was. Nhuri sat on the other side, leaning against me while she ate. Hard to believe Khundorn was really dead. For so long he had loomed over my life, holding me captive and trying to force my will. I almost wished it had been my own hand that wielded the knife.

Sitting in the dirt in this rough company with Jolaina and Nhuri on either side of me, eating plain food, watching the fire and listening to the excited voices around me, I was sharply aware of feeling happier than I ever had in my life. Certainly freer than I had ever felt in the Palace of Maktesh! Then Nhuri sighed, groaned and dropped her head in my lap. With a sudden stab of pain I wondered what had been done to her by those men while I was helpless to save her. In that instant all my happiness fled.

After we had wolfed down a huge pile of grain cakes and gobbled some simple fare from an enormous stew pot, Vondran played on his ferril and sang a succession of plaintive old songs. Much to my surprise, Dharlan seemed to know them all. She joined in with her deep, rich voice, singing with such spirit that others turned to watch her. I could see admiration reflected in their eyes. Never before had I seen Dharlan as separate from myself. She had always been there in my life as my nursemaid, even before my birth. Though she had raised and trained me, having far more responsibility in that than my sickly mother, still I always felt I had power over her life and had seen her as part of myself. Now, suddenly, I saw her from a distance — a strong, handsome woman who had a secret life of her own, private, separate and totally unknown to me. These were certainly not the songs I remembered from my childhood.

When they finished, Jolaina brought Gairith over to meet me. The man had been watching me strangely. Now he made a deep bow and asked with mock solemnity, "Lady, did you like the little surprise present I put in your tub?" Then he and Jolaina instantly dissolved into helpless laughter. When they could finally speak again, they told me the tale of the tub and how he had hidden her in it and how they had first met in Zanzairi when the carriage that held me prisoner had passed so close Jolaina could have reached out and touched me.

Later, with Shamu adding her part, Jolaina told us all the story of her escape and everything that had happened since I had last seen her. She even showed us the scar from her wound. With trembling fingers I reached out and touched the rough puckered flesh. From Shamu's words I understood just how close I had come to losing Jolaina to death and what pain it had cost her to ride out in search of me.

At the very end of the evening, with the Wanderers beating an accompaniment on drums or pots, Veridas danced for us in the same red dress we had followed like a banner out of the Parade Grounds. "For Zarna Aranella, who is a free woman this night!" she called out boldly. Watching her with her head thrown back, her dark hair flying and her limbs flashing in the firelight, I marveled at her tireless energy after the strain of that long hard day. I was exhausted, slumped

179

against Jolaina, barely able to keep my head up and Nhuri was fast asleep in my lap. But Veridas was well worth watching. She was bold, fierce, sensuous and beautiful, moving like a dancing flame in her red dress. In all my years in Maktesh, I had never seen anything like her.

Noya

I keep glancing at Aranella and glancing away again, afraid the whole story is clearly written on my face, wondering if she already knows, trying to see by watching her words and motions what kind of a person she really is. I am pained by my deceit and it drives me back into the shadows. In my whole life among the Hadra I have never lied to anyone or even tried to conceal the truth. Though we can shield our thoughts, we cannot hide our feelings from other Hadra and so, from an early age, even as we learn to speak, we learn to speak the truth. Now I find myself caught in a web of lies and deceptions. It hurts me in the deepest part of myself. Jolaina keeps speaking of how different the Hadra are from other mortals and this is one of our differences. We live in a web of knowing, a deep sea of connection to others, a sea of truth and trust. Words are only the surface of it.

My silence is choking me, but the truth would be too cruel. Besides, it is not mine to say. It is up to Jolaina to speak, not me. I cannot betray her in that way, not even for my own comfort. Yet every time Aranella looks at me I find myself looking away in shame and confusion, unable to meet her eyes, feeling my Hadra soul twisting inside me.

I cannot find it in my heart to like the woman and I wonder if my dislike grows from my own discomfort so that I wrong her doubly. Oh Garlian, it is a big world out here that you sent me into and a very confusing one. So much of it I was completely unprepared for. At this moment I wish you were here to give me counsel or better yet, here in my place. Perhaps you would know how to act in this swirl of confusion. And in spite of all this, I cannot bring myself to regret what has happened between me and Jolaina. No, I cannot wish it undone though the pain of her distance cuts like a knife. Nothing has ever touched my soul in quite that way.

Aranella

Free! I was free! The shock, joy and amazement at suddenly being freed was so great I could hardly comprehend it. I would find myself longing for freedom as I had so many times in those past few months, only to remember again that I already had it.

That night, lying in the luxury and shelter of Jolaina's arms, I kept falling asleep out of shear weariness and exhaustion. Then I would wake again full of delight. Recalling with pleasure where I was, I would lie there in the dark, listening to her breathing and feeling her body next to mine or I would pull her close against me, kissing the back of her neck and stroking her hair, even as she slept. Sometimes she would wake and we would begin caressing each other with eager hands until sleep swallowed us up again. Nhuri slept on a mat on the other side of me so I could reach out and touch her for reassurance whenever I wanted to. I needed to know that she was really there with me.

The next day we made our plans for a triumphal re-entry into Maktesh and talked endlessly of how it could be accomplished. Vondran kept saying it needed to be soon, that I had been out of power far too long. Other factions would already be struggling for power in the wake of Khundorn's death. Jolaina, as usual, was full of ideas. So was Dharlan.

This was a side of her I had never seen before. Her eyes shone with excitement, her words were full of passion, and when she spoke others listened. The Wanderers also had ideas and advice. So did the folk of the Thieves Guild. Only Noya, Councilor of Zelindar, seemed distracted and distant, oddly silent. Perhaps she was longing to be back in her own beloved city.

As we were talking excitedly, I intercepted a strange look between Jolaina and Noya. It felt as if a rock had dropped into my stomach. I said nothing at that moment, but I set out to watch them. Soon there were more looks and it became clear to me that something had happened between them in my absence. A flash of anger threatened to tear me apart, but I kept a calm exterior. Of course it was not possible to fool Noya or the other Hadra, not with their cursed skill of reading minds. When there was a pause in the talk I asked Jolaina and Noya both to step aside with me.

It did not take Hadra mind-powers to read the guilt and confusion on both their faces. Neither one of them would look me in the eye. My terrible hurt made me cold and hard as a blade. I had been betrayed by the woman I trusted above all others in the world. "What is it between you?" I asked, looking from one to the other. "I can see it, smell it, feel it. I am no fool, Jolaina." My voice was like ice. She was looking down at the ground. "Look at me Jolaina. Tell me, are you and Noya lovers?" I could hardly get the words out of my mouth.

With that Jolaina raised her head and looked straight at me. Our eyes locked. All of her pride, her honor and her fierceness blazed in that look, but her words were gentle. "I am truly sorry, Aranella, for the hurt I have caused you. I love you now and I always will. I have loved you from the very first moment I laid eyes on you. But what happened between me and Noya was between us and the will of the Goddess. It happened when the world had turned upside down and we did not know if we would live out the week or even the next day.

I cannot, in all honesty, wish it undone. Yet tomorrow I would risk my life for you all over again, no matter what the cost or the fear and would never have a moment's peace again till you were safe. No matter what else was happening, I never forgot for one moment that you were a prisoner in their hands and I used every tool that came to hand for the purpose of freeing you."

Unable to meet her stare, I was finally the one who turned away. I had thought she would grovel and beg forgiveness and was not even sure I would grant it. I had not expected her to face me down that way.

Jolaina

And so it has been said much sooner than I wished and with nothing to soften the blow. There is no way in this tangle of people and obligations to really talk, to find a place of truth and honor and compassion between us, to convince her of my love in spite of what she sees as proof to the contrary. This has been a hard day of trying to keep our feelings in check and plan for what needs to be done.

And now I cannot sit up all night, talking and holding Aranella and giving her reassurance as I might like to. Shamu has given me a draught for the pain and I can already feel sleep tugging at me, claiming me, blurring my thoughts and my vision, slurring my words . . .

Aranella

That night I could not sleep. Sleep evaded me like a fish darting through the water. Except for the sentries, everyone else in the camp was asleep. Even Jolaina lay with her arm heavy over me and her leg thrown over mine, breathing loudly, almost snoring. *How could she sleep so easily after what she had told me?*

I lay awake, staring up through the leaves into the starry sky, the rat of jealousy gnawing holes in my brain, *How could she have done that? How could she?! How could she have forgotten me in the arms of another woman while I was a prisoner in the hands of our enemies with my life at risk? And after all I had done for her, chosen her above all others, chosen her to be my life's companion when she was nothing but a Kourmairi farm girl with no future before her except drudgery on her father's farm. If I were a true Zarn and really had Zarn powers I would not put up with it. I would have her put to death in an instant for this treason. When I returned to Maktesh and was back in power again, I would see her sorry for what she had done and show no mercy.*

That was how part of my brain ran on and on. The other part wanted me to fling my arms around her, sobbing and begging her to tell me none of it was true, that she loved me best and always had and had never loved anyone else. I lay there stiff and sleepless, trying not to thrash around and waken the others, doing neither one thing nor the other, neither sleeping nor rising, listening to Jolaina's breathing with my heart breaking. I should have been rejoicing at being free. Instead I was a different kind of prisoner, trapped in the prison of my mind, tortured by my own thoughts. *How can she sleep that way while I lie awake in torment? How is it that she does not feel my pain?*

I did not really plan it or intend it. I would never have done such a thing deliberately. It almost happened of itself, one thing unfolding into the next. The moon had risen and was filling the camp with ghostly light when I heard Nhuri stirring in her sleep and then calling softly to me. I slipped out of Jolaina's embrace and stood up. Nhuri needed to relieve herself and could not do it there among all those rough men.

I walked her a little way from the center of the camp. When I met the Hadra sentry there I told her what we were doing. She let us pass with a warning to be very careful and stay close by. I went beyond her to a place where Nhuri could do her business in privacy. As I waited I heard a horse nickering softly beyond us in the dark.

That was it, my answer! I would simply ride away in the dark and take Nhuri with me. I could not face seeing Noya and Jolaina together. I could not imagine what my life would mean without Jolaina in it. What did I care about being Zarna of Maktesh? What would that mean to me with Jolaina gone? I would find some other life. I would make a new life for myself and forget the past. Underneath all these thoughts was the loud refrain, *And then she will be sorry . . . then she will be sorry . . .*

Anyone could have stopped me with the right word. I had no plans, no food, no direction. Instead all the doors fell open. Like a fish hooked on a line, I kept being drawn forward on this dangerous path. When I went to the horse it was one of Amairi's guards who stopped me, not one of the Hadra. I drew myself up and ordered him to saddle and bridle the horse for me and to be quick about it, saying I had to go on an errand for Jolaina. Though he must have thought it strange, he had long training in obeying commands and not questioning his "betters". No Hadra would have let me go off that way in the dark. Besides, she would have known I was lying. But this man was of Maktesh. How could he think to say no to the Zarna? He made my horse ready and so set my fate in motion.

Driven to thoughtlessness by the pain and madness of jealousy, I set out into the night with Nhuri mounted in front of me. I had no thought but to go as far as I could from Jolaina and the grief she had caused me. For a while there was a great sense of relief from finally taking some action and no longer lying trapped at her side, stiff and sleepless.

The night air was cool and damp, a pleasant relief after the heat of the day. There was even enough moon to see by. I rode along in silence, lost in my own private fantasies. *I could go to a Kourmairi village and ask for shelter there and become a peasant woman as Jolaina's mother had been. I could meet with other Wanderers and ask protection of them as Amairi had done. I could go back to Maktesh and rule as my father had, angry and cruel and without mercy. Then I would denounce Jolaina and she would be a fugitive again, regretting her betrayal while she fled for her life. Whatever had made me think Jolaina's vision of a different way to rule could work? Perhaps they were right and she really had bewitched me. We had been such foolish young women, she and I, thinking we were going to change the world together. And look at what the world had done to us, wrenched us apart and put another woman between us.*

Then Nhuri asked me for the third time, "Where are we going, Nella? What are we doing out here in the dark?" This time her words finally reached through to me because she added, "Nella, Sister, I am frightened. Those men are searching for us and I never want to be in their hands again." Her voice shook and she shivered in my arms. Suddenly some sanity returned to me and with it a horror of what I had done. What was I thinking of? Where was I taking this child? Bad enough to be risking my own life with this madness; worse yet to be taking my little sister into more danger as if she had not had enough already.

"We are going back," I said softly, trying to reassure her. "I only wanted to do some thinking." But when I turned the horse I saw it was already too late. I had not heard them. I had been too lost in my own private imaginings. They had been stalking me, probably for a while. I could see them clearly in the moonlight, blocking my way. There were several, five or six or more, not enough guards to mount a raid on our camp, but certainly enough to recapture one fool of a woman, out alone with a child. I suppose they had hoped I would ride far enough from the others so they could capture me without my alerting the camp with my cries. Like an idiot, I had obliged them.

I spun my horse around and kicked him into a gallop, gripping Nhuri tight against me. I could hear the pounding of hooves in back of me and one man shouting, "Take them alive. Zuron will pay much for those two." Remembering Jolaina's story I turned toward the woods. When the way grew too thick I abandoned the horse and ran on into the moonlight-splattered darkness, pulling Nhuri along with me. I expected to hear them crashing through the woods in back of us. When we had gone some distance and my fears had somewhat subsided, I realized that the only sounds were ours. Panting and trembling, I slowed to a staggering walk.

We seemed to be on a small path or maybe an animal trail. If I kept my head low the way was not too hard for me, but I could feel that Nhuri was rapidly tiring. I knew I did not have the strength to carry her and keep on going. I was about to sink down in despair when I saw what appeared to be a small hut in front of us. With the trickery of moonlight and shadow it did not look to be much more than a rock heap, yet some light was seeping out from under a door.

I knocked and knocked and there was no answer. No matter how I tugged at it, the low stone door seemed immovable. Nhuri had crumpled by my feet and was whimpering like a child of three. This was the end of the road for us. We could not go on. I would have climbed in a window or down a chimney to find some shelter for her, but I could not see any openings into this strange stone hut. I stepped back again to look and suddenly a woman was standing in front of me.

Startled, I sucked in my breath. Nhuri looked up and gasped. It was as if the woman had appeared out of nowhere. She was tall and dark skinned, as dark as Jolaina with silver hair that hung over one shoulder in a long club of a braid. A glossy black raven sat on her other shoulder and she had a huge toad cupped in her hands. She looked neither old nor young nor any age exactly. Her voice, when she spoke, sounded more creature-like than human, strange and rusty as if it did not get much use. "Shokarn, your people have driven mine almost to extinction. Now you have pursued me even here. No doubt your hounds will follow. What are you doing here in my woods and what do you want?" There was nothing kind or welcoming in her voice.

I was too desperate to care. Holding out my empty hands I croaked, "Sanctuary!" My voice sounded almost as rusty as hers. "Please, if not for me then for my sister; she cannot go on. I can go back out and lure them away. It seems they are determined to have me, one way or the other. Perhaps if they have me they will let her live."

"They will not have either one of you, not while I live. I have been expecting you, Aranella. Get up and stop crying, Nhuriani. We have no time for that now. We have too much work to do."

"How did you know . . .?"

With a shake of her head she pushed against the stone door and it swung open easily. "No time for that now. Go inside. You asked for sanctuary, Zarna, and there it is." When I hesitated she gave me a shove to get me moving.

Pulling Nhuri with me, I staggered in, too frightened to object and too amazed to question more. The raven fluttered from her shoulder over to a perch at the end of the bed. The toad she set on a rock ledge among some ferns. Inside the hut was lit by a single lamp. At a quick glance it looked more like a piece of the woods with a roof over it than like any room I had ever seen. In spite of myself, I shivered with distaste. This strange woman was watching me closely with an expression on her face I could not fathom, only that it had some mix of triumph and amusement. "My name is Ouvrain and I am a Witch. I know far more about you, Aranella, than you will ever know about me." As she said that she gestured toward a large, dark bowl filled to the brim with water. It was sitting on a black cloth in the middle of a small round table. Glancing at it, I saw dizzying movement across the surface of the water that made my stomach lurch.

"What . . .?"

"Not now — later. There is no time now for explanations. We have much hard work to do if you are to stay free of them. And they will be here soon. Sit on the floor, both of you."

Nhuri was trembling, looking around fearfully. I pulled her down beside me. Then Ouvrain blew out the lamp and suddenly we were in total darkness. In a compelling voice, she went on, "Link hands with me and shut your eyes. Take a deep breath to clear your minds." Ouvrain's hand gripped mine with surprising strength, Nhuri held tight to my other hand. Soon I could feel an amazing flow of power between the three of us. "Now, with all the strength you have, think of vines, rocks, brambles, tree roots, briars and thorns. Then weave them together, tighter, thicker, see them covering this hut, covering everything, covering everything. Thicker! Think harder! Put all of yourselves into that thought. Now hold tight to that no matter what you hear. Hold tight! See the vines covering everything . . . everything . . . everything . . . See this hut disappearing from sight, see it becoming invisible to human eyes."

My head ached from the effort. Bright colors flashed behind my closed eyelids. Then Ouvrain began to hum, a strange terrible sound that grew and grew till I thought my skull would crack with it. Though the ground under me felt as if it were shaking and heaving, I held to that image with all the force of my mind; vines and brambles weaving together to cover everything. I could feel Nhuri pressed tight against me. Finally, over the terrible hum, I heard the sounds of men's voices again and the dreadful baying of hounds.

Amairi

*All I have done since I have been here in this camp is write
and eat and sleep, not as much sleep as I might have wanted
though, for I was anxious to get all that part about
Midsummer Day set down in my little journal. I knew we were
planning to move on soon and who knows when I will have
the next chance. Though I no longer have to write to save my
sanity it has become a habit to keep a record of things, at least
when life allows me to.*

The camp is in a great uproar of agitation and anxiety this
morning. Aranella has disappeared. She apparently ran off on
her own, taking Nhuri with her. Some Wanderers and Hadra,
under Morghail's direction, are out searching for her. There is
even some fear that this may be a trap for Jolaina so she has
been persuaded not to go. Far too dangerous for her out there.
Instead she is pacing around in an agony of guilt and worry.
I gather she and Noya had some kind of attraction between
them and Aranella found them out. Truly I think there are
more important things in the world right now. Perhaps I only
say that because all that sort of thing seems so unimportant
to me at the moment.

With Ethran having set up the camp, and Nastal and
Morghail and Ablon here a good part of the time, I am surrounded by lovers or potential lovers. None of that seems to
matter to me now. That fire in the blood that burned so hot
for a time has vanished back into the ashes and I am quite
content to sit and write and watch the games of others. Even
Nastal's loving is a kind of burden now. Perhaps I should say
especially Nastal's. She seems to think it gives her the right
to manage my life. Sometimes she forgets that I am not a child
to be managed in that way. Indeed, when I was a child, I was
already managing for others.

Somehow I do not share everyone's anxiety for Aranella.
In my heart I see her coming back safely, my way I suppose

of "smelling the wind". Still my heart aches with pity for Jolaina as I watch her pacing up and down. Noya also looks tense and drawn. I have tried to tell them what I "see", but they are too eaten up with guilt and fear and in no mood to listen.

Vondran says we need to be quickly gone from here. This is not a safe place to be. Yet we cannot leave until Aranella is found. Though he keeps his silence on it, I see the anger in his face. Stobah, however, is under no such restraint. She says loudly and indignantly as if to the whole camp, "Curse her for a fool! After what we risked to rescue her, she puts us all in danger with her mindless folly. Why should a Zarna's life be worth any more than that of other folk? I say we should leave her to her fate."

I think she would have gone on and on in that vein if Vondran had not shouted angrily, "Enough Stobah! That is not helping anything!" I had never before seen him lose his composure in that way.

Stobah glared at him but abruptly shut her mouth. Then, in an aside to the rest of us she muttered, "I was only saying what so many here have been thinking."

It was a curious camp gathered there, with Hadra and Wanderers and folk of the Thieves Guild mixing freely with my farm-boy guards. Even one of the shepherds from the Parade Grounds was with us, a man who appeared to have some connection with Jolaina. Every one but me seemed to be doing something useful, so I told my men they had to make themselves helpful in the life of the camp. Argus hung around the cookfires doing one chore or another until Mhirashu finally taught him how to make bread. Gorinth assisted Danil and Douven with the horses and Yorant left on the search with Morghail.

In the evening, when the activity of the camp slowed down and it was too dark to write, I found myself drawn to talking with Vondran at the fire circle. As I settled down beside him, he said with a wry grin. "Talk to me of anything but Aranella's disappearance unless you know where she is or have some important new information."

"What should we talk of then, since that is all that seems to be on everyone's tongue? For what it is worth, my feeling is that she has not come to harm nor will she."

"For what it is worth, I think your feelings are well worth listening to. I think you know much more than you know you do. Now tell me something; I gather those men are from your family lands. How are things going at home?"

"Very badly and that is no longer my home," I snapped back, answering him sharply to hide my pain.

"And I suppose you are going to tell me that you care not one bit what is happening there."

I was about to make another sharp retort. Instead I heard myself saying, "I care more than I can say." Then, all in a flood of words, I found myself telling him everything Argus had told me.

At the end of my recital he said thoughtfully, "Perhaps it is time to go home and take charge there." At his words fear lurched up in my chest. I shook my head vigorously, but he went on, "You do not have to do it in the old way, Amairi. You do not have to be the Shokarn overlord, but there are many people whose lives depend on that land. They are at the mercy of your brother's wastrel ways. They do not have the power in their hands to change things."

"And neither do I. It is up to Nhageel now. Besides it is all too painful. How could I go back? Oh Vondran, think of it, my parents grew sick and died and I did not even know they were ailing. I was not there to help and comfort them in their last hours, to say good-bye, to make their funeral, to speak for them." Suddenly all the grief I had been holding back erupted and I found myself crying in his arms, sobbing wildly. He held me close against him for a long time. Even after I had calmed he kept his arms about me so that the space around us felt like a little island of safety in all the pain and chaos of my life.

Aranella

So they have gone to get dogs, I thought with a shudder. *There is no escaping them now.* Then, very close, as if he were in the same room, I heard a man say, vexed and puzzled, "They must have come this way. Hounds do not lie." And another answered, "Then where are they now? There is nothing here but vines, brambles and rocks. Nothing human could live in that thicket." I was shaking with fear, expecting at any moment to be recaptured.

"Hold on to the image," Ouvrain hissed in my ear. Having no choice, I did as she said. I held onto the image with all my strength, shutting out the sounds from outside and straining to maintain my center, though after a while it felt as if my head was going to crack open with the strain. Suddenly the hounds were moving off, yipping, baying and howling as if on the trail again. Soon the shouts and footsteps faded into the distance. After listening for a while in silence, we released each other's hands. Mine were wet with sweat and painfully cramped from holding so tight. I sat up with a deep sigh, worked my fingers loose and then rubbed my temples to ease the pain. Ouvrain lit the lamp again. Nhuri was swaying slightly. She looked dazed, as if awakening from a dream or a trance. Ouvrain was grinning with satisfaction and appeared totally in control of herself.

I stood up, shaking all over. "We must go back to our camp at once. I should never have left."

The witch shook her head. "A little late to think of that now, Zarna. Not safe on the road, not till night falls again."

With those words she pushed open the door and I blinked in the daylight that suddenly flooded the room. So much time had passed! She turned and gave me another of those strange looks so full of meaning. "And when you go, leave the child with me. She will be safe here."

"No! Never! She belongs with me," I burst out, hugging Nhuri against me protectively. "Besides, they will come back. They will find her here."

"No, it was you who left them a trail. Without you they cannot find their way to my hut. Aranella, you have work to do out in the world. You cannot do it carrying this child on your back. It endangers you both."

"How do you know who I am? It is time now for some answers, Ouvrain."

"Is there anyone in this region who does not know who you are?"

"So, you use the witch's trick of answering a question with another question."

"I saw you in my bowl. I have been watching for over a week as you came closer and closer. But that is the past. Let us look at the future." She shook the water in the lustrous dark bowl, spilling a little on the floor.

I looked into the bowl and could only see water that quivered with shapeless colors. Staring at it made my stomach crawl. I shivered with revulsion. Then Nhuri came to stand at my side. "Look," she said eagerly, pointing into it. The surface misted and then cleared. When it did I saw myself riding openly in the streets of Maktesh on a big black horse with Jolaina riding proudly beside me. Crowds of people were waving and cheering wildly. Even if it was only an illusion, at least it made me feel a little hopeful for that moment. I was about to say, *Is that really the future?* when I noticed other riders beyond Jolaina, Noya among them. So, that cursed woman had followed me even here. In the bowl picture she turned suddenly and Jolaina smiled at her, a smile full of

194

acknowledged affection. Quickly I passed my hand through the water, shattering the reflection.

"Jealousy is bad magic," was all Ouvrain said to me for breaking the spell that way. Then she nodded toward the bowl. "They may call that one a witch all they please, but their accusations will not make her one; Jolaina is a warrior and a fine one, but she is no witch. And you, Aranella, you are a born leader, but you have no gift for spells. Now that one," she said nodding at Nhuri, "She has the gift and with a little training she could do very well. We could not have held that spell without her. I cast the spell and she held it with only a little support from you."

"What do you mean a little?" I asked indignantly. "I gave it every once of strength I had."

"Yes, indeed you did, but I am speaking of talent now, not effort. Even with no training the child has skill. Think what she could do with training."

"Is that why you want to keep her here, to make a witch of her?"

"There are so many answers to that question. I want to keep her alive because she is valuable. Out there she is in danger. Here with me she is safe. You are going about the risly work of changing the world and it makes her a target. As far as making her into a witch, that I cannot make or unmake. She is one already, the question is of training. Trained, her life will be safer and she will be much better protected. All those around her will also be safer. An untrained witch is a danger to everyone, as unpredictable and uncontrollable as lightning. And then another answer with a question; is it so bad to be a witch?

"Surely there are worse things to be in the world. In terms of harm to others surely being a Zarn is one of them. Think of your father and all the suffering he caused. You have no cause to look down on Witches, Aranella. But ask the child if she wants to stay. In the end it is her choice. Even if death waits on the other side of the door, I hold no prisoners here and no reluctant students."

Silently I looked Nhuri in the eye, my question loud but unspoken. "Leave me here Sister," she said with a sigh. "I am too weary to run anymore. I have no strength left for it. You have work to do and I am a burden and a danger. Besides, Ouvrain has something to teach me. Maktesh has room for only one Zarna, but that Zarna may well have need of a witch. And I have a need to be something in my life besides the little sister of the Zarna."

"Well, well, indeed!" Ouvrain nodded her approval. "The child has a will as well as a talent. And who knows, she may be right. One day the whole game could turn on the strength of her spells. Leave her here with me. You will know when it is safe to come back for her."

I saw the look of clever malice on Ouvrain's face and suddenly I understood. "You did it; you made it happen. You used my jealousy to draw me here like a trap or a web of sorcery. You cast a spell because you wanted Nhuri in your grasp. Tell me the truth, Ouvrain."

"Ah yes, the truth indeed, but which truth do you want? There are always so many. Asking a witch to tell the truth is like asking the wind which way it will blow next. But yes, I saw the chance in my bowl and I used it. And you, Aranella, you left the door open for me, wide open!"

She was grinning at me, very pleased with herself. I had been tricked and used. I wanted to put my hands around her throat and shake the life out of her.

"Not so," she said smiling even wider, as if she had read my mind. "I have done you and yours a great favor today. Let us hope, if the time ever comes to repay it, you will know how to do it adequately."

I could see I was outmaneuvered. "So be it," I said with a curt nod. "Now how can I get safely back to camp? Or do you mean to keep me here as well?"

She shook her head. "Why should I keep you? You are not

the one I need. Karst, the raven, will take you to my friend Branith. He will lend you the use of a horse and see you safely to your camp. But you will ride back on different roads than those you came by so those men cannot catch you if they are watching and waiting for you there. We must be very careful."

At the thought of those men, I shivered with fear, not at all sure I really had the courage to go out into the woods again. How could I have been such a reckless fool? Much as I disliked Ouvrain, her small hut suddenly seemed like safety to me, a safety I wanted to cling to at that moment. But of course that was not to be.

I think Ouvrain must have sensed my fear. There was an edge of malicious amusement in her voice as she went on, "I must warn you that Branith is a strange man, little used to the company of women or, for that matter, any company at all. He may not speak, yet he is a good guide, very skilled at getting through unseen and he would do anything for me. We have an old debt between us. First I must see where they are camped."

With those words Ouvrain shook the bowl and passed her hands over it, mumbling something to herself or to some invisible entity. When the water stilled I could dimly see our camp. She seemed to know immediately where it was. "Good, that is easy enough to find, just on the other side of this forest. And tell your people from me that they need to move on quickly to some safer place; it is too dangerous there. In truth Aranella, alone you would never find your way back safely, but with Branith you will have no problem. Take him this note from me." As I watched the water cleared and I saw Jolaina pacing up and down with a terrible look of distress on her face. "There is your Kourmairi puntyar, in an agony of worry about you," the witch said, looking over my shoulder.

"Have no fear, she will quench her worries easily enough in another woman's arms," I answered bitterly.

"Put a rein on your jealousy Aranella, and get it in hand," Ouvrain said dryly. "It will not likely serve you well. You must have lived a very pampered life and always had your own way if you have never had cause for jealousy before." Jolaina was talking intently to someone I could not see. Then, for just a moment, she turned and looked straight at me as though she could see me. She appeared so distraught I cried out and reached for her. Instantly the image blurred and vanished. "You see what you have done with your jealousy, you have put them all in danger. Listen Aranella, you are her first lover and her only real love. Do not begrudge her a little experience in this life."

"What do you know of any of it?"

"Only what I see in the bowl, though the water tells me more than just pictures. The water can also read the heart."

I shrugged and turned away. Now I wanted to be gone from there, away from the grating sound of Ouvrain's voice. More than anything in the world I wanted to be safely back in the camp I had left in such anger. And in truth I needed to be away from Nhuri also, Nhuri who had abandoned me so easily for this stranger. This promised to be a long day. I began pacing up and down nervously, probably matching Jolaina's anxious pacing on the other side of the bowl. I filled that small space with my restlessness until Ouvrain said with sharp impatience, "Sit down and drink some tea. It will calm you." I was foolish enough to trust her and the tea not only calmed me, it put me straight to sleep.

The next thing I knew Ouvrain was shaking me awake. "Get up, quickly! Get ready to go!" she urged. "For now there is just enough moonlight breaking through the clouds to be able to follow Karst. If you ride hard you will be there well before midnight. Remember, tell your people to move on in the morning."

Now that the moment had finally come I felt unprepared. "But how will I find my way back here? How will I ever find Nhuri again?"

"She will be safe here with me. You will know when the time is right. You will find your way here when you are meant to. That is the best I can tell you at this moment. Now go re-take your city without worry for the child on your mind."

To my surprise Ouvrain's words sounded almost kind as she folded her note and put it in my hands. Nhuri threw herself in my arms, "Be safe Aranella, and send for me soon. It is hard to part again so quickly. But I will stay here for now and learn from Ouvrain all she has to teach."

"Is that really what you want, Nhuri, of your own free will?" It felt like another loss, another betrayal, but it was my own fault. I had brought her to this place.

Nhuri nodded and Ouvrain said sharply, "I have not put a spell on her if that is what you are asking. The child has her own needs and her own abilities as well, very different from yours." It would have been so easy to hate this woman who had tricked me and saved our lives and now was laying claim to my sister.

"I never, never want to fall into the hands of those men again. They . . ." Nhuri suddenly stopped speaking and stood staring down at her feet, a slow flush creeping up her face.

Comprehension dawned and with it rage burned up through my body. "What did they do? Did they hurt you, Nhuri? Did they . . ."

Ouvrain grabbed my arm and shook me. "Out! Now! This is not the time. Go!" The raven flew over and landed on her shoulder. Then the witch pushed me out the door and quickly followed. The bird cocked its shiny black head toward her as if asking a question. "Branith," Ouvrain told it. "Find Branith." With those words she lifted the raven from her shoulder and set it on my arm. "Take Aranella. Find Branith."

Jolaina

Oh to have had her and to have lost her again and all through my own fault! I can still feel her arms around me, feel her kisses up the back of my neck and on my lips, feel her body pressed against mine in sleep with her breath matching mine and her legs between my legs. And now she is gone, lost, perhaps hunted as I have been.

If only I had been able to lie to Aranella. But how could I lie to her when she knows me almost as well as I know myself? She already knew the truth when she asked the question. Would she have believed anything less? I am angry for what has happened between Noya and myself. Yet I know I could not have prevented it and did not want to and even now cannot regret it — though I regret with every cell in my body the pain we caused by our passion. There was a spell between us, and for that matter there still is, though for this moment its fire is buried under the ashes.

I wish they would let me go to look for Aranella. They are all adamant about it, Vondran especially, saying that not only will I endanger myself, I will endanger Aranella and the rest of them as well, so I must trust the Wanderers to find her and bring her safely back. Oh, but it is so hard to do nothing! And I had just made a pledge to her that if she were ever in danger again I would not rest until I found her. Now I can only pace up and down, driving everyone else to distraction.

Noya

It is very hard for me to watch Jolaina in such pain, pacing about like a caged animal. I want to go to her and put my arms around her for comfort, though which of us I would be comforting it is difficult to say. Instead I do nothing. Guilt stands between us like a block of ice. I can barely even look at her. Yet I cannot look away for long. Nor can I say those threads of connection have been cut. They still run hot to the core of me. No doubt that is what caused this trouble to begin with. So hot guilt and frozen passion are all mixed in me. I suppose on the outside I look hard and cold and contained, but inside, a river of molten metal runs up and down my back, my blood, my body. Inside I am like the fire-mountain that my mother told me stories of when I was little.

Aranella

That was surely one of the strangest nights of my life; first struggling to follow a crow through the gloom of the deep forest and then riding behind a silent man in the dark on a path I could not see. When the Karst finally swooped down to land on the roof of Branith's little hut I was surprised. It looked to me more like a bundle of sticks than any real dwelling place. Full of fear, I hesitated to knock, but the crow cawed loudly and banged on a pole with its beak.

Though I could see shafts of light seeping through the cracks, there was a long silence. Then the blanket that covered the doorway was drawn aside by a man who himself looked like a walking bundle of rags. He brushed back the greasy hair that hung down in front of his soot-grimed face and glared out into the night, seeming more angry than startled to see me. I took a step back and with trembling fingers reached out to hand him Ouvrain's note. I thought he might ask me to read it for him as he did not look like a man with reading knowledge, but he glanced at it by the dim light of his single lamp and then nodded to me.

All in silence Branith saddled the two horses that were tied near his hut and helped me mount. Then he fastened a rope from his horse to the horse I rode and we set out with Branith in the lead. I could safely have fallen asleep and indeed I dozed off at moments only to be awakened each time with a start. The moon had clouded over. I had no idea how he knew his way. Perhaps he was more wolf than man. Perhaps the horse was his guide. He never said a word to me, not that whole time. When we were close enough to hear distant voices he stopped, turned back, tapped me on the arm and nodded. As soon as I slid off the horse, he turned with it and vanished in the night as if he had never been there. I did not even have a chance to thank him.

A little moonlight had broken through the clouds again so I could see where to put my feet. Following the light of the fire I went toward the camp, calling out softly, "Otta, Otta." I did not want the sentries to take me for a hostile guard, creeping up on them. Suddenly Jolaina was upon me, sobbing, "Oh Aranella! Aranella!" She was hugging me, then shaking me, then hugging me again. "You fool!" she hissed in my ear. "I risked my life over and over to save yours and then you run off in the night like that, frightening us all. You could have been killed! They would not even let me go to look for you. Vondran said it was probably a trap. I thought this time you were gone for sure. If you had not come back by this morning, I would have gone after you no matter what they said. Oh Aranella, how could you do that to me?" With those words, she crushed me so tight against her that I had to struggle free in order to breathe.

"You are right; I am a fool. If not for Ouvrain the witch I would be dead for my foolishness and so would Nhuri."

Jolaina shook me again. "Where is Nhuri? Why is she not with you? Has something happened to her?"

I shook my head. "No, nothing bad. She stayed with Ouvrain for safety and to learn some things she had a need to know. And do not shake me again Jolaina. I may fall over. I am far on the other side of exhaustion."

With that she pulled me over to the fire and made me sit. Soon others were crowding around. I could see Noya's anxious face among them. Then Vondran was pushing his way toward me through the dappled moonlight, anger plain on his usually calm visage. Unable to face his stare I said quickly, "Ouvrain

202

said to tell you this is not a safe place to stay, that we should be gone by morning."

"It does not take a witch to tell me that, Aranella. If not for you we would have been gone from here yesterday." He turned quickly and said to Ethran who had been following him, "Break camp. Get everyone ready to leave. We need to be out of here before the hour is up. They may follow her to this place."

"There is no chance of that. Ouvrain sent me back by a different . . ."

Vondran whirled on me, his tone savage. "Zarna, do not tell me how to run my camp. I only hope you are worth all the trouble you caused us, saving you not once but twice."

I answered without thought, "You only saved me once. I returned with no help from you the second time."

"And with your mindless folly you endangered everyone who went to look for you as well as all the rest of us who waited here in camp. You had no thought for anyone, not even your sister. Thank the Cerroi none of us died this night because of you. I only hope you will rule differently enough from other Zarns to be worth the bother of saving you at all."

No one spoke to me that way. No one! I felt the flush of anger rush up the back of my neck and into my face. My tongue burned to make a sharp cutting retort. I even had a moment of wishing the man some harm. Then I tried to think of how Jolaina would advise me and instead said firmly, "I deeply regret whatever trouble I may have caused, Vondran, but you *know* that I rule differently from other Zarns. That is not even in question."

"Well, see that you continue so that we have not wasted our lives in this venture." Without another word Vondran turned and walked away. At that moment I did not want to rule in a new way. The old way would have done me well enough. I would gladly have given the command and seen him swinging from a rope in front of the palace as my father would have done for such insolence. No one, not even Jolaina had ever spoken to me that way in front of others. In the next moment the smoke of my anger had cleared. I knew he was right. I had deserved his scolding for my thoughtlessness. Contrite and exhausted, I went to gather my things and help break camp. Whatever Jolaina, Noya and I had to settle between us would have to wait until we were in a safer place.

The hardest thing that night was facing Dharlan. Though she came to help me, she also had her own stern words to say. "Aranella, I have been your nursemaid since you were a little child. You were so willful then that we seldom tried to bind you to any rules. Instead we rejoiced in your freedom and your spirit. Perhaps we have all spoiled you; me, your father, your mother; indulged you too much, giving way to your willfulness. Now I need to tell you clearly, Lady, there is more to being Zarna than having power. There is a great responsibility to others, the obligation to give up your own private needs when something must be done for the larger good. You have shamed me this night. Do not do so again."

"Goddess help me, Dharlan, I would never have planned to do such a foolish thing and that is the truth. The doors fell open before me; the invitation was held out; I think Ouvrain spelled me."

"What a shabby excuse for being such a fool. A Zarna can have no such excuse. She has too much power. She needs to have the wisdom to see what harm or good her actions will cause in the wider picture and act accordingly. After all, Aranella, you are not a simple peasant girl with only the safety of your sheep to think about."

I nodded and this time kept my silence. In less than an hour we were all on the road again, going as quickly and quietly as we could through the first gray light of dawn. I was so weary I could hardly stay awake to sit on my horse.

Noya

We rode hard and in silence, making only short stops to rest the horses until we finally stopped to eat sometime after midday. Vondran led the way and set the pace, also setting the tone which was one of grim silence. Sometimes he sent Larameer or Morghail ahead or back to check for danger and would confer briefly with them. Otherwise there was little talk among us. If any broke the silence he would flash us a warning look and we would quiet instantly. Not even Stobah dared to make her clever and acidic remarks. Amairi's troop of guards seemed to accept this new leader without question and more often looked to Vondran rather than Amairi for commands. We Hadra rode together as if seeking shelter with each other from the harshness of Vondran's stormy weather.

It seemed to me as if most of the Wanderers were deliberately shunning Aranella, their cool manner so different now from the warmth and openness with which they had first greeted her. Vondran's curtness in the last camp had seemed intentionally cruel. Though I had my own anger at her for running off, it was so mixed with guilt and empathy that I began to feel a little pity instead for how she was being treated and finally some anger toward the Wanderers for their harshness.

I do not know if Aranella cared or even noticed any of this. She rode her horse like a sleep walker. Jolaina stayed on one side of her and Dharlan on the other to watch over her and keep her safe. Jolaina would have taken her up on her own horse, but Vondran said sharply that it would slow us down. Mhirashu stayed close by, the only Wanderer who did not seem to join in the shunning.

When we finally stopped to eat, tempers were short. The Wanderers, usually kindly and easy going, snapped at each other, seeming all out of sorts and not so different after all from other folk. Then the mood shifted suddenly because of Mhirashu. Dharlan had just asked if we needed to keep up such a hard pace, no doubt feeling it not only for Aranella, but for herself as well. Vondran had answered curtly, "It is the Zarna's fault. If not for her foolishness we could have ridden at a much easier rate. As it is we stayed in that dangerous place much too long. Now we must go at this punishing speed to make up for it."

At those words Mhirashu came and stood in front of Vondran with her hands on her hips and her head cocked to one side. "Think to the Cerroi, man, and listen to your own words. Did some god appoint you judge and executioner? How can you judge another's ways and understand her actions when you have not lived in her skin or seen life through her eyes?"

I saw anger cloud Vondran's face. "You think to lecture me on the Cerroi, Mhirashu, me of all people!"

Though he stared up at her, she held her ground, shaking a finger at him. "Yes, you of all people! You are the one who should know better, but I see you are not above human failings after all and certainly not above being reminded of the Cerroi. Remember you are not Zarn here, you are only leader because we follow by consent. Never forget that Vondran."

I could feel anger boiling up in him. He seemed about to burst out with furious words. Then, abruptly, his face cleared and changed. He sighed deeply and his mood shifted. With a shrug and a wry grin, he said, "Well that is the beauty of the Cerroi, it all comes round in a great circle and in the end it always comes home. And yes Mhirashu, I am not above it, only sometimes I think I am." He coughed, shook his head and seemed to be struggling with something. Then he nodded to Aranella, looked her straight in the eye, and said with clarity and dignity, "I hope you can forgive the cruelty of my words and my great illusion of superiority. You have certainly been no more wicked or foolish than any of the rest of us have at some moment or other in our lives, those times when pain drives us more than sense. And as Mhirashu has so generously pointed out, I also have my own failings." Now a little grin tugged at the corners of his mouth.

Aranella took a deep breath. Her expression had gone from anger to hurt to surprise to pleasure. There was an edge of tears in her eyes. "Thank you for that Vondran, but I think I truly deserved your angry words." She spoke softly, making a slight bow in return. Then she stood up slowly, took another deep breath, swept our circle of faces with her eyes and said in a clear, heartfelt voice, "I ask pardon of every one of you for the danger I have exposed you to by my rashness and for all the trouble I have caused. Believe me, I have had all this day to think on it. And I want to thank you all from the bottom of my heart for the many brave and dangerous and difficult things you did to rescue us. Nhuriani and I will be forever grateful and remember you always in our prayers." Then she flashed a smile on us all that could have melted a heart of ice and sat down to cheers and applause, mine included.

Aranella had won us over. I suddenly glimpsed the Zarna who could rule a city in a new way and gain the love of her people. Jolaina hugged her impulsively and several Wanderers said little words of kindness and reached out to touch her. Now that the silence had been broken, the meal progressed with a much different tone. Since the normal easy banter of the Wanderers had been restored, the rest of us felt free to talk and laugh and join in.

The ride that morning had been painfully tense. The mood in the afternoon felt somewhat different. Vondran was no longer a smoldering mountain of anger. Since he seemed more approachable I thought to ride next to him for a while. I wanted to see what I could learn of Wanderer ways and knowledge. Some of the other Hadra also moved up near him and Pathell chose to ride on his other side. With a nod he gave over his command to Morghail and turned to answering all our questions in an easy and companionable way.

But no matter how friendly we all seemed at that moment, no light banter was exchanged between Aranella and myself. I rode with a knot of tension in my chest, knowing that the three of us, myself and Jolaina and Aranella, had to talk of what lay between us. I both dreaded this and hoped it would be soon, but there was no chance of it that night. Aranella was so exhausted she was asleep almost the moment that we stopped.

Aranella

As Zarna I had never had to feel the sting of disapproval. Just the opposite. Until my capture by Khundorn, I had always been surrounded with adulation. This ride with the Wanderers, under the lash of Vondran's harsh tongue, had been a most educational time. It had given me much to think on, such as how it felt to be the Hadra, despised and maligned by most of Garmishair; and what it had been like for Jolaina to be hated and hunted in that way. With the exception of Jolaina, I had probably never apologized to anyone before in my life. Now Vondran had set me an example of how a leader could be both humble and proud at the same time, could be strong and also confess weakness. There is much to be learned from this man who looks to be no better than a street beggar and yet carries himself like a Zarn. I must say I am very glad that he relented for the afternoon. I felt as if I had gotten enough lessons for one day. It was a pleasure to have the Wanderers befriend me again. I had been feeling chilled to the core in spite of the relentless heat of the day.

I thought that Jolaina and Noya and I would have to have some sort of reckoning that evening. I was anxious for it to be done and over with, but that was not to be, at least not then. Instead I fell flat out as soon as my mat was unrolled and did not waken till I felt Jolaina shaking me the next morning, saying, "Time to rise Aranella. Everyone is already up." My first thought was of Nhuri. I reached out for her next to me and then looked about frantically. With a sinking heart I remembered in that instant where she was. Punishment enough for my recklessness, worse punishment than any scolding by Vondran or shunning by the Wanderers could possibly be.

We rode fast all that morning, but without the terrible relentless pressure of the day before. Those we passed on the road were mostly Kourmairi, farmers or village folk who called out greetings or asked for news of Midsummer Day. Then one or the other of the Wanderers would explain in all seriousness that Khundorn had been vanquished and the Zarna would soon be returning to Maktesh in triumph. All the while shivers would be running up and down my back. Of course no one could have recognized me in those ragged clothes with soot rubbed on my face and my yellow hair hidden under a scarf.

By the middle of the day, the heat had grown too oppressive for horse or human so we stopped for a long rest by the banks of a stream. Some walked into the water fully dressed and others rode their horses into it. Most, however, stripped off their clothes with no apparent embarrassment and dropped them on the shore in careless piles while they dashed in laughing and splashing. In that one moment I saw more naked flesh than I had seen in all of my life in Maktesh. I did not join in the sport but sat watching somewhat enviously from the shade of a tree.

That evening, as we took our bowls to wash them in the big pot of hot water by the fire, Jolaina, Noya and I crossed paths as if by accident, though the Wanderers would probably have said it was the workings of the Cerroi and the Hadra would no doubt have credited their Goddess for that meeting. Noya stopped in her tracks and Jolaina put her hand on my arm, saying, "This silence between us has gone on long enough, Aranella. We need to talk, all three of us together, before it turns to stone or ice."

I looked back and forth between them. Jolaina had rescued me from Khundorn's clutches. After I had come back from my foolish flight, she had ridden at my side, helping me when all the others had turned away. I was no longer so angry with her. Now I thought it was Noya, the outsider, the intruder, *the Hadra,* who was at fault and had caused all this trouble. In my head I had been saying the word *Hadra* in the same tone of contempt that the Shokarn used for the word *muirlla,* though I suppose I myself might be considered a muirlla by some. Then I blushed deeply for I suddenly remembered that *Noya the Hadra* could read all my thoughts.

Noya looked me in the eye and said coolly and levely, "Just remember Aranella that this *Hadra* worked harder than anyone but Jolaina to save you and risked as much and cared as much that you were free. That needs to be understood between us before anything else is said. And if there is nothing else that binds the three of us together it is that we are all muirlla, all of us. And one more thing; I saw Jolaina's anguish when she thought you were lost out there. If you wanted to hurt her deeply then you most certainly succeeded, perhaps even more than you had meant to."

I opened my mouth to say something cutting and bitter. The look in her eye stopped me. Instead, to my surprise, I found myself nodding. "All of that is true, Noya." Then I added quickly, "And we still need to talk."

Jolaina grabbed up a blanket, slung it over her shoulder and took us each by the arm. Then she walked us to a quiet spot away from the others where she spread it out on the ground. After a moment of awkwardness, we all three sat down on the blanket in a sort of rough triangle. No one said a word. We were staring at each other, not touching and not talking. The silence stretched on and on as we each waited for the others to speak first.

Finally Jolaina burst out, "Oh Aranella, I cannot win back your love by betraying or denying a part of myself or by denouncing Noya. And I cannot prove I love you by pretending she is nothing in my life, nor can I beg you for your forgiveness. I am more sorry than I can ever say for the pain it cost you. But I am not sorry for what happened and I cannot tell you I regret it.

"Yet I can tell you this: at great danger to myself I have tirelessly plotted and planned and worked to save you. I risked my life over and over, lost sleep and blood and nearly died of an unhealed wound. No matter what else was happening in my life I could never ever for one moment forget that you were a prisoner in their hands.

"So now you must take me as I am. Flawed or foolish or too wild; you must decide. But I tell you Aranella, you are truly the love of my life, the person that I want to be with. About that much I have no doubts." Then she stopped abruptly and sat staring off, looking into some far distance I could not see, sitting very still as if holding her breath.

I could not answer. My heart was like a rock. There was a stone in my mouth; no words would come out. I thought we might all stay that way forever, frozen like statues. Strangely enough it was Noya's voice that finally reached through to me. Very gently she said, "I know your heart is hurting, Aranella. I am very sorry for that. And so is Jolaina. Please believe me that neither of us meant for it to happen this way. No one planned it; no one would have chosen it; and yet now we have to live with it. We may all have aching hearts, but we also have a city to win back and a world to change. We are bound together by events far bigger than ourselves."

Suddenly pity broke through my shell of hardness — love and pity. I was flooded with love for Jolaina. No matter what she and Noya had shared, she was still the great love of my life. And yes, she had risked everything to save me. If not for her, I would likely be dead or in the hands of torturers. Now she was there waiting for my verdict, this woman who was my beloved, my companion, my lover and advisor and closest friend. I saw the pain in her face and I was finally able to let it touch me.

A Zarn would have had her beheaded or hung or worse for such a betrayal. But I was not a Zarn; I was the Zarna Aranella, trying to make a new way. With a deep sigh I said at last, "Oh Jolaina, I chose well when I chose you. What other woman on this earth would challenge and defy and torture and torment me as you do, and at the same time force me into a new way of thinking? We have too much to do together in this life to be enemies. And I love you too much to hate you or to be a stranger. Whatever happened Jolaina, I still love you and always will."

She let out the breath she had been holding. Then she turned to look at me and tentatively put a hand over mine, saying in a shaky voice, "I hope someday you can forgive the pain I caused you, Aranella."

And so we made our peace, Jolaina and I. We had too much to do together in that city not to mend our fences and there was too much between us not to be lovers again. About Noya I did not feel so forgiving. I hoped she would soon be riding back to Zelindar. With any luck, we would never see each other after that.

That night, as I lay trying for sleep, I thought of my father as I had not thought of him in years. Usually when he came to mind it was as the Zarn of Maktesh, with his cruelty and his abuse of power. Then I would feel anger and bitterness for the guilty weight I had to bear as I tried to undo all the damage he had done and find some new way of ruling. This time I just thought of him as the man who been my father, the man I had loved in spite of everything. I remembered how he had let me have my own way, encouraged my every skill, even allowed me to have Jolaina in my life as lover, friend and companion. He knew that people spoke scathingly of his muirlla daughter behind his back, yet he bore his shame proudly for me. Others hated him and rightly so. He did terrible things. But I know he loved me. There was some corner of his heart that was capable of love. He loved me and my mother and my little sister and, Goddess help him, I think he even loved my idiot brother who died at his hands, or at least his command so that I could rule undisputed.

Jolaina

Though Vondran and Aranella had grudgingly apologized to each other at Mirashu's insistence there were still hard feelings between. Once, when had we stopped to eat, I came on them in the midst of an argument. The Zarna was quite a startling sight — hands on her hips, feet apart, her face soot-smeared, her clothes ragged, her bright golden hair all in tangles and darts of anger flying from her eyes.

"Can you never see me as a person, Vondran? Am I only a thing to use, a handy tool to wield for your desired ends?"

"Aranella, you are our best hope for a good monarch in Maktesh — or at least one who will do the least harm — and perhaps the only person in Garmishair who can prevent an outbreak of civil strife."

"Faint praise. Somehow that does not seem very flattering or even very human; it is like saying the best table or the best chair for some purpose."

"True enough, Zarna. I have no great love for monarchs, no matter how kindly disposed. And you have certainly given me no reason to love or trust you. Besides, am I not also a tool for you? It cuts both ways you know, this knife of use."

I was about to intervene when Amairi stepped between them. She put her arm through Vondran's to draw him away, saying, "Zarnas are not made of stone, you know. They have human feelings just like the rest of us and can be hurt by words as easily as other mortals. Even Wanderer chieftains have feelings. Why are you pretending to be so hard? Have you something to prove to Aranella about your leadership or something to prove to the rest of us because of her?"

Under the layer of road dust I saw Vondran's face redden. "You know I am no chieftain," he blustered with a shake of his head. "I am only leader of this camp, nothing more."

"Then why is it that every Wanderer camp leader comes to consult with you?"

I could not hear his mumbled answer because Amairi laughed at that moment. When they were out of hearing, Aranella said angrily to me, "That is how he is. He will apologize for his meanness in one breath and then he is at it again with the next. Oh, Jolaina, I want to be home in the palace and sleep in my own bed again. I am sick of wandering about on hot dusty roads, sleeping on the ground and taking orders and insults from a man my father would have hung for insolence. I wonder if there will be any place for us in Maktesh. Will those solemn, hard-faced men who were my advisors still take commands from a woman? Or will they have elevated someone else to the place of Zarn in my absence? Perhaps everything was already lost when Khundorn made his move. Amairi is right, I have feelings just like other humans. Right now I am very weary and very frightened."

"Vondran may not always speak with kindness, but he is most eager to see you safely back on the throne and he bends all his efforts in that direction. For my part, I will do everything in my power to protect you." When I folded her in my arms, she leaned her head against my shoulder. For that moment, at least, she allowed herself to cry and be held like any ordinary woman. I whispered softly in her hair, "We will soon be home Love, very soon, as fast as the road can take us there; then everything will be alright again," I said it over and over to reassure Aranella. I am not so sure I believed it myself.

Part III:
Maktesh

Noya

With Vondran rushing us along, we were making our way
to Maktesh with all possible speed. The heat of midsummer
was dreadful, the weather exhausting and relentless. Day
after day the sky remained a bright hard blue with not a scrap
of clouds visible. Heat waves made the land itself appear to be
melting. Dust filled the air, getting in our eyes, mouths, and
noses, making a fine coat of irritation on the sweat that
always covered us. Even the leaves on the trees and the road-
side weeds hung limp and wilted. Flies were everywhere, a
cloud of torturers that followed us mercilessly. They were
especially cruel to the horses who had no hands to slap them
away.

Never in my life had I experienced such weather. I found
myself longing painfully for the cool sea breezes of Zelindar

and my daily swim in the river or the ocean. I tried to keep my complaints to myself, yet even those who were accustomed to this climate said the heat was exceptionally fierce. The men cursed and grumbled. The Hadra looked at me accusingly. Aranella was sharp, spiteful and haughty, at least to me. And Jolaina would not even speak to me or look in my direction though I knew it hurt her to be so distant. I found myself wishing fervently that I was riding home instead of going on to Maktesh as fast as the horses could carry us there.

Where possible we traveled at night, in the early morning or in the evening. In the heat of the day we tried to rest and let the horses graze, though sometimes we could find neither shade nor water and so had to go on under the cruel sun. Due to his knowledge of the roads and his natural ability for it, Vondran had again assumed leadership of the whole group. We were driven forward by his sense of urgency. He kept saying, "We have lost precious time, it may already be too late." For my part, I could not imagine going any faster. If the fate of the Hadra had not been so connected to Aranella's fate I would not have cared one pence whether or not she regained her throne.

On the fifth afternoon, after a fitful restless sleep, I woke to the sound of thunder. All around me sleepers were jumping to their feet, cheering and shouting, waving their arms at the heavens. The sky was rapidly filling with dark clouds that were crowding out the blue and a cool breeze had sprung up like a blessing. "Quickly, on your horses," Vondran was shouting. "We may need to find shelter."

After the blistering heat, I thought we should be glad enough to ride in the wet, but the rain, when it came, was neither gentle nor kindly. It was a violent summer storm, as merciless in its own way as the heat had been, with raging winds and lashing rain that made riding quite impossible. We were only too glad when Vondran found us shelter in a Kourmairi farmer's barn. The farmer, Marn, was headman of his village. And the barn, being collectively owned, was large enough for us all to crowd into, even with our horses.

In spite of the Zarna's wet bedraggled state, Marn recognized Aranella instantly from having seen her at public appearances in Maktesh. Bowing deeply and plainly afraid to look at her directly, he muttered, "Lady, we have prayed for your safety and lit many candles for you, but never dreamed to see you here among us. You honor our humble space with your presence." Then, struck shy and dumb with the wonder of having the Zarna under his roof, he hovered nervously around the door until Vondran beckoned him to come sit with us. He did this with several more deep bows after first calling out to the villagers to bring us tea and food.

Soon we were all sitting flank to flank, drinking hot tea and eating good country bread and cheese with our wet clothes steaming around us. We told our stories and chatted with the Kourmairi as if we had all known each other for years, while outside the storm roared and raged, and rain drummed loudly on the roof. I will say this for Aranella, she was as gracious and kindly as could be, thanking the Kourmairi many times for their generosity and refusing their offers of anything special or different from the rest of us. I saw another side of her and wondered if some of my view of the woman had not been clouded by the poison of jealousy.

Vondran soon led the talk around to the possibilities of war and the need for gathering a large force loyal to the Zarna so Aranella could safely re-enter the city. Marn listened attentively to our account of the Midsummer Day adventure. Then, at the end, he said diffidently, "If I may be so bold as to speak here, though you have rescued the Zarna and will return her to Maktesh, hopefully in triumph, that has not ended the war. I know the Zarn of Eezore is still recruiting farm boys in the countryside. The Zarns' failure at Midsummer will only delay their plans a little, but I think they soon will push on, even without the help of Maktesh."

219

This was followed by an excited babble of talk, then Vondran said loudly, "What we need is someone to ride to Eezore and tell Zarn Ozmaryn that if he does not call off the war and persuade the other Zarns to do likewise, then his city will suffer the same fate as the Parade Grounds on Midsummer Day."

Jolaina jumped to her feet. "Is that possible or only a threat?"

"Very possible," Ochan of the Thieves Guild said grimly. "But it would take some preparation and Eezore would be a very hard place to live in afterward. Such destruction cannot be started and stopped like turning a faucet on and off. I am not sure if the Zarn or the chaos would be worse to live with. It is not a thing to threaten or to undertake lightly. But yes, it could be done." He was nodding thoughtfully, then a sudden gleam of malice came into his eyes. In the dim, steamy light of the barn his face took on a malevolent air as he leaned forward and hissed, "Yes, with some planning it could be done. Let the high and mighty Zarn of Eezore beware. He is not as safe as he thinks. His war might come home to him in his own city or even right to his own palace."

Still standing, Jolaina swept the room with her eyes. "But who could take such a message to the Zarn? Who would he listen to? Zarns do not like being told what to do. He might easily kill the messenger before such a message could be delivered."

"I might be able to do . . ."

"Not you, Vondran," Mhirashu said instantly. "You had best keep your face out of that city. They probably blame you for their Midsummer Day disaster. Besides, a Wanderer does not go to confront a Zarn." I started to stand up and she whirled on me. "Do not be such a fool, Hadra! There is no one the Zarn would better like to have in his hands than the Councilor of the Hadra. Even with your powers you cannot stand against all his guards. You would make a fine trading chip in his deadly game if you walked right into his hands."

Suddenly Amairi was on her feet. "I am the best one to go. I am Shokarn Uppercaste and so can speak to him more easily from that place of power. Also I have a little troop of guards loyal to me who might accompany me on that journey. I am not a leader who is needed elsewhere or whose life can be used for ransom. I have no husband, children, family to protect, nothing to bind me. Let me do this thing for all our sakes." There was a storm of protest from those who loved her, especially Nastal and Morghail. With a cry Nastal threw her arms around Amairi's legs and tried to pull her back down. Amairi ignored her, standing solid as a rock. Looking from one to the other of us she said in a strong, clear voice, "I am the best one to go."

Vondran was staring at her, strangely quiet. Finally, looking her right in the eye he said, "You know Amairi, if he decides to kill you we cannot save you. By the time his city is in ruins it will be too late for you. If you do this, you and those who go with you are on your own. And, Goddess help you, you will be facing a very angry man with the powers of a god. No one would dare to speak for you or try to stay his hand." There was terrible grief in his voice as well as a sort of weary resignation. "And even if we were to all agree on this plan, it must wait till we retake Maktesh and the Zarna is back in power."

Toki added quickly, "And you must give us time to set things in motion. The Thieves Guild are skilled at magic and surprises, but we must have a little time to prepare."

I looked at Amairi and thought *She is probably riding to her death and she does not even seem to care.* It almost seemed to be her deliberate intent.

After that we talked and argued and discussed possibilities and ate and drank while that storm slowly abated. Long before the sun came out again I knew the cards had already been dealt. Amairi would be the one to take our message to the Zarn. Nastal, of course, spoke to go with her. Her little band of guards also volunteered along with some of Aranella's men. Veridas of the Thieves Guild promised to be their guide.

Amairi

I find myself embarrassed and somewhat confused by all the attention suddenly heaped on me. They all praise me for my courage in going to Eezore to face the Zarn. But it is not courage, at least not courage as they understand it. This is a thing I do more for myself and less for others. But how can I explain? No, I cannot explain, nor do I want to. Better to suffer the embarrassment and let them think whatever they please. For me, going to Eezore is something very dif- ferent. It gives me a thing to do, a place to go, a person to be, some purpose and clarity in the great confusion of my life. If I can do that, go to Eezore and change the course of war and peace and come back alive, then I can never again be Elvaraine, the beaten wife, nor will I any longer be Amairi the Wanderer. There is some new self waiting on the other side of this trip to Eezore, some new self that even I do not know, some part of myself ready to emerge after the rest has been burned away by danger. Oh, but under my brave words lies the dragon of my fear, coiled in the darkness, waiting. I know I will meet her on that road, over and over.

Vondran also has some part in my wanting to leave and prove myself, though of course he knows nothing of it and I would speak of this to no one but these pages. I have grown much too fond of the man. When he is close to me, my heart beats louder and aches in my chest, my breath fails me and I find myself liable to say foolish things that I instantly regret. If this is love then I have never been in love before, not with anyone. I am not even sure I like the feeling or would chose it if I had the choice.

When I see Nastal, watching me with her heart in her eyes, I sympathize and I pity her. I would gladly free her of that bondage if I could, though I know she would not want me to. As for Vondran, he has more than enough women tangled in his life or chasing after him already, Mhirashu and Shamu among them; so many women wanting to play mother and lover to this man who is wise and gentle and seems both so strong and so hurt, yet is so very resistant to love. What would he need me for? Better to leave quickly before these feelings force themselves out into the light of day and make me their fool. Perhaps it takes less courage to go to Eezore and face the Zarn than to stay here and face loving Vondran and all that it would mean in my life.

Noya

Now that the storm had broken the spell of the heat, our focus was on gathering people for a triumphal re-entry. As we went through towns and villages, Vondran called people together and Jolaina spoke to them. She was the bridge between the Kourmairi of the countryside and the city of Maktesh. Sometimes Gairith the shepherd spoke. His very commonness made people listen. Then, if the reception was favorable, Aranella herself would appear briefly to wild cheers and many bows and we would gather up more folk for our moving camp.

Ethran and Dharlan had already gone on ahead to prepare the way in Maktesh. Ethran knew secret Wanderer ways into the city. Dharlan had connections through a vast network of servants, nurses and cooks, people working in the Great-Houses who could tell her everything we needed to know about who held the power in the city, who to contact and how best to organize Aranella's reappearance. Meanwhile Douven and Shamu had ridden off in one direction while Ablon had gone with Larameer and Rhondil in the other with the news that the Zarna was returning in triumph.

Some of the Kourmairi town folk and villagers understood very well what it would mean for their lives and their futures if someone like Khundorn came to power instead of Aranella. They rushed to offer us whatever help and support they could. For most of the others, however, coming with us to Maktesh was a holiday or a great adventure, a sudden welcome change from the boredom of their lives. Whatever the reason, we were gathering a huge mass of people wherever we went. It was as if the whole countryside were rising up and flowing along with us. Aranella would be carried into Maktesh on an irresistible rising tide, of that I had no doubt. Whatever happened later would be full of treachery and danger, but for that moment, at least, I was sure of our victory.

In spite of that, I felt more and more uneasy the further I went from Zelindar. It was as if the thread of my life were being stretched out thinner and thinner, almost to the breaking point. In the midst of that huge and growing mass of people, I had a increasing sense of loneliness and a longing for home. It helped to talk to Pathell and Tenari and Zanti and the others; it gave me some comfort to remember that we were all Hadra together.

Jolaina

The evening before we reached Maktesh, we joined a large Wanderer encampment with several campfires. Dharlan and Ethran were to meet us there with news of the city. As they had not yet arrived, I took myself off to a small fire circle at the edge of the camp. I was in a strange solitary mood and had no wish to join in the excited talk about Maktesh or be at the center of speculations and decisions. Until we had more information I had nothing new to add. It had all been said already, I had heard it all already, and it wearied me.

Instead, I took my place in the Wanderer circle by the edge of the woods, a stranger among strangers. There I found myself sitting next to a man who appeared to be blind. His face was oddly scarred and puckered and he was dressed in ragged clothing. It surprised me to see that part of this clothing was a soiled and much worn guard jacket. From the talk around me I gathered that the man's name was Perth and that he had just come into the camp with some Wanderers from the north. Leaning toward him, I asked in his ear, "You look to be a soldier and a guard. How do you come to be among the Wanderers?"

"First off, stranger, you should ask how I came to be blinded for that is what led me to the Wanderers, but it is a very long story and would wear out your ears."

"Tell it!" the Wanderers called out. "Tell us your story Perth. We have all night and a good story is always welcome at a Wanderer fire." Finally, after much urging, Perth cleared his throat, spit into the fire and began, "I had gone to a tavern with my guard troop, but I was in a rank foul mood. Once there I proceeded to get myself very drunk very fast. Truth be told, I am not a kindly drunk. It makes me even more quarrelsome than usual.

"One of the tavern wenches there was pretty enough to catch my eye. I kept thinking she fancied me too, yet every time I tried to put an arm around her she pushed me away rudely, fanning my anger all the more. There was another wench at the tavern who seemed to be keeping an eye on her, an ugly, mannish thing who acted more like a man than a woman. I would never have tried to get my hands on her except perhaps around her throat. At some moment she was even bold enough to lean over and say in my ear, "Man, this is a warning. Leave her alone if you know what is good for you."

"*Well,* I thought to myself, *I am a man and a guard. No woman is going to give me orders!* Oh, but that was then and this is now. How different it all seems, sitting here and telling the story. As it was, of course, her threat only added to my interest, heated my loins so to speak. At some moment I saw my chance. The one I fancied went into the back cellar by herself to fetch some wine and I followed her there. Intent on having my way with her, I blocked her path and grabbed her arms. 'Stop teasing woman, and give me a kiss.' I told her forcefully. 'There is no harm in that.' I had had enough of being played with.

"She was having none of it and gave me no kiss at all. Instead she screamed loudly, bit my hand, kicked my shin, pushed me away and ran past me. Furious, I turned to go after her and was met by the other one, blocking my way with something in her hand. 'Leave her be!' she yelled at me.

"At that moment, my anger sealed my fate. 'Out of my way!' I shouted in a rage, trying to force my way past her. With a cry she threw something in my face. It burned so that I screamed and screamed. Soon people came running with water to pour over me. It was already too late. The lye had eaten away my sight and seared my face. Since that moment to this I have seen nothing but shadows.

"It was my wife and daughters who brought me to the Wanderers. I said I would go mad if I had to live home with them day after day, sitting still in one place all the time and being fussed at by women. I like to roam. Soldiering had suited my nature. I was the one who always asked to be sent to far places when others wanted to stay close to home. My wife often said I only came home to make new babies. She cried and cried when she had to leave me with the Wanderers. What with my blindness she thought she finally had me home for good. But I know my four daughters will not miss me at all. I wanted a son and cursed them all too often for being girls. To me they were only something in the way. And now look at me, I am no better than a girl and in the way myself.

"Before, my eyes were my life. The other men called me 'eagle eye'. I was the one who noticed everything, who saw things at a distance, who never missed my shot. I was always a fair swordsman, but it was with the bow and arrow that I excelled. With that I was an artist, a genius. I brought down whatever I shot at, deer, rabbit or man. The other men always praised me. They bragged on my prowess, set me up in contests and bet on the outcome. I only wish I had all the money now that was won on me. After my blinding those same men who had been my friends and comrades shunned me, as if it were my fault, as if I had somehow shamed them, as if my blindness was contagious and they might catch it. I was even let go from the guard without pay. That was a great blow to me. Next to the blinding itself it was the worst imaginable happening. Suddenly I wondered what I had been fighting for and why.

"When it first happened I wanted to kill myself. I could not imagine living blind; better to be dead. Several times I tried to turn my knife against my own life and cursed my cowardice when my hand shook so badly that I could not do it. But the Wanderers accept me as I am. Among them I am no more and no less than any other. And something is happening to me from living among them. I find myself changing, more every day. Besides, it is true what they say, that other senses sharpen when you lose your sight. So I have decided to live and experience what there is to experience in this new condition of mine. If it grows too hateful, I still have the option to leave this world by my own hand.

"Before my blinding I would never have sat and talked to a woman this way. I thought women were only good for making sons, satisfying the flesh and cooking the meals. When I had my sight, there were so many things I was blind to that now I am beginning to see. Now that I am blind it is as if my sight has gone inward. I find myself thinking deeply about things that never crossed my mind before. Perhaps I never even thought before. Like an animal, I simply acted. I drew my bow and shot as I was told with no thought for who was on the other end of that arrow — that it might be a person not so different from myself, with their own needs and their own life to live. And, as I said, I was very good with that bow. Not many of my targets lived to tell of it, very few in fact.

"I still remember my last shot. We were in pursuit of Jolaina, the Zarna's muirlla and advisor. Khundorn wanted her captured and held as a pawn in his game to dethrone the Zarna. By the luck of the draw I was one of his men, though I could just as easily have been on the other side. Truth be told, I never had any great love for that man and now I hear he is dead. No regrets from me, I can tell you that.

"That Jolaina — she was certainly clever and very fast. She slipped right through our hands, she did. Perhaps she really was a witch, just as they said." As he spoke my name I found myself shaking with rage or fear or both. I leaned back into the shadows so none could read my face, very glad there were no Hadra in the circle to read my thoughts.

Oblivious to my reaction, Perth went right on, "She had led us a wild chase into the woods and would probably have gotten clean away if not for me. Thinking that she might circle back to the horses, I rushed back while the others were still crashing through the woods, shouting and blundering about. And there she was, just as I had imagined. Smart that one, she had cut the other horses loose and was just making off on the last one. I would have gotten her right between the shoulder blades and brought her down for sure if she had not leaned forward at just that moment. Instead my arrow caught her in the shoulder and she went galloping off. Got clear away, she did. And I can tell you we had quite some time collecting our horses afterward. It took much cursing and many hours; some we never found.

"At that time I cursed my luck. The others mocked me for missing my target and I bloodied Barsto's nose for him. With his loud mouth, he was the worst of the lot. That was when I went and got drunk in the tavern and so walked right into my blindness and my fate. Afterward I cursed Jolaina as if she had been the cause and wished her a painful death from her wound. Now I am not so sure. As I said, I am changing. I find myself thinking of her often and hoping she survived. It would make me glad to think she had escaped and is living her life somewhere. She was a bold one. I did not like her ways, but it was hard not to admire her spirit. I wish I knew for sure."

Out of my long silence I suddenly said, "She is alive soldier. You need not fear for her."

"But how do you know? Are you sure? Have you seen her?"

I put a hand on his arm. "I know because she is sitting right here beside you listening to your story."

There were exclamations of surprise from around the circle. Jerking free of my hand and throwing his arm up in front of him, Perth yelled, "Jolaina!" while at the same time whirling to face me as if he could really see. Then he dropped his arm and said with resignation, "Will you kill me now that you know? What a fool I was with my loose tongue. I am certainly at your mercy at this moment and you would have every right to . . ."

"And what purpose would that serve? I have need for many things in this life right now, but vengeance is not one of them. You are quite safe here with me. Just rejoice that we are both alive to tell our tales."

"I suppose I am too pathetic now even for vengeance."

At those words I wanted to shake him. "You said you would be glad if I lived and so be glad for me, not sorry for yourself. You caused me a great deal of pain, I assure you, more than you could possibly imagine. I almost died of the fever from that wound. But what would it serve me to harm you now? You are not the same man who shot me. If someone handed you a knife and told you to stab me through the heart right now, would you do it?"

"Of course not," he said, drawing back with a shudder of revulsion.

"There, you see, you are a different man. How could I wish you harm? Besides, we are both sitting at a Wanderer fire circle. It was the Wanderers who took me in as they did you. They fed and sheltered and healed me. Should I repay their great kindness to me by shedding your blood at their fire? Would I ever be welcome among them again if I did such a thing? Peace brother, let us make peace between us now." Very gently, so as not to startle him, I put my hand on his arm again.

He nodded. Then he took my hand between his and pressed it with gentle force, saying, "Peace between us, Lady, and let all the Wanderers be witness to it. May neither of us ever again raise a hand against the other." There was cheering from the Wanderers seated in the circle and the others who had gathered to listen. I had been so intently focused on Perth I had almost forgotten them. With a sudden wry grin, he said, "Well, Jolaina, I have accidentally told you my story. Now, in return, you must tell me yours, everything that has happened to you since our last ill-fated meeting."

I was deeply engaged in telling Perth the tale of my flight and Aranella's escape and all that had happened on Midsummer Day when I heard Vondran calling my name. Then Ablon rushed up, saying, "Jolaina, we have been looking for you everywhere. Dharlan and the others are already here."

"Later," I said, tapping Perth on the arm. With that I stood up, nodded to the rest of them and followed Ablon back to my duties.

Amairi

We will soon be back in Maktesh. Is that not what we all have worked for and risked our lives to make happen? I should be overjoyed. Instead I find myself filled with dread, feeling as if it is no longer my city, as if, in fact, I will be a stranger there. I have just taken this moment of time to read back through all I have written here. Now it is with a heavy heart that I set aside my little book of writing and go take my place in the circle to listen to Dharlan and Ethran and the others. Part of me wants to turn and run the other way, back to the freedom of my days among the Wanderers.

Jolaina

The news from Maktesh was certainly encouraging. It was Dharlan who was the spokesperson, sitting very straight and speaking out with a bold, loud voice that carried to all in our circle. "I have made contact with Bardaith and several of his advisors, men who have been running the city in Aranella's absence. They are hoping for her quick return and still believe she is only one who can reunite Maktesh without bloodshed and civil strife. I believe they are very ready to hand the power back to her. Bardaith is planning a grand welcoming ceremony and is eager to talk to Aranella and Jolaina both on how to best accomplish their mutual goals." To my amazement, Dharlan sounded almost like an official of the court rather than a woman who had spent her whole life being a nursemaid.

I mostly listened quietly, asked a few questions and said little. Then I went to bed early, but I could not sleep. Most of that night I lay awake, tossing about with my mind churning. We would be in Maktesh by the next day and my head was full of unanswerable questions and disturbing thoughts.

Going back to Maktesh now, I was very different from the young woman who first came to the city, a girl really, a girl of fourteen, so proud to have been chosen by Aranella to be her companion. I had grown into a woman there, seasoned and a little cynical now from all I had seen. That meeting with Perth was wonderful in its way, and the pledge between us was like the closing of the circle, like the Cerroi working its way in our lives. But it also reminded me of how deeply I had been affected by being the object of such lethal hatred.

Now that we were almost back, I found myself wondering what I, a dark-skinned Kourmairi, was doing in a Shokarn city. In a city where most of the Kourmairi are slaves or servants, my own people see me as one of the Shokarn Uppercaste. And why not? I dress like them, talk like them, work among them every day. And yet secretly I do everything I can for the Kourmairi, everything possible to change and ameliorate the conditions of their lives. But they, of course, know little of this and are neither thankful nor grateful for I am no fool. I do not make public that part of my work. And so the Kourmairi see me only as a Shokarn tool.

The Shokarn, on the other hand, only tolerate me because I am Aranella's advisor and under her protection, her pet as they see it. Some of them even curry favor with me because I have power in court. But to them I am always a Kourmairi and always will be. Sometimes they even call me "the Kourmairi." They never forget it and they never let me forget it either. They have their subtle and not so subtle ways of reminding me that I am the outsider in their midst. I did not feel it so keenly before. I was too busy doing my work to care and of course I always had Aranella. Being hunted down like the worst of criminals and having to run for my life has changed me, marked my heart, done something to my spirit. It is not that I was naive before. Living under the old Zarn I knew, of course, that the Shokarn used killing and torture as a means of keeping or gaining power. It was just that foolishly, I had never expected to be the object of their plots.

I was always well aware that I was not loved, not as Aranella was. I had never tried to be. If something hard or unpopular needed to be done I took the blame, leaving Aranella free of it so people could love her and the ugly thing could still be done. It was a strategy we had worked out and agreed upon between us. Now, suddenly, it hurt, like leaning on a knife, a knife that was turning in my heart.

I think every city needs an outsider who is not caught up in the old web of family ties and obligations and the inevitable games of power, and so is able to see past all that to what needs doing. I was just not sure I wanted to be that person any longer. Traveling with the Wanderers, feeling their easy love, their camaraderie and acceptance, has made me long for that in my own life. Yet I knew I could never be a Wanderer; it is not in my nature to be ruled by the Cerroi, or for that matter, to live forever on the road.

Maktesh has been my home now for twelve years. If I do not go back there and take up my position as resident outsider, where else could I go? Certainly not back to being a Kourmairi in a Kourmairi village. Nor can I go live among the Hadra. I do not have their powers. And, as I have already said, I could not be a Wanderer. There is no place where I would not be an outsider. And if I left Maktesh, I would be an exile from there as well, longing always for this city that I both love and hate, and especially longing for Aranella and my place at her side. And what of the Zarna herself? Could she rule without me? We were like some strange twins, light and dark, holding the power between us, juggling it. But I could not be her shadow-self anymore. Something would have to change, that much was clear. And what of the men who now held power in Aranella's name? Would they be willing to give it back or would they expect her to be a figurehead behind which they ruled in secret? And would I be disposable, an inconvenience to their plans? They needed the Zarna to unite the city, but did they need me? Or would I be the hated witch, the bad influence, the very convenient scapegoat? And so I tossed about and thought and struggled through the night. It seemed I had no sooner fallen asleep than Dharlan was shaking me awake again.

Noya

I am sitting here alone, late at night, with my book and my candle, writing and thinking. The others all seem to be sleeping but I cannot. Some little rat of wakefulness gnaws at my mind.

Poor Amairi. Though she tries hard to hide it, I know she is full of fears about returning to Maktesh, fears so strong I can feel and hear them as clearly as if she spoke the words aloud. And yet she is brave enough to ride forward with us into the face of fear. Well, I have my own fears too, fears of riding into that city that despises the Hadra, riding openly and publicly into the place of the enemy and leading my sisters there, a place where people may point and stare and call us ugly names. Besides, I have never been in any city except our own Zelindar, a city where things are done in Hadra style and Hadra ways are what is considered normal. What am I to expect from this place? Will we know how to behave among these people? Will Jolaina and Aranella suddenly be ashamed of us for our differentness? Besides, I know only too well that Aranella has no great love for me and this, after all, is her city.

But enough of all this late night maundering. I must keep reminding myself that we Hadra are here for one purpose and one purpose only, to stop the war from coming back to Zelindar. Nothing matters compared to that. If we can accomplish that goal, then a few days of strangeness and discomfort are easy enough to endure. Besides, look what Amairi has pledged herself to do with no power of protection. Now that is true courage.

Jolaina

Home! We were coming home! All the doubts of the night before were suddenly swept away in the morning light. It was a glorious day for our return. The rain had settled the dust and cooled the air, there was a light breeze blowing, the sun was shining and the sky was a bright clear blue. We all rode toward Maktesh, full of hope and high spirits, laughing, shouting, singing, calling out to each other, gathering more and more folk as we went forward. Aranella rode at the front. I rode on one side of her and at Aranella's insistence and with much urging from me, Dharlan rode on the other. Amairi and Noya rode on either side of us, five women at the head of this vast moving river of people, five women who together had changed the course of events.

At some moment Aranella turned to me, grinning triumphantly. "We did it, Jolaina! We are back! When we left I was a captive and you were a fugitive and Khundorn was about to take power. Now we are back to stay!"

"Yes, we did it!" I nodded, grinning back at her, full of a sudden fierce, wild joy. "We did it, you and I, but not alone. We did it with the help of all these others." I turned in my saddle to look back. As far back as I could see there was a

mass of people riding after us, a vast weaponless army of
friends and comrades, strangers and lovers, that covered the
land.

I shared Aranella's joy, but there were also many thoughts
going through my head that I did not voice at that moment,
questions about what the future held. Getting safely back to
Maktesh might only be the beginning of our journey.

Amairi

The Wanderers, whose ordinary clothes were mostly drab,
shabby and roadworn, sometimes even ragged, all seemed to
have some sort of festive garments hidden away that they
pulled out for this momentous occasion. I, of course, had
nothing of my own to wear, but for the great day itself Shamu
lent me a lovely tunic of soft lavender, embroidered in gold
thread. In fact she insisted that I wear it, saying, "We should
all look our best in honor of this return. We must be a grand
and memorable sight." But I kept on my guard uniform pants
as they were easier to ride in than any skirt. Shamu herself
was in pale blue with blue flowers braided into her dark hair.
Vondran was looking quite handsome, all dressed in green. For
a change, his wild red hair was brushed into some sort of
order, held back by a woven band of green and gold around
his forehead. Even Stobah had decked herself in a startling
blue-beaded orange blouse that she combined with a purple
skirt. They all looked very different from their ordinary selves.
The most astonishing transformation of all was Morghail.
Dressed in elegant black, he suddenly looked like a proud,
slightly shabby Highborn. Seeing him that way, I wondered
again who or what this man really was.

I would have been glad enough to ride among the

Wanderers, but Jolaina called me up to ride at the front with herself, Aranella, Dharlan and Noya. When I hesitated Stobah gave me a push. "Go! Go!" she said impatiently. "Take advantage of the moment. It is not often that glory calls. When it does you should not keep it waiting."

While we milled around preparing to leave I grew impatient with all the fuss, only wanting to be on the way. I thought I could just as well have ridden in back with the others. But when I was mounted next to Jolaina, riding at the head of that huge mass of people, my heart suddenly swelled with pride. I felt very honored to ride at the front with Aranella and Jolaina in that line of brave, resourceful women and proud of having earned my place among them. Yet even in the midst of all that excitement I felt Eezore pulling at me, drawing me northward, waiting there for me like some deadly and alluring lover.

We did not have far to go before we were met by groups of people coming out to greet us. I had expected to see some armed opposition or perhaps even to find the gates shut and guarded. Whatever opposition there was had melted away, making itself invisible at that moment. The gates had been flung wide. To cheers of welcome, we streamed into the city in the triumph of a great bloodless victory.

Jolaina

All around us banners had been raised and were fluttering in the breeze. Behind us rode the rest of the Hadra and the Wanderers, openly appearing at our side. In back of them came the great mass of Kourmairi along with a lesser number of Shokarn, friendly with each other, at least for that moment. When we came within sight of the city walls there was a roar of sound and people rushed out to greet us, led by Bardaith. Our own guards had to come forward and ride alongside us to keep us from being crushed by good-will as we were swept into the streets of the city.

After that we scarcely had time to eat and bathe and change out of road-dusty clothes into something more suitable before the ceremony in the great square began. Zeeli helped me comb out my tangled hair. Then she braided it in many small braids to loop up in formal court style. For this grand occasion and at Aranella's urging, I put on my gown of deep purple with the white lace sleeves. Even though it was designed with a split skirt for easy movement, I suddenly felt very constrained and conspicuously overdressed being back in court clothes again after the easy freedom of the road.

One of the questions from my sleepless night was quickly answered when Bardaith, along with some of his men, drew me aside. "You must speak to the people this afternoon, Jolaina. It cannot just be Aranella. If you are to continue in a position of power here, then people must see you and hear you. You need to be more of a public presence than you were before. You left here a hunted fugitive. Now you must take back your place. In fact you must make a new one if you are going to help Aranella, and we both know how much she needs you. You must do this for your own survival as well. These are dangerous times and much hangs in the balance. You can trust me, we have old history between us. Know that I will help you in any way I can. I am very glad to see the Zarna back and more than ready to lay this burden down." I heard the sincerity in his voice and it touched my heart. When he laid a hand on my arm and looked into my eyes it was all I could do to hold back the tears. The other men around him were all nodding their agreement.

So one fear had been laid to rest, for the moment at least. Another instantly rose in its place. I was no public speaker.

Aranella was the one who always shone in the public eye. Now I would have to summon up a new and very different kind of courage from that which had carried me all through this time of hardships.

Amairi

Surrounded by a rejoicing populace, I was absorbed in watching the events in the vast city square, when a drunken man bumped against me rudely, then recoiled in mock horror. "What are you then, a man or a woman or some in between creature like those filthy Hadra?" he drawled contemptuously as he looked me up and down with scorn. I suppose it was the pants from my guard uniform that had drawn this unfavorable attention. The man stank. His fine clothes were shabby with wear and neglect. He looked far gone into drink, not just that day but for many long days before it. I was backing away in disgust when the shock of recognition hit me. "Nhageel!?" I sputtered. It was half a question and half an exclamation.

At the same moment he said in amazement, "Elvaraine, is that really you? You are so changed, Sister. What are you doing in half of a captain's uniform? I thought you dead on the road somewhere."

Suddenly I was filled with rage for all that had happened. "And no thanks to you that I am not," I shouted into his face. "How could you marry me to that pig of a man? What did you think would happen to me after years of his beatings? Or were you too drunk and debauched to think of anything at all? Did you sell me to him for drinking money? What has happened to our family lands? Who is caring for things now? Certainly not you, that much is clear."

"Lalaini manages quite well without me, or so she tells me

when I come home from my pleasures. And who are you to criticize? You ran off and left your home and your husband and have become a whore or a Wanderer or something even more disgraceful."

At his spiteful words, my conscious mind clouded over and rage possessed me utterly. I lunged at him, grabbing for his neck. Drunk as he was, he offered only feeble resistance. With the terrible strength of my anger I had my hands around his throat. I was pressing hard and shaking him violently while some evil pleasure buzzed up through my body and into my fingers. Just as his pasty pale face was beginning to turn purple before my eyes, my arms were roughly grabbed from either side. I came back to myself hearing Vondran shouting my name over and over. Suddenly I was aware of Morghail yelling, "Stop! Stop! Let him go, Amairi! You are killing the man!"

As soon as I released my grip, Nhageel slumped to the ground with a groan, limp as a sack of flour. With a hard grip on my arm, Morghail forced me to turn and face him, asking sharply, "Amairi, who is this man that you are trying to kill and what has he done to you?"

"That is the brother who forced me into my husband's bed so he could take over the family lands."

Vondran was shaking his head. "Well, you certainly have a serious score to settle with the man, but killing him may not be the best way, especially here. It puts your own life in jeopardy and endangers the rest of us. Strangling your own brother at the Zarna's celebration of return is probably not a good homecoming nor a wise step for your future. Besides, you have a mission . . ." He looked around at the crowd that had gathered, shook his head again and said no more on the subject, but gave Morghail a nod. Between them they hauled Nhageel to his feet. Two men quickly came forward. They began asking questions and appeared to be his friends.

Vondran pushed Nhageel into their hands. "Here, take this man away and sober him up. He is disrupting the celebration by insulting women and he is very lucky to still be alive." I hoped Nastal had not witnessed this scene. She was quite capable of finishing the job with Nhageel without even consulting me.

After this I was even more eager to get away from Maktesh before my past life caught up to me, entangling me in its snares. I was very much afraid that people would begin recognizing me or asking questions and putting the pieces together. Perhaps I was even more afraid that my own fears would catch up with me. I had hoped to leave before I was immobilized by terror at the thought of what I was about to do. But I knew I could not leave yet, not till after the celebration and the banquet and the ball. Luckily my little scene with Nhageel had ended before Aranella made her dramatic appearance and so I was free to give that my full attention.

Noya

Aranella and Jolaina had both invited me to speak that day to the people of Maktesh, urged me to in fact. I vehemently refused. It was only because of Bardaith's persistence that I even agreed to sit on the platform along with some of my sisters. Personally I wanted to vanish into the crowd as Vondran had insisted on doing when there was talk of having him honored. Shaking his head, he had told Bardaith firmly, "Best for no one to know the part we played in all this. Wanderers are not supposed to choose sides among the Zarns or mix into the affairs of stationary folks. For us it is far better to be invisible than to be honored."

When Bardaith kept after me I finally said — in what

Pathell later told me was a rude and bristly manner — "I refuse to sit up there and be stared at by people who only see us as freaks and monsters."

Bardaith nodded. He took no offense. He merely smiled and answered in a very reasonable tone, "And how will that ever change, Noya, if you do not appear before them as human. An opportunity like this will probably never come again, not in our lifetime, with you Hadra here and all the people of Maktesh assembled together. These people will remember everything that happened on this day. Later they will tell and retell the story, even to their as yet unborn children and grandchildren. And one of the things they will surely remember is seeing the Hadra sitting on the platform with the Zarna and members of the Council.

"They are afraid and ignorant. They have heard bad stories about you. Let them exercise their curiosity. Let them stare. In fact, let them stare all they want, it cannot really hurt you. Surely you Hadra have faced worse dangers. And it would be best to look friendly, Noya, instead of rageful. It helps in calming people's fears."

In the end it was Pathell who forced my decision. I was about to make some further protest when she said decisively, "Noya, whether or not you are on that platform, I plan to be sitting there along with some of the other Hadra. I think we would much prefer to have our Councilor there with us." So, in spite of my objections, it was from the platform, smiling and trying to look friendly and feeling as uncomfortable as a cat walking through water, that I watched the events of that momentous afternoon.

Aranella told me that as Zarna of the Hadra I should wear something appropriate for the occasion. She and Jolaina had both offered to lend me anything I fancied. I could have had my choice of all sorts of elegant garments in velvet brocade or sheer silk or even lace. Though Zeeli fussed around trying to help me, everything I tried on in front of the long glass made me look stiff and awkward, a stranger even to myself.

As the clothes piled up on the bed and I kept shaking my head, I felt guilty of ingratitude, but nothing suited. Finally, in desperation, I pulled the last of the clothes from the bottom of my pack and shook them out. They were very wrinkled and quite shabby compared to fine court clothing. But they were mine and they smelled of home — a long tunic in bands of brightly-patterned homespun and soft loose dark pants, gathered at the ankle. After I put them on, I stared for a long moment at the woman in the mirror. Then I mouthed to her in silence, "The Zarna of the Hadra is ready." Even Aranella applauded when I turned. "Yes, perhaps that is best after all," she said in a tone that could have had many shades of meaning.

Jolaina

It was all Bardaith's idea. He was most intent on Aranella making a grand and very visible re-entry. "The royal carriage is how she left this place, hidden away as a prisoner. Let her reappear altogether differently."

As if our triumphal ride into the city that morning had not been enough, he had requisitioned the biggest and most beautiful black horse in the royal stables for her and had it decked out in finery and flowers. Mounted on this splendid beast, in a robe of milky blue-green that shone and shimmered in the sunlight like moving water, with a circlet of flowers and ribbons wound around her jeweled crown, Aranella was certainly a sight to remember. I thought my heart would burst in my chest. Never had I seen her look more beautiful.

Aranella had been trembling with excitement and nervousness when I helped her dress. Once mounted she seemed to regain her regal presence. The horse pranced and arched its neck proudly while she rode with her back straight and her head held high, bowing slightly from side to side and actually waving to the cheering crowds, something surely no Zarn before her had ever done. The people went wild, Highborn and commoner alike. There was no question that they welcomed their Zarna back. Bardaith and I rode on either side of her; guards and City Council members flanked her for safety. At Bardaith's insistence Noya and some of the Hadra, along with Amairi and Dharlan followed close behind us, but for that moment all eyes were on Aranella.

When we reached the central platform of the city square I could see that it was surrounded on all sides by masses of brilliant flowers and latticed over the top by more flowers and ribbons. Bardaith and I helped Aranella to dismount and escorted her up to the royal throne, a huge seat of red velvet decorated with gold ornaments. For this occasion it was also decked with flowers. Once seated there she suddenly looked very small and frail to me, much too slight to carry such a burden. I trembled and my heart went out to her, full of love and concern. Then I found myself looking around anxiously, scanning the crowd for any possible threat.

As soon as all that strange assortment of dignitaries had been seated, Bardaith bowed in front of Aranella, holding out a large key on a golden chain. "Your city welcomes you home, Zarna Aranella. We bless the day that has brought you safely back to us." With those words he ceremonially laid the chain around her neck so that the key shone brightly between her breasts. When she thanked him, all those watching cheered and shouted a thunderous welcome. Finally, as the uproar subsided, Aranella rose. I could see she was about to speak when a murmur ran through the crowd, heads turned, the murmur increased and then the cheering began again, this time even louder than before.

Aranella

This was it, the moment we had all worked so hard and risked so much for. Yet for me something was missing, or rather someone. Nhuri! Nhuri should have been there beside me, sharing this moment of triumph. They had all persuaded me that there was no time to spare, that I had been away from Maktesh far too long already, that any more delay was at the risk of civil war. Bardaith, Jolaina and Vondran had been adamant about it. Even Dharlan had insisted. I had bowed to their wisdom, yet my heart ached for Nhuri's presence there beside me on the platform.

With Jolaina on one side of me and Dharlan on the other I listened to the cheering of the people. Jolaina signaled several times for silence while I thought of what I was about to say. The noise had almost subsided when a new wave of cheering broke out. I glanced up in time to see a crow fly overhead. The crowd was parting for someone. I could not see who it was until suddenly Nhuri stepped out of the mass of people and walked straight toward me. Behind her I noticed Ouvrain quickly disappearing in among the forward edge of watchers, not the Ouvrain of the woods, but Ouvrain dressed as a grand lady. Nhuri looked very solemn and much older than her years, walking through that shower of applause with her head held high, looking straight ahead. Only when she got closer did I see the slight trembling of her chin.

As she reached the platform and climbed the steps I opened my arms wide. Neither of us said a word. She walked right up to me, then turned to face the crowd while I wrapped my arms around her and she pressed close against me. The crowd abruptly fell silent, so silent I could hear the sound of the crow's wings as it flew back to Ouvrain. In my surprise I found I had forgotten all of my carefully prepared speech and so had to speak straight from the heart. With tears in my eyes I began, "Now that we are together again we can mourn our losses and begin to rebuild what was damaged by greedy men. With my beloved sister here beside me I can once more . . ." Suddenly, with a sob, words failed me. I quickly beckoned Jolaina forward to speak in my place while I tried hard to compose myself. The tears were running freely down my face.

Jolaina

To my amazement I saw Nhuri walk across the square and up the steps to join Aranella on the platform. When Aranella wrapped her arms around the girl I suddenly felt as if things were complete again, the pattern restored. In the next instant I saw Aranella beckoning me. With a lurch of my heart I understood that I must be the one to speak because at that moment she could not.

Bowing in all directions, I took a deep breath and made myself begin, trying to find my deepest, strongest voice, the one that would carry to the far edges of the great square. "Thank you to the people of Maktesh for this glorious welcome. And thank you to Bardaith for your kind words and for keeping the door open for our return. Hopefully there will be no more plots from men like Khundorn, wanting to drag Maktesh into a disastrous war. I want to repeat here what you probably have already heard, there will be no war against Zelindar, Mishghall and the coast. The Hadra are not our enemies. Some of them risked their lives to help us rescue Aranella and Nhuri from death or worse at Khundorn's hands. And some of them even sit here beside us on this platform. They are here in the city as our guests for a short while before they return to their own city and their interrupted lives. I trust we will treat them with the greatest courtesy.

"As for the Kourmairi of Mishghall, we can make treaties and alliances with them for trade and access to the coast. We do not need to wash their streets in blood or send our sons there to die or come home as broken cripples in order to sail Maktesh ships out of Mishghall's harbor. In fact, due to our part in stopping this war, we are in a position to make very advantageous terms with that city, something I will be glad to see to myself.

"Due to the unfortunate events of the past few months there has been much unrest and uncertainty in Maktesh. I trust that is over. Now we must work together, Shokarn and Kourmairi alike, to give Aranella our full support and to help mend the rips in the public fabric. Thank you good people of Maktesh for lending me your ears and now may we all join together for merriment and feasting and celebration." Drenched in sweat, I bowed again. Just as I was stepping down to a thunder of applause, I thought I caught a glimps of Manyier in the crowd, clapping along with the others. The sight of him made me smile.

My knees were shaking from that speech. I could not have said another word. In fact, I could barely stand. Luckily Bardaith was there to grab my arm. "Well done, Jolaina, and well said," he whispered in my ear. "Just what was needed." My comrades from the road quickly crowded around to congratulate me. I nodded and smiled, glad that was over for now though I could see before me many other occasions for such speeches. I could only hope I had covered my fears well enough that day and that the terror would lessen as time went on.

When I had the chance I leaned over and whispered to Aranella, "I think I saw Manyier out there in the crowd, clapping with enthusiasm for my speech."

"Good. Maybe he is over being angry and will come back to us. I miss him. He was like an uncle to me when I was growing up." Her smile warmed my heart and for that moment I forgot my nervousness.

Noya

Being displayed on the platform that day may have made us seem less strange to the people of Maktesh. In no way did it make Maktesh seem less strange to me as I made my way through the city later. I had grown up in Zelindar where enough always felt like plenty, so now plenty felt like too much. The excesses of Maktesh sickened my soul and my spirit. And the dreadful poverty, right there in plain view, shocked and amazed me. How could the wealthy folk of the city bear the sight of such misery around them and do nothing? With my Hadra empath powers I felt it all. When I questioned Jolaina, she said things were changing. Then Aranella added that it was much better than it had been under her father's rule. I shook my head. For me their "better" was not good enough. Hard to imagine what it must have been like before.

Our ways and customs were so very different from those of Maktesh that we Hadra came together often to mutter among ourselves. Danil would say, "I hate to see how they ride their horses and how they treat their women — not so different really." And Nairin would add, "This place is full of sickness and the supposed healers are the sickest of all." Then Pathell would shake her head in disbelief. "How odd to be in a place with no mind-touch. There is so much constant noise and at the core of it such a thick block of deadly silence." Not having mind-touch with others forced us to seek out each other's company and keep close contact in the midst of city crowds.

In truth, I had odd feelings the whole time we were in that city. People watched us strangely. I heard the words witch or muirlla or puntyar much more often than I heard the word Hadra. For the most part they were polite enough, though I sometimes felt them drawing aside fearfully as we passed on the street. To ourselves, in our Hadra city of Zelindar, we were ordinary. Here we were something peculiar, as if we had pointed ears or lived forever, something not quite human, or more than human, or both. No doubt the people of Maktesh were grateful to us for helping to bring their Zarna safely home. I thought they might have been just as grateful to see us leave. We were too much for them. Jolaina, the Kourmairi muirlla, was hard enough for them to swallow, but there was only one of her and they were already used to her. Now, suddenly, there were all these peculiar Hadra in their city streets, a small but potentially dangerous invasion.

For myself, I was ready to get back on the road. Restless to be home, I was very much afraid of what we might find when we got there. I had heard rumors from the Thieves Guild that there might be wild men on their way to Zelindar, fortune hunters, not guards under anyone's command. Aranella had invited us to stay for more festivities, but I was sure she would be as glad to have me gone as I would be to leave.

Aranella

Later, at the palace banquet, Nhuri was more like her child self again. She came to my side and stood leaning against me with her arm around my neck. While we fed each other special morsels of food, she chattered about all that had happened since I had last seen her. At that moment my ears were only for her, but when she heard a friend's voice calling she went instantly to the girl's side. Then another friend

249

called out to her, and then another. In that way she went from place to place at the table, favoring different people with her presence. Not even Dharlan had the heart to remonstrate with her for her lack of manners.

I watched Nhuri for a while, my heart full of delight mixed with a slight tinge of jealousy. Then Bardaith claimed my attention. Soon I was deep in conversation with him and two other men of the City Council. We were talking about plans for the future when I felt called to look up. Ouvrain was standing across the table, watching me intently. She looked quite imposing in a long black velvet gown with silver trim. Her club of silver hair had a blood-red ribbon braided in it along with a row of tiny blood-red roses. The crow sat on her shoulder in the midst of that noisy crowd as calmly as if it were a creature of the city. Heads began to turn in her direction. A murmur of whispers rose.

I nodded and beckoned to her. As Bardaith and the other two men stepped away, Ouvrain came around the end of the table to stand beside me. Refusing my offer of Nhuri's empty seat, she said nothing and merely continued to stare at me. Finally I felt obliged to speak, if only for politeness' sake, or perhaps out of nervousness. "Thank you for keeping Nhuri safe. How did you know it was time to bring her back?" I spoke softly, not wanting everyone to hear.

Ouvrain answered in a bold loud voice, "I watched in the bowl, saw what was being planned and knew it was important for her to be here. And I thought it was better to bring her to Maktesh. I certainly did not need you making a trail to my house again. Besides, I myself wanted to have some part in these great events. And Nhuri needs to take her place here and be visible, the sooner the better."

"She has grown in our time apart." I felt a pang of envy seeing Nhuri so much in Ouvrain's pocket.

"Yes, she has grown, and in more ways than one. The important ways are not the ones that show. She has her own very special powers, Zarna. Remember that in case you ever

250

think to . . ." Though she let her words trail away, the implication was clear enough.

I wanted to shout at her that my brother's death was no fault of mine. Instead, keeping my silence and my temper, I stared her down. She looked away first, but there was a little smile of malice at the corners of her mouth.

Jolaina

The banquet hall of the palace was all light and color. Hung with bright banners and more garlands of flowers, it was ablaze with lamps and candles. A restless, noisy, brightly-dressed crowd moved about there, unable to sit still for long. I was delighted that everything was going so smoothly when this homecoming could have been full of troubles. Yet I was weary beyond belief. Asleep on my feet, I was trying my best to stay alert. Aranella beckoned me over several times to sit by her. Tired as I was I did not want to sit down, not just yet. I was not hungry, and besides I wanted to keep watch on everything.

There was a constant flow of people and platters in and out of the kitchen along with overflowing pitchers and huge steaming bowls and heaping bread baskets. Musicians strolled about, stopping here and there to favor someone with a tune. People moved from table to table, greeting friends and catching up on the great news in a constant buzz and rumble of excitement. Noisy toasts were made; glasses were raised and emptied. Guardsmen chatted with friends when I would like to have seen them standing alert and silent. Altogether there were too many people in motion all at the same time.

And everyone wanted to be near Aranella — to get her attention, welcome her back, congratulate her, touch her, offer her gifts, ask her for some favor. Though there were guardsmen all around her, still it made me uneasy and I kept glancing over at her. Suddenly there was a commotion by the kitchen doors; the crash of a platter and some angry curses. Distracted, I looked that way for just an instant. It was then that I heard Ouvrain's warning cry.

Aranella

As Ouvrain made her way back to her place on the opposite side of the table she turned several times to glance at me with malicious triumph. When she sat down she smiled with that same expression, clearly very pleased with herself. Then, all in an instant, her face totally changed. With a look of horror she sprang to her feet again and screamed, "Watch out! In back of you!" She was staring straight at me.

Even as she shouted I was already turning to see what had startled her and so was able to slip sideways and dodge the knife that had been aimed at my back. The man fell forward, his long, sharp knife plunging into the table and sticking fast in the wood. Two guardsmen were on him in an instant, one with an arm around the his neck. He fought back fiercely. I was knocked down and trampled in their struggle. Then strong arms grabbed me up and Koshar put herself between me and those men. I reached out and grabbed Nhuri against me while Hadra sprang up all around to protect us.

Everything seemed to be happening at once. I heard Ouvrain scream Jolaina's name and Bardaith shout to close and guard the doors. The man who attacked me cried out in pain and slid to the floor, covered with blood. When I glanced at him I was shocked to see that he wore Manyier's face. In a panic I turned to look for Jolaina, terrified that she might have been stabbed. At the same time I heard Ouvrain shout, "Noya, point to the others!"

I could not move, I was packed in too tightly by my protectors. "Jolaina! Jolaina!" I called out desperately, unable to find her anywhere. Finally I saw her rise only a short distance away. There was a knife in her hand and blood on her sleeve, but she seemed unhurt as she turned and plowed her way toward me. Others quickly moved out of her way.

Noya

Too little air. Too much noise and food and talk and drink. The smell of cooked meat was sickening to my Hadra senses. It was hard to talk. It was even harder to answer when people spoke to me. I was in a daze, half asleep, trying to shut it all out and wishing I were somewhere else. For comfort I pictured myself riding up into the hills above Zelindar or running down to splash in the Escuro river, any place where there was wind and fresh air and not so many people talking all at once, saying one thing and meaning another.

Suddenly I sat up, alert and frightened, all my senses instantly sharp. I felt it just moments before it happened. Even so I was not sure what was coming, only that there was some great danger. I should have felt it sooner. We all should have, all of the Hadra. But I think the constant commotion, the overloading of the senses, had dulled our powers. When I saw the man lunge at Aranella I understood in that instant that we were under attack.

Quickly I leapt up, wanting to rush to her defense. Then I saw I was not needed. Two guardsmen felled Aranella's attacker before he could harm her. Hadra were on their feet all around her, shielding the Zarna with their bodies. Now the room was in an uproar. Just as I began looking around frantically for Jolaina I heard Ouvrain shout to me, "Noya, who are the others? Point to them!"

Sweeping the room with my eyes I could suddenly see them as if they were outlined in red. Their intentions gave off a heat and a strange glow. How could I have missed them before? It was not like reading their minds, it was more like seeing them.

"There!" I shouted, pointing my finger at a man very close to Nhuri who seemed to be trying to creep forward. Then I swung around and pointed at two others in the middle of the room who were standing very still, trying not to draw attention to themselves. And then I turned and pointed at a big man who was running for the door.

I felt like the finger of death. Swords and knives flashed suddenly. The man near Nhuri was quickly overpowered and killed. The other two put up more of a struggle. Then they were also brought down and killed. Some of the guards were wounded in the fight. The big man crashed through the door with a howl of fury and escaped into the night.

When Bardaith called out to me, "Any more?" I scanned the room again and shook my head. "Not here at least," I called back to him. At that moment the backwash from all that sudden death caught me like a cresting wave and I passed out cold, falling into instant darkness.

Jolaina

Alerted by Ouvrain's shout, I saw the motion out of the corner of my eye. All of my combat training came into play in that instant. I grabbed the man's wrist and snapped it so that the knife went flying. Then I swung him by his arm so that he landed on his back with a crash that knocked his breath away. Before I had time to hesitate or he had time to move, I had my own knife in my hand and his throat was cut. When I looked into his face I saw that it was Rhenfel, Jalmoth's assistant in the combat yard, the man who had taught me how to fight. My hands and those fancy white lace sleeves were all covered with his blood.

Retching I stood up quickly and glanced around, afraid

there might be another of them coming at me. Then, over all the screams and shouts and turmoil, I heard Aranella's terrified voice, calling my name. I pushed my way through the crowd, afraid of what I would find. People backed away from me in haste. I had almost reached her when there was an uproar by one of the doors. I turned to see several guardsmen staggering back with cries of pain or actually flying through the air. Then Jalmoth hurled his body at the door, burst it open and flung himself through it with a roar of rage. Though guardsmen ran after him I did not think they were likely to catch him nor likely to be very eager to try.

When I reached Aranella she fell into my arms and hugged me so hard I thought my bones would crack. I groaned with relief at seeing her safe. As I pressed against her I could feel our hearts pounding in unison. For just that moment no one else in the world existed. Then Bardaith was at my side. "Noya says we have all of them except for Jalmoth. That one got away."

"I know," I said with a nod, "I witnessed his exit." Then, remembering that I was supposed to be a leader there, I wriggled loose from Aranella's embrace and jumped up on the table. I had to bellow to make myself heard over the commotion. "People of Maktesh, please listen! The danger is over now and the Zarna is unharmed. We need to stay calm before we hurt each other by accident. The plot was foiled. The assassins are all dead except for Jalmoth. He escaped, but I trust we will find him and that no one in this city will give him shelter."

From that height I could see that a place had been cleared for Noya on one of the tables. She was gray-pale and lying very still, but there was no blood visible anywhere. Nairin and Tenari were working on her while the other Hadra formed a loose circle of support and protection around them. My heart gave a lurch of fear, yet there was nothing I could do for her at that moment. She was being well cared for and I was certainly no healer.

Quickly I pulled Aranella up beside me on the table so she could be seen by the crowd. Aranella raised her arms and gradually the room quieted. Then she began to talk using all her charm and all her power, casting her words out into that room like a spell. I can remember nothing of what she said, but she kept people's rapt attention while Bardaith had some guards take away the bodies and scatter sawdust to soak up the blood. As soon as that was done the doors were opened and people were allowed to leave. The banquet was over. There would not be any more celebrating that night.

Aranella

The panic had quieted. There were no more shouts or screams or scuffles at the door. The bodies had been quickly taken away and some sort of order restored. The guards and some of the servants were moving about, calming people and facilitating an orderly departure while the rest of the servants cleared away the chaos of our partly eaten meal. My throat was raw from trying to make myself heard. Bardaith was standing back to back with me and when I stopped speaking with a little croak at the end of my words he took over for me, his mellow calming voice filling the hall.

I looked about at what was left of our banquet and though with some bitterness, *This will certainly be a night everyone will remember and tell their grandchildren about, but not for the reasons we had hoped.* There were five men dead and one ruined, at least in Maktesh. And what had it all been for? Was there another Khundorn hungry for his chance, just waiting for opportunity? Or had these six been their own plot, angry enough at having a woman ruler that they were ready to seize this moment and willing to risk losing their lives in the venture? Well, unless Jalmoth was caught we would not know, at least not for a while. Whatever their purpose they had very nearly succeeded. It was clear that Jolaina and Nhuri and I had been the targets. I was enough my father's daughter to be glad these men were dead, wish Jalmoth dead along with them and even think they had died much too easily. But it grieved me deeply that Manyier had been one of them, their leader perhaps. That hurt my heart. If only we had kept one of them alive we might have leaned what this was all about. Then I thought of the methods we would have had to use. No, I was not that much my father's daughter.

Suddenly I was overwhelmed with weariness. My knees buckled. I slid down until I was siting at the edge of the table. It seemed safer at that moment than a chair and I was very glad to feel Bardaith's legs pressed against my back. Nhuri came instantly and leaned against me. Her face was streaked with tears. "Oh Aranella, he almost killed you."

When I put my arm around her I could feel her trembling. "But he did not succeed," I said firmly. "I am alive and you are alive and Jolaina is alive. That is all that matters now." I hugged her close and stroked her hair. I did not mention that one of those men had been coming for her but I think she knew.

I was feeling strangely calm, almost cold. I suppose I might have been shaking with fear or even hysterical after what had happened. Some women would have been. But I had almost been ex- pecting it. Everything had been too smooth, too easy. I suppose I had felt something evil lurking there under all the flowers and banners and music and shouts of welcome and good wishes. Now the worst had happened. We had lived through it. It was over, at least for the moment and I could breathe a sigh of relief.

Finally I became aware of my feet. Those lovely red velvet slippers with the gold buckles that had so pleased me earlier in the evening now hurt dreadfully. I kicked them off. With that I had a glimpse of myself as from a distance. I could see how I, the Zarna, must look at that moment. My beautiful crown of flowers and jewels had fallen off and been crushed underfoot. My hair had tumbled down wildly from its formal arrangement and was hanging in tangles around my face. My fine gown was torn, rumpled, blood splotched and hiked up around my legs. My sheer white stockings were in shreds. And still people kept bowing and wishing me well as they passed, their faces distressed and full of sympathy. I thought they might well burst out laughing as soon as they were out the door. I know I probably would have.

I had not sat on the edge of a table that way since I had been a child. At that thought, for just a moment, I was back to being a child once more and what went through my head was, *Dharlan will be very angry at me for messing my dress again.* That struck me so funny that I threw back my head and laughed aloud. Once I started I found I could not stop. Everything struck me as funny, my appearance, the look of shock on people's faces, the tattered remains of the meal, even the thought of those bloody bodies suddenly dropped right in the middle of our banquet. In her sternest voice Dharlan told me to stop. That made me laugh all the more. Next Jolaina grabbed me by the arms and shook me, but still I could not stop. Even her pained, anxious expression struck me as funny. At last she raised her hand to slap my face, but discovered she could not. After all, one does not strike the Zarna's face and certainly not in public. Her hand hovering out there in space with no place to land seemed even funnier.

Finally Ouvrain appeared at Jolaina's shoulder, her face very serious. Looking me straight in the eye she shouted, "Stop!" in a voice of command and clapped her hands once like thunder. I stopped instantly as if someone had poured cold water over my head. She grabbed one of the passing servants and said, "Bring her a glass of water quickly."

258

Jolaina moved out of the way. I made a little nod of acknowledgment to Ouvrain and said quite formally, "Thank you Ouvrain for saving my life. A few more seconds and that knife would have found its mark." Then a glass of water was placed in my hand. As I drank it I could feel my sanity returning.

There was none of the usual mockery in Ouvrain's face when she answered. Instead she looked distressed and was shaking her head. "I am so sorry Aranella, it almost was too late. I should have known sooner, much sooner."

I frowned, puzzled by her words. Then a sudden thought struck me. "How did you see the knife? Manyier was behind me."

"I never saw the knife until it struck the table. I am a witch; I can see things. I saw his intent and I would have seen it much sooner if I had not been so busy playing foolish power games with you instead of scanning the room for danger as I should have been doing."

I stared at her in silence. When I made no answer she went on. "It is a hard, lonely life being a Witch at this time in the world. All the glory is behind us now, long gone. We are hated and feared and there are so few of us left there is little comfort to be had from our own kind. Besides, most of us have grown bitter and are hardly able to give comfort anymore. Sometimes I think it is only little games of malice and power that keep me alive. I scolded you for jealousy, yet I myself am eaten up with envy.

"Then a child like Nhuri comes along who has such talent that it gives me hope. To my shame I was competing with you for her allegiance, mocking you when I should have been guarding you both from danger. I hope you can forgive me. I know I will have a hard time forgiving myself."

Stunned by the tone of her speech, I reached out my hand in a gesture of conciliation. "Well this day has certainly been full of surprises. One never knows what to expect. The man I thought to be my friend has turned out to be my enemy. And now the woman I think of as my enemy may turn out to be my friend."

"Aranella, I was never your enemy, only your teacher."

"My teacher?" I found myself bristling with anger again.

She nodded, smiling but with only a little mockery this time and no malice. "As you no doubt are mine. Yes, I have already leaned much from you. Some day perhaps we can even be friends though we might be too much alike for that. And you will need friends in this time to come, ones you can trust, ones who have been tested. Who knows what lies ahead. What you are trying is a very dangerous game as you can see. Khundorn may only be the first of many. You and Jolaina and Nhuri might continue to be in danger for a long while yet."

I was sure that was true. I was not sure Ouvrain was the one I wanted guarding my back. Just then I felt Nhuri tugging on my arm. She asked urgently, "Can we find a place here at the Palace for Ouvrain to stay? There is so much I still have to learn. I only came home this soon to be here for your return. She said it was very important."

"Ouvrain? Here?" I probably did not sound very gracious. I was just about to get Noya out from under my roof. Did I have to accept Ouvrain in her place? I was not sure which was worse. I looked over at Jolaina. She was watching me intently and gave me a slight nod. Then Dharlan spoke up in that bold, new way she had, saying, "Lady, let me go find her a room in the east wing and make her comfortable there."

So the three women I loved most in the world wanted this. Who was I to stand against their will? Even a Zarna cannot stand alone. I nodded, giving my consent without a word spoken. It seems it had already been decided without my help. Then I turned to the witch and said stiffly, "Be welcome in my home, Ouvrain."

I had expected to see a look of mocking triumph on the woman's face. Not so. Her expression was very serious and her voice almost solemn when she answered with a slight bow, "Thank you Lady. You will never regret this and Nhuri has much to gain from it. And I will not forget my promise to watch over her and keep her from harm and you as well."

I bit back whatever sharp answer I might have made. Instead I shrugged and said, "Ah well, as the Hadra are so fond of saying, *as it must be.*" Not graciousness yet, but at least not open hostility.

By then the hall had almost cleared. The wounded guards had been attended to. The Hadra had taken Noya, still unconscious, up to their rooms. Accompanied by guards, Nhuri had gone with Dharlan and Ouvrain. Just as she was leaving Ouvrain turned back and said to me, "Take care Aranella. Pride and stubbornness are good qualities for a Zarna, necessary even, but if not tempered with humility then they are a great danger, to yourself as well as others. You have too much power over people's lives to let your will go unchecked." Before I could say a word in answer she was gone and I was left staring after her, speechless.

Soon Bardaith and Jolaina along with several more guards accompanied me to my chambers. Before they let me go in they sent the guards ahead to search the rooms. They were taking no chances. Once my safety was assured I said I wanted to be alone for a while. They both protested, but I insisted. They offered to send Zeeli to help me undress. I shook my head. Finally they consented to leave me after making sure the windows were fastened from the inside and having my promise that I would keep the doors locked and let two guards keep watch just outside and not leave until Jolaina came back. In effect a prisoner in my own rooms. "Yes, yes," I said impatiently. "I will be fine. I just need a little silence and solitude to reflect on everything that has happened."

It was with a sigh of relief that I locked the doors behind them. When I heard their footsteps fade away I struggled out of my ruined clothes, brushed out my hair, put on a loose robe and sat down at the desk with my head in my hands. So much had happened so fast and too many questions buzzed in my head. Were the deaths that night the end of it or were there more plots hatching? I did not want to be forced to rule as my father had with torture and fear, but what if I had no choice? And what of Jolaina? Before she had been all mine, my true-heart and my partner in all these ventures. Now, since Noya had come into our lives, I could feel her confusion and her divided loyalties. Could I still trust her? And what of Ouvrain? Did she really mean me good or ill?

After a while I shook my head and said aloud, "Well, we are back in Maktesh and I have been returned to power as Zarna, but nothing is the same. Things are shifting and changing in ways I do not yet comprehend. There are forces at work under the skin of appearance that I need to understand if I am to keep my place at the helm of this city." Suddenly I found myself wishing that everything could just slip back to the way it had been before.

I have taken this moment alone to write this last part of my account and to re-read all of it, looking for the patterns that can give me guidance. What I have set down in these pages is the truth as I know it and there is much here that does not make me proud. As I have already written far more than I intended to, I mean for this to be the last of it. Let it be joined to the other accounts and let people see that the Zarna is just as human as other folk.

Aranella, Zarna of Maktesh

Amairi

Danger can come from anywhere and at any time. That much could be learned from what happened that evening. I only went to the banquet because Aranella and Jolaina expected me to be there. They said they wanted to honor me. I had to beg them not to draw more attention my way. As it was, I slipped away quite early to begin making preparations for a quick departure and so was lucky enough to miss the attempted assassination and all that followed. I think if I had witnessed that much violence I might well have lost the courage to go on with my own venture.

By the afternoon of the next day I was ready to leave for my appointment with fate. I had my own little troop of guards, the ones I had stolen from Horvath, as well as some men like Cedrun and Tornald who were loyal to Aranella. The only women besides myself were Nastal and Veridas. Nastal, of course, had insisted on coming. Veridas was to be our contact with the Thieves Guild since Toki and the others had already gone on ahead to make things ready. I could only hope their clever and deadly preparations would not be needed.

As we were leaving, Aranella and Jolaina tried to press on me more food and clothes and supplies than we could possibly carry. They wanted to send still more men with me "for safety". I kept explaining I had no intention of fighting and a larger force would only look hostile. Finally Aranella hugged me good-bye. I was aware again of how small and slight she was to be carrying so much weight on her shoulders, hardly more than a girl under all those fancy clothes.

When we were mounted and ready to ride, Vondran, Morghail, Noya, Ethran, Shamu, Ablon and many others crowded around to wish me good-bye. At that moment I felt loved as I never had before in my life. To my surprise, Vondran even pulled me forward and kissed me hard on the mouth. "Come back safely to us, Amairi." With that he put a little purse in my hands. "The money from your jewels. Use it for whatever you need on this trip." Then he pressed my hands between his own and gave me a strange, unreadable look before quickly turning away.

As we made our preparations to leave, none of us said the

word Eezore in public as being our destination. We even made a great show of departing eastward from the city as if going to my family's lands. For the first part of the afternoon we kept riding east. After Yorant and Argus hung back several times and ascertained that we were not being followed, we finally turned north to Eezore on a narrow, little road known only to Veridas.

Noya

I woke up with a fierce headache that lasted most of the day in spite of Nairin's pills and teas and herbal remedies. I needed to be out of this city soon, away from this world where you could suddenly be forced to choose between killing or being killed. I found it hard to look at Jolaina. She had suddenly become a stranger, someone I hardly knew. She had taken a man's life as easily as slicing a melon.

We Hadra got angry with each other, but the worst we could do was unspeak one another or withdraw our affection. And our quarrels did not usually last long since we were empaths and could all too easily feel the other's pain. If we thought a Councilor was unfit we could call for a vote and seek to persuade the others. It certainly would not cross our minds to try and kill her. And yet I myself had become a killer last night with my pointing finger. The men I pointed at had died. This was all too complicated and confusing, too much to try thinking about with a throbbing head.

It was the afternoon of our second day in the city. People were beginning to gather in the great hall of the palace, waiting for the music to begin. Bardaith had said the festivities should continue so as not to show weakness in the face of that attack, but I certainly had no heart for it. Amairi had already left on her mission to Eezore. The rest of the

Wanderers had faded away, going back on the road, except Douven who was staying to visit with his sister and Shamu who had stayed to be with him.

I was already weary of being in Maktesh. Thinking to find the other Hadra, I hoped we might walk together by the river. It was the one place in that city where I could feel some sense of ease and comfort. Just as I was wondering how we could slip away from the dance without seeming rude, Douven rushed up to grab my arm. He was breathing hard from exertion and sweat was beading his forehead. Shamu was with him, looking very anxious. Hardly waiting to catch his breath, Douven burst out, "Toki sent us to warn you. This time it is no longer a rumor, this time it is the truth. A band of men calling themselves the 'Mad Dogs' have set out to invade Zelindar. They are inflamed by stories of treasure and do not care if the Zarna opposes the war. Horvath, the one who leads them, is reputed to be the maddest dog of all."

"Horvath?" I said, shaking my head in wonder. "The man who was once Amairi's husband? How strange if we are destined to meet again this way."

"How many?" asked Danil, crowding against my shoulder. The rest of the Hadra were soon pressing around us having been drawn by my thoughts or my fears.

"Two or three hundred, Toki was not sure."

"Have they already left? Will they be there before us?" Koshar asked anxiously.

"Not if you let me be your guide," Douven answered. "I know a Wanderer way that would get you there much faster, even faster than the way we came." Then he stopped abruptly, blushed, and shook his head. Looking embarrassed and confused, he stammered, "No, I should not have said any-thing . . . it is a secret way . . . I was not supposed to know . . . First I must ask Vondran. It is forbidden to lead Ganja on those roads." From the distress in his mind I gathered that Larameer and Rhondil had once taken him on

265

that route when they were not supposed to and then sworn him to absolute secrecy.

"Forbidden but necessary," Shamu said quickly, "And Vondran is not here to be asked. I am Wanderer born. I can give permission as well as he can. I would show them the way myself if only I knew, but you are the one who has followed that secret road. Besides, I myself am a much better healer than guide. You say you never lose your way; do what you can Douven. Get them to Zelindar as fast as possible."

"Will you let me be your guide?" Douven asked again, staring at me intently.

"Only if you let us heal your leg in payment," I answered with sudden inspiration.

He glared at me in silence for a moment as if I had trapped him in a bad bargain instead of offering him freedom from a life of pain.

Shamu slipped her arm around his waist. "Tell her yes," she said firmly. "Not such a hard word, Douven. Just say it, say yes. And I am coming too. You will need my help."

"Yes," Douven and I said at the same moment. Then I whirled around and snapped impatiently, "Danil, Koshar, get the horses. And no saddles or bridles. This time we ride back as Hadra." Even as I spoke the words they were already rushing out of the great hall. Jolaina and Aranella had joined us. There was an increasing buzz in the hall as the news began to spread. I heard the words *Mad Dogs* and *Zelindar* repeated several times in that rising tide of voices.

Jolaina said urgently, "Let us send some guards from this city to help protect Zelindar. We owe you that much at least for all the help you have given us." What I heard in her head was, *I should be going with you too. You will need me there.*

"No," I said quickly. "No Jolaina, thank you for your kind offer, but you do not understand. We cannot have armed men fighting other armed men in front of our city. That would not guard us. It would only harm our own powers of protection."

I could sense Aranella struggling hard with her emotions.

Then she took a deep breath and said with seeming calm, "Jolaina is free to go with you if she wishes and to take as many men as she needs. After all, we owe you a great debt."

As I answered, I looked Aranella right in the eye, wanting to speak straight from my heart to hers. I knew what that offer had cost her. "Thank you, Aranella, for your generosity, but Jolaina is far more useful to us here, keeping the peace in Maktesh and making sure no new Khundorns rise to take his place, especially after what just happened. With our powers we can probably handle a few raiders. What we cannot survive is an invasion."

At exactly the same moment I felt Aranella's anger and Jolaina's hurt. From Aranella's mind I heard, *She can take Jolaina away from me just like that, any time she wants to.* And from Jolaina's I heard, *She is done with me. She is going home and does not need or want me anymore.* When I turned to Jolaina she would not meet my eyes. I tried to send her some message of love with my words. "And thank you Jolaina for your courage and concern. I will take that with me for strength." In my mind I added, *And hold it always in my heart.*

Suddenly Nhuri was there among us, looking up at me and speaking very seriously. "I wish I could go with you, Noya, and help guard Zelindar with my witch powers, but Ouvrain says they are not strong enough yet."

I tried not to smile at her earnestness. Young as she was I knew she already had powers of her own. "I doubt that your sister would want you gone again so soon. She has just gotten you safely home."

Nhuri put her hand in Aranella's. In a quick gesture of fierce protectiveness Aranella put her arms around the girl and pressed her close.

I nodded to them all. "We Hadra are sorry to have to leave so suddenly, but with this new threat we need to be on the road for home as quickly as possible." I felt my lie of politeness vibrating in the air around me and half expected someone to shout "Liar!" or point an accusing finger at me for those false words. In truth I was only too glad to be leaving Maktesh. I was only sorry such terrible danger to Zelindar was my excuse. And so, gathering up all the supplies that were offered, we made our escape that very evening.

Just as we were about to leave, Jolaina threw her arms around Douven and said, "Go safely my brother. Go with all my love and come back with your leg healed if that is your desire." She still would not look at me, but riding away I could feel her eyes staring holes into my back. Even on the road I was not sure if I was more eager to be home or more eager to be out of that city that had so little place in it for Hadra. And yet, with every step, the separation from Jolaina tore at my heart. I kept my silence on this. Sheilding my feelings from the other Hadra, I tried to turn all my thoughts toward the west and home.

Jolaina

I am sitting here late at night, thinking and writing by the light of one small oil lamp, remembering everything that happened in these past few months that were so full of danger and excitement. In setting all this down on paper, perhaps I can make some sense out of it at last. From the darkness, from beyond the circle of lamplight, I hear Aranella breathing softly in her sleep. Nhuri is safe in her room with Dharlan asleep nearby. There are guards outside our door, something we never had before.

We three have been welcomed home and Maktesh is ours again, but not without a terrible price. For the first time in my life I have killed someone, a man I knew and liked. I will learn to live with it, but things will never be the same for me again. Now it is time for me to reacquaint myself with this city and find my real place here, whatever that may be.

They are all gone now, all those strangers who for a while were my whole world. Vondran and his band of Wanderers have slipped away like smoke on the morning wind; Amairi and her little troop have gone to meet their fate and perhaps their death in Eezore; and just this afternoon Noya and all the Hadra departed in a great rush with my brother Douven to guide them, not even waiting for the morning light.

When Noya left there was a frozen silence between us and I could not even look her in the eye. I know Maktesh is where I need to be, where I want to be. I am very glad I did not have to go to Zelindar. And yet I can feel my heart stretching thinner and thinner as the distance between us grows and Noya rides westward toward the coast and whatever fate awaits her there.

Jolaina of Maktesh

Name List

City of Maktesh:
Aranella — Zarna of Maktesh
Jolaina — the Zarna's lover and advisor
Nhuriani, Nhuri — Aranella's younger sister
Ralyn — Aranella's younger brother
Dharlan — Aranella's nursemaid who also becomes her friend and companion
Bardaith — advisor to the old Zarn, then to Aranella and Jolaina
Manyier — also advisor to Zarn and teacher of Aranella and Jolaina
Amairi/Elvarain — abused Uppercaste wife who becomes a Wanderer
Horvath — Amairi's abusive husband
Nhageel — Amairi's younger brother who takes over the family estate
Lalaini — Nhageel's wife
Thairn — coachman for Horvath and Amairi
Yani — Elvarain's maid and Thairn's wife
Khundorn — the man who plots to overthrow the Zarna and make himself Zarn
Jalmoth — an instructor in martial arts for the palace
Rhenfel — Jalmoth's assistant

Hadra from Zelindar:
Noya — Councilor for Zelindar
Garlian — former Councilor
Pathell — Noya's right hand in this venture
Vranith — Noya's estranged lover

Hadra who accompany Noya and Pathell on journey:
Danil — skilled with horses
Nairin — healer, knowledgeable with plants and herbs
Mitru — guide and pathfinder
Koshar — tough and determined

Zanti — strong empath
Tenari — Noya's childhood friend

Wanderers:
Vondran — the leader of the Wanderer band
Mhirashu — another leader of the band and sometimes Vondran's lover
Ethran — Amairi's lover
Morghail — former Shokarn
Shamu — healer, looking to find settled place
Ablon — Shamu's son
Stobah — sharp-tongued and bitter
Nastal — new member of the Wanderer band, in love with Amairi
Douven — Jolaina's brother
Larameer — Wanderer guide and Rhondil's lover/companion
Rhondil — Wanderer guide

Thieves Guild:
Toki
Ochan
Veridas — girl who dances in red dress, also the guide on Midsummer Day

Others:
Gairith — wandering shepherd
Gwain — Gairith's cousin
Marn — Kourmairi Headman

Glossary

Yarmald Peninsula — all land west from the edge of Garmishair to the ocean, home to the Hadra and Koormir

Escuro River — most important river in Yarmald running north to south, bordered by several Hadra and Koormir settlements and by the city of Zelindar

Garmishair — all land east from Yarmald to the Rhonathrin Mountains, ruled by the Shokarn from their four city-states but including many Koormir towns and villages

Pellor, Nhor, Eezore, Maktesh — going from north to south, the four Zarn- ruled cities of Garmishair

Zarn/Zarna — Shokarn rulers of the cities

Shokarn — white-skinned ruling class of Garmishair, ruthlessly aggressive to their Koormir neighbors

Uppercaste/Highborn — upper caste among the Shokarn

Muirlla/Puntyar — insulting Shokarn and Kourmairi words for women who love women

Hadra — a new people who have just come into existence a hundred years before. These women have special powers and are all lovers of women. They live in their own separate cities and settlements in Yarmald but are at peace with the neighboring Koormir (see origins of the Hadra)

Kersh — powers possessed by the Hadra

Zelindar — main Hadra city located in South Yarmald on the coast

Zildorn — most important building in any Hadra city or settlement, a combination archive, meeting place and ritual space

Koormir/Kourmairi — dark-skinned native people of Yarmald, free in Yarmald but often slaves or servants to the Shokarn in Garmishair

Essu — spring and fall festivals descended from old Koormir rituals of planting and harvest. The Essus are now shared with the Hadra and are the only place where Hadra and Kourmairi mix freely.

Mishghall — main Kourmairi city located on the coast north of Zelindar

Muinyairin — fierce, nomadic riding people of the Drylands

Drylands — crescent of desert between South Yarmald and Garmishair

Wanderers — nomadic people living in wagons who run the main trading caravans between Yarmald and Garmishair

Cerroi — circle of fate that is at the center of the Wanderer system of ethics and beliefs

Ganja — mildly contemptuous Wanderer word for anyone not a Wanderer

Draiga — Hadra word for all those who are not Hadra

Thieves Guild — well-organized association of thieves operating in the Zarn-ruled cities and having a loose connection with the Wanderers

The Origins of the Hadra

The Hadra have a unique history in the region. They have only been in existence as a separate people for about a hundred years. Their origins date back to a comet, locally known as the Great Star, that was circling the planet. Many of the girl-children born at the time of the comet's passing were born with powers which later came to be called Kersh. Among these powers: the ability to speak mind-to-mind with each other; communication with animals; extra strength for physical work; and perhaps most important for their lives, the power of physical self-defense. Force used against them returns to the sender; conversely they cannot physically harm or compel another as that harm will come back to them.

As the first Hadra were growing up they were often ostracized in their own communities for their differences that others perceived as strangeness. When they were about seventeen, they came to the notice of the Zarns, patriarchal rulers of the four Shokarn city-states of Garmishair, and were seen as a threat to the Zarns' absolute power. The Zarns declared a death edict on the Hadra and hunted them down with the intention of exterminating them, but because of Hadra powers they were not so easy to kill. The Hadra eventually found each other, gathered together and fled toward the coast to escape the persecution of the Zarns. Eventually they made settlements there and founded the city of Zelindar. This is all described in the books *Daughters of the Great Star* and *The Hadra.*

Originating from the three different racial groups in the area — the Koomir, the Shokarn and the Muinyairin — the Hadra now live in their own separate settlements and cities in Yarmald near the coast. Contact with the neighboring Kourmairi is friendly but limited. If the Hadra want to have children they go to the spring or fall Essus, the big festival celebrations that they share with the Koormir. There, at night, they have anonymous sexual contact with men. Only girl children come of these unions. These girls will be raised by two mothers, a birth-mother and a bond-mother and they will have the Hadra kersh.

The Hadra language is a slightly altered and differently accented form of Kourmairi with the addition of many Shokarn and Muinyairin words and as well as many new words that originated with the Hadra and pertain to their life and powers.

In this present account, war with the Zarns again threatens the Hadra and the peaceful coast of Yarmald.

About the Author

Diana Rivers lives in the hills of Arkansas on women's land, in a house she designed that was all built by women's hands, including her own. She has a girlfriend who lives across the creek, two cats and many characters that keep her company, a wonderful view, a little vegetable garden that she tries to remember to weed and water, and now, in spite of resistance, a computer which is often her friend but sometimes her enemy. She used to write short stories that were published in feminist magazines until the Hadra come galloping into her life and demanded her full attention. *Clouds of War* is the fourth Hadra book and she has finished writing the next one. Every time she says that she will not write any more Hadra books, some character starts talking in her head, telling her a story she cannot resist.

CLOUDS OF WAR by Diana Rivers. 288 pp. Women
unite to defend Zelindar!   ISBN 1-931513-12-0 $12.95

OUTSIDE THE FLOCK by Jackie Calhoun. 220 pp.
Searching for love, Jo finds temptation. ISBN 1-931513-13-9 $12.95

WHEN GOOD GIRLS GO BAD: A Motor City Thriller by
Therese Szymanski. 230 pp. Brett, Andi, and Allie join
forces to stop a serial killer.   ISBN 1-931513-11-2 $12.95

DEATHS OF JOCASTA: The Second Micky Night Mystery
by J.M. Redmann. 408 pp. Sexy and intriguing Lambda
Literary Award nominated mystery   ISBN 1-931513-10-4 $12.95

LOVE IN THE BALANCE by Marianne K. Martin. 256 pp.
The classic lesbian love story, back in print!
                                             ISBN 1-931513-08-2 $12.95

THE COMFORT OF STRANGERS by Peggy J. Herring.
272 pp. Lela's work was her passion . . . until now.
                                             ISBN 1-931513-09-0 $12.95

CHICKEN by Paula Martinac. 208 pp. Lynn finds that the
only thing harder than being in a lesbian relationship is
ending one.   ISBN 1-931513-07-4 $11.95

TAMARACK CREEK by Jackie Calhoun. 208 pp. An intriguing story of love and danger.   ISBN 1-931513-06-6 $11.95

DEATH BY THE RIVERSIDE: The First Micky Knight
Mystery by J.M. Redmann. 320 pp. Finally back in print, the
book that launched the Lambda Literary Award winning
Micky Knight mystery series.   ISBN 1-931513-05-8 $11.95

EIGHTH DAY: A Cassidy James Mystery by Kate Calloway.
272 pp. In the eighth installment of the Cassidy James
mystery series, Cassidy goes undercover at a camp for
troubled teens.   ISBN 1-931513-04-X $11.95

MIRRORS by Marianne K. Martin. 208 pp. Jean Carson and
Shayna Bradley fight for a future together.
                                             ISBN 1-931513-02-3 $11.95

THE ULTIMATE EXIT STRATEGY: A Virginia Kelly Mystery by Nikki Baker. 240 pp. The long-awaited return of the wickedly observant Virginia Kelly.   ISBN 1-931513-03-1 $11.95

FOREVER AND THE NIGHT by Laura DeHart Young. 224 pp. Desire and passion ignite the frozen Arctic in this exciting sequel to the classic romantic adventure *Love on the Line.*   ISBN 0-931513-00-7 $11.95

WINGED ISIS by Jean Stewart. 240 pp. The long-awaited sequel to *Warriors of Isis* and the fourth in the exciting Isis series.   ISBN 1-931513-01-5 $11.95

ROOM FOR LOVE by Frankie J. Jones. 192 pp. Jo and Beth must overcome the past in order to have a future together.   ISBN 0-9677753-9-6 $11.95

THE QUESTION OF SABOTAGE by Bonnie J. Morris. 144 pp. A charming, sexy tale of romance, intrigue, and coming of age.   ISBN 0-9677753-8-8 $11.95

SLEIGHT OF HAND by Karin Kallmaker writing as Laura Adams. 256 pp. A journey of passion, heartbreak and triumph that reunites two women for a final chance at their destiny.   ISBN 0-9677753-7-X $11.95

MOVING TARGETS: A Helen Black Mystery by Pat Welch. 240 pp. Helen must decide if getting to the bottom of a mystery is worth hitting bottom.   ISBN 0-9677753-6-1 $11.95

CALM BEFORE THE STORM by Peggy J. Herring. 208 pp. Colonel Robicheaux retires from the military and comes out of the closet.   ISBN 0-9677753-1-0 $12.95

OFF SEASON by Jackie Calhoun. 208 pp. Pam threatens Jenny and Rita's fledgling relationship.   ISBN 0-9677753-0-2 $11.95

WHEN EVIL CHANGES FACE: A Motor City Thriller by Therese Szymanski. 240 pp. Brett Higgins is back in another heart-pounding thriller.   ISBN 0-9677753-3-7 $11.95

BOLD COAST LOVE by Diana Tremain Braund. 208 pp. Jackie Claymont fights for her reputation and the right to love the woman she chooses.   ISBN 0-9677753-2-9 $11.95

THE WILD ONE by Lyn Denison. 176 pp. Rachel never expected that Quinn's wild yearnings would change her life forever.   ISBN 0-9677753-4-5 $12.95

SWEET FIRE by Saxon Bennett. 224 pp. Welcome to Heroy — the town with the most lesbians per capita than any other place on the planet!   ISBN 0-9677753-5-3 $11.95

Visit
Bella Books
at

www.bellabooks.com